The Tinfish Run

The Tinfish Run

Ronald Bassett

HARPER & ROW, PUBLISHERS

New York, Hagerstown, San Francisco, London

FIRST U.S. EDITION

ISBN: 0-06-010233-0

LIBRARY OF CONGRESS CATALOG CARD NUMBER: 76-50167

77 78 79 80 81 10 9 8 7 6 5 4 3 2 1

For a glossary of Naval lower-deck terminology and technical terms see the end of the book (p. 249).

For a brief account of the fortunes of convoy PQ17 also see the end of the book (p. 262).

Author's Foreword

In 1939 the British Navy was the largest and undoubtedly the most professional in the world, but still needed massive reinforcement in ships and men to meet the challenge of the next six years. The Navy's peacetime strength on paper was misleading. Approximately half of British warships had served in, or had been designed for, the First World War. Although a number of these had been reconstructed or refitted to a standard of reasonable efficiency, many were obsolescent or positively obsolete. The other half, built between the wars, was a mixed bag of good and indifferent. Some, like the County Class cruisers and the later destroyers, were superb vessels and beyond criticism. Others, designed and constructed during an era of parsimony and cheeseparing, were fit only for 'showing the flag' and were woefully inadequate for modern sea warfare, too lightly armed and armoured for fighting, too slow to run. The price of their inadequacy would be paid for by thousands of sailors' lives.

Pre-war cinema audiences were smugly enthralled by the spectacle of battleships in line ahead, wallowing majestically, with snow-white decks, mighty guns and fluttering ensigns. With God and such a navy on our side the cliffs of Dover were surely secure from the evil designs of lesser breeds. The Navy had begun the war with fifteen operational capital ships — battleships and battle-cruisers — but only two were of post-1918 vintage, although five more were near to completion. Of this total of twenty, five were to be sunk by enemy action, one of them at anchor.

It was a war in which battleships could seldom be deployed with advantage. Their bulk and relatively slow speed made them exquisitely vulnerable to air and submarine attack, and they could not be exposed without an escort of smaller vessels and air cover. Yet, on the surface, only a battleship could challenge a battleship, and while the enemy retained such monsters the Navy must keep its own. As a result, except for occasional brief forays, capital ships were kept locked within fortified anchorages, absorbing thousands of Naval personnel who might more usefully have been employed elsewhere.

A far more gruelling, dangerous and widespread war was fought by the smaller ships of the Navy — the cruisers, destroyers, frigates, corvettes, trawlers, and so many converted merchantmen that it is impossible to describe them. It would also be invidious to suggest that one type worked harder, achieved more, or whose function was more important, than any other. From the River Plate to Murmansk, Hvalfjord to Hong Kong, they took the war to the enemy wherever they found him, kept secure our ocean lifelines, succoured our armies and provisioned our allies. They did all that was asked of them, and more for good measure.

This book is about a destroyer, HMS *Virtue*, and the men who served in her. Very many readers, now middle-aged and greying, will remember a great deal about destroyers, but for a younger generation a few words of description will be of value.

By sea-going standards, destroyers were small ships, in tonnage ranging from about 900 to 2400 tons, having been developed from the earlier and even smaller torpedo-boats. They were fast, narrow, light, of shallow draught and consequently requiring sensitive handling, tending to pivot, when turning, at a point somewhere below the after funnel — or roughly amidships. Crew numbers varied from 130 to 300, depending upon the vessel's size, and accommodation, particularly in the older and smaller ships, was confined.

Initially, the destroyer's primary armament was the torpedo, designed for use in high-speed attacks against an enemy battle formation. Even during the First World War, however, opportunities for major fleet actions were rare. The U-boat was a far more serious problem, and by 1918 the destroyer's most important role was that of convoy escort.

The combined threats of U-boats and aircraft were recognised before 1939 and, within the limitations imposed by the Navy Estimates, a number of preparations were made. Among these was the progressive modification of eighty elderly destroyers to more nearly meet the demands of escort duties.

Contrary to popular opinion, the destroyer was not an efficient or economical escort vessel. It had been designed for totally different circumstances. Its torpedo facility was superfluous, its low-angle guns useless against aircraft, and its high speed seldom utilised, being confined to about twenty knots when engaged in submarine detection. Thus its massive engines were space-consuming deadweight requiring, with the ship's other refinements, a disproportionately large crew and specialist skills.

Subsequent purpose-built escort sloops and corvettes were smaller but less cramped, slower but less complex; they could be built more quickly and cheaply, were operationally more economical, and they were more seaworthy.

Modifications to the old destroyers varied from vessel to vessel and were still continuing when the war began. A few had structural alterations, others had torpedo tubes replaced by anti-aircraft guns, or existing low-angle guns removed to increase depth-charge accommodation. A small number remained materially unchanged.

The 'V & W' Class destroyer *Virtue* was launched in 1917. She was of 1100 tons, measured 300 feet, and accommodated a crew of 125. Because of the removal of her forward boiler to increase fuel capacity and thus endurance, her speed was reduced to a matronly 25 knots. Her modified armament was two 4-inch guns, one 3-inch AA gun, two 2-pounder AA guns — known as 'pom-poms' — and 118 depth-charges.

To the uninitiated these technicalities are probably of little meaning. In simple terms, *Virtue* had been shorn of almost all offensive capability, no longer a fanged ocean greyhound bred for savage pursuit but a slower-plodding sheepdog in which stamina, watchfulness and patience were more desirable qualities. But the sheepdog could still bite.

What of the men who crewed *Virtue*?

The Navy's lower-deck strength was mixed in origin.

The hard core was the peacetime regular service of men serving seven-, twelve- or twenty-one-year engagements, well trained and experienced. Some of them had enlisted to escape unemployment during the early thirties, had become quickly disillusioned, and waited only for the day they would achieve their discharge. For them the war had imposed a viciously unjust extension of a penal existence. Others had adapted more philosophically and had re-engaged after completing their initial engagements. All of them, however, referred to themselves as 'Active Service' ratings.

These were supplemented by recalled reservists, many of middle-age, who had hoped their seafaring days to be over but now had to resume a spartan regimen for which they were often physically unfitted. Next were the men of the Royal Naval Reserve and the Royal Naval Volunteer Reserve, the first being trawlermen and merchant seamen who, if undrilled, contributed valuable experience. The second were amateurs with more enthusiasm than expertise, referred to as 'Saturday Night Sailors', but who generally adapted quickly and with good humour.

The most massive reinforcement in manpower, however, involved the 'HO' — the 'Hostilities Only' rating, the product of national conscription.

It would be untrue to suggest that many HOs accepted their compulsory commitment with any emotion other than resignation. They came from every conceivable background, from the slums of Glasgow and the clubs of St James's, the industrial towns and the green shires. For most, the Navy was the last career they would have chosen, and they had not chosen it now. They could not guess what was expected of them and, for almost all, the messdeck was a shuddering experience.

Someone once said that the Navy's wartime role consisted of 'periods of intense monotony alleviated by moments of intense excitement', but this is true only if the word 'monotony' is understood to mean week after week of heaving green sea, bitter cold and stinging rain, debilitating fatigue, poor food and cramped quarters. Soldiers and airmen, whilst their locations may have been remote and their duties arduous, usually had the consolation of a NAAFI canteen and similar off-duty distractions, and respite, even if brief, from a war environment. They were seldom long separated from civilian influences and those warming glimpses of domesticity without which values become blurred, language coarsens, and mental processes become locked into formalised channels.

The sailor was a member of a small, closely quarantined, all-male community and, whether or not he cared for his fellows, he could never escape from them, never enjoy a few moments of solitude, never be free of noise and motion; for every minute of his day and night the ship's engines throbbed, generators hummed, the deck under his feet was never still. He performed his personal ablutions without benefit of privacy, and his most intimate possessions must be revealed to common gaze. Nothing could be held hidden; even the letters he wrote were scrutinised. For the newcomer, the exposing familiarity of Naval life was punishing, but mercifully his more sensitive instincts soon became blunted, and he cared progressively less.

A few weeks of bullying by Gunners' Mates could not make seamen out of clerks, labourers and bus-drivers, and many HOs never did become seamen. However, they brought new logic, different perspectives, to a Navy which justified many of its procedures only by the fact that they had always been done that way and nobody had considered an alternative. Some HOs became officers and made invaluable contributions in technical fields.

There was yet another source of manpower, small but significant. The war was not going to last for ever and, the Admiralty determined, there must be laid the foundations of a post-war Navy, as drilled and polished as the old order. One day, even if distant, there would again be Spithead reviews, gleaming brass, Royal Marine bands on the quarterdeck, Mediterranean cruises, immaculate uniforms, and all the practised pomp and ritual that had made the Royal Navy a thing of awesome beauty and the darling of the British public. For this reason the enlistment of boys was continued.

Entry was open to boys of good character from the ages of 15 years and 3 months to 16 years and 6 months, the engagement being for twelve years of man's service, which commenced at eighteen. Thus many youngsters, anxious to be seen in uniform in a predominantly uniformed world, committed themselves to upwards of fourteen years' service with hardly a thought for the consequences. They either survived to curse their impetuosity or were killed before achieving, or barely achieving, manhood.

Boys' Service training was carried out in HMS *Ganges*, Shotley, near Harwich – in Naval terminology a 'stone frigate' – until the establishment's vulnerable location was abandoned for another on the Isle of Man. This was HMS *St George* – in happier days Cunningham's Holiday Camp, but now stripped of all frivolities and as bleak and austere as only the Navy could make anything. Long terraces of flimsy, single-room chalets accommodated a thousand boys segregated into eight divisions, each division embodying several classes of varying seniority. Divisional titles were Anson, Benbow, Collingwood, Drake, Exmouth, Frobisher, Grenville and Howe.

The nominal commander of HMS *St George* was a superannuated commodore who, however, was seen only at Sunday Divisions or periodically by more serious defaulters; only the commodore could order corporal punishment.

Executive command was exercised by a commander, subordinate to whom were the divisional officers, all lieutenant-commanders, while at a more intimate level were the instructors, chief petty officers, who had not been chosen for either tolerance or intellect, and whose attitudes towards their charges were uncompromising, unfeeling, and occasionally little short of brutal.

For the officers, Boys' Training was a backwater in which their careers would stagnate, and the appointment was often a penalty for some act of inadequacy, or conduct not quite becoming. Their interest was therefore superficial; they delegated supervision to the instructors and turned a blind eye towards levels of oppression that would not have been tolerated in a school of correction.

This is not to say that the boys were submissively innocent of any delinquency. They came, in the beginning, from two distinctly different backgrounds. Roughly half were 'ship boys', which meant that they were from orphanages and training ships, such as *Arethusa*, and had been off-loaded on to the Navy at the earliest permissible age. They were thus comparatively juvenile and with only a vague knowledge of the world beyond their orphanage gates, yet familiar with an institutional way of life and less critical of circumstances. The other half had enlisted from normal civilian life, and most were a year or more older — a significant margin in this age group. Most, too, had experienced employment and had earned two or three pounds a week. Some boasted of sexual experiences, had a taste for tobacco; they included a sprinkling of grammar-school boys, occasionally officers' sons. The gap between these two groups, in the beginning, was wide, and some distinctions never disappeared but, during the fourteen or sixteen months that followed, the gap narrowed until, on completion of training, it was scarcely perceptible.

New intakes of boys, at four-monthly intervals, were referred to disdainfully as 'Nozzers' and considered distinctly inferior by their seniors. For their first five weeks they were strictly quarantined from the main establishment, and during this period had heads shorn, were medically and dentally tormented, inoculated, vaccinated, taught rudimentary drill movements and the requirements of a confusion of pipes and bugle calls, and introduced to icy communal showers, a rope's end, and a baffling list of punishable offences. In all too brief leisure moments each sewed his full name into sixty-one items of uniform kit — a tolerable task for a Lee or a Hay, but a swingeing one for a Montgomery or a Wigglesworth.

Launched at last into the main stream of training activity, he discovered that he was a Boy 2nd Class, and his pay was 5s 3d per week. Of this, however, he would

15

receive only one shilling; the balance was retained 'in credit', to accumulate, subject to deductions by Authority to cover breakages, boot repairs, haircuts, and items of lost or stolen kit. The final diminutive residue could be drawn upon only when proceeding on home leave — three times a year. With the shilling in his hand he must provide himself with a modicum of toiletry necessaries, a postage stamp if he had someone to write to, and provide for 'going ashore'; he was permitted an afternoon's freedom three times a fortnight and on return was thoroughly searched for forbidden purchases.

He was forbidden to smoke, to be tattooed, to wear a ring, a watch, or any item not of service issue, to have hair longer than one inch, to use obscene language, to be out of bed after 9 p.m., or in bed after 6 a.m. He must never walk within the boundaries of the establishment, but always trot. Every minute of his day was occupied; he climbed, vaulted, rowed, boxed, drilled, swam, hauled guns, spliced ropes, hoisted flags, flashed signal lamps, heaved lines, washed and darned his clothes, wolfed his food and was always hungry. He became a Boy 1st Class with his pay increased to 8s 9d, which meant an extra sixpence weekly, placed on his proffered cap. He broadened, hardened, developed cunning, fought a continuous war of subterfuge and evasion against the instructors and, when he was out-manoeuvred, retribution was vicious.

For lesser offences, Punishment No. 10a, imposed for seven or fourteen days, entailed loss of both pay and shore leave, and a necessity to report to the Regulating Office at numerous, inconvenient times each day. This regimen was included in the more demanding Punishment No. 8a, but which also required defaulters to be double-marched on the parade-ground for one hour daily, each with a rifle held aloft — a gruelling penance that was not halted on occasions of physical collapse.

Finally, for more serious offences, of which smoking was the commonest, a boy was ordered twelve 'cuts' applied to the buttocks by a heavy cane in the hands of a detested 'crusher' — a regulating petty officer — and supervised by an officer. Prior examination by a surgeon was required to assess the defaulter's fitness; the cuts left the buttocks blackly bruised, scored and often bleeding. Prostration was not uncommon.

The beau idéal upon which all Naval boys were expected to pattern themselves was John Travers Cornwell, Boy 1st Class, aged sixteen, who had died at his gun at Jutland and earned a posthumous Victoria Cross, and there were men still serving who could tell of Jackie Fisher and Jellicoe, of coal-burning ships, Zeebrugge, the Harwich Force and the Dardanelles. They had medal ribbons to prove it and grim stories to share, but in a quarter-century there had emerged a range of new weapons — radar, asdic, radio location, acoustic mines, long-range aircraft and the submarine wolf-pack — which had made sea warfare infinitely more complex, more diabolically scientific.

Only the men of the lower deck, from whatever background, had changed little. They experienced the same emotions — fear, love, hate, homesickness, moments of happiness and moments of despair. Sometimes they got drunk, brawled, blasphemed; often they laughed, occasionally they cried.

The Tinfish Run

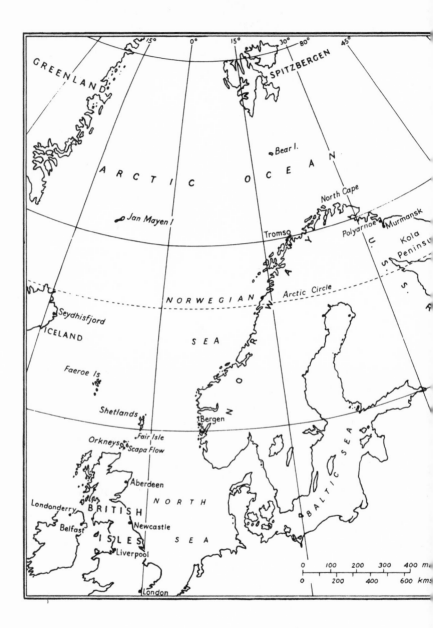

One

Aft of the bridge of the destroyer *Virtue*, Ordinary Signalman Ludd wiped his nose on the back of a gloved hand. He clung to the flag locker as the ship wallowed in a long swell, and wanted to be sick. It was June in the year 1942, but he was chilled to the bone; he was also tired, apprehensive, and eighteen years old. Somewhere beyond the see-sawing, rain-hazed horizon to the northward was Iceland. Not that he cared. At the moment he wanted nothing but the conclusion of the forenoon watch, the stale warmth of the messdeck, and a hour of delicious oblivion in the hammock netting.

'What yer looking for, Ludd,' the Yeoman of Signals had told him, 'is another destroyer like this'n — the *Vagrant* — two escort trawlers, and a Flower Class corvette, the *Pennyroyal* — so keep yer eyes skinned.' Ludd's eyes felt as if they had already been skinned. Yeoman Shaw lowered his voice. 'The Old Man don't like being challenged first, see, but the *Pennyroyal*'s got radar and she'll have our bearing long before we're visual.' Who saw what first was a matter of complete indifference to Ludd, but if it was important to Commander Hayes-Mailer, who sat in his high swivel chair on the bridge with binoculars raised, then presumably he, Ludd, ought to give some thought to it.

'All right,' the Yeoman concluded. Almost everything he said was prefixed by a preparatory 'all right'. 'I'm jes' going below, boyo, for the last met. report—' For his rum, Ludd guessed, and cringed at the thought. *Virtue*'s bows plunged sickeningly, and the sea exploded over a deserted fo'c'sle deck. Jesus Christ.

Ordinary Signalman Ludd had been at sea for only six days; it had been long enough to shatter his illusions. A destroyer, the Drafting Office in Devonport had told him — a pierhead jump from Liverpool — and they had grinned at each other knowingly. He had shrugged, feigned nonchalance, but had been secretly pleased. His earlier companions had been drafted to battleships and heavy cruisers, which were reputedly nothing more than floating barracks. A destroyer, now, was something different. He had experienced a moment of disappointment at discovering that the ship he was to join carried the innocent name of *Virtue*; he would have preferred a *Bulldog* or a *Panther*, but one couldn't have everything.

It might have been different had it not been for that outrageous last night in Liverpool, into which he had been led like a lamb to slaughter. He had barely lowered his hammock from his shoulder when a figure had raised itself from a mess-stool. 'Ludd? Bleedin' shave off.' There was a chuckle. 'Yer Lobby Ludd, an' I claim the *News Chronicle* prize!' Another chuckle, then, 'Did they pay yer in Depot before yer left, Lobby?' Telegraphist Bungy Williams had uncoiled from his seat speculatively. 'Yer from Walham Green? *Walham Green*? Shave off. Yer a townie o' mine.' He paused. 'Well, nearly.' Bungy

Williams leaned forward confidentially. 'I've got these two parties lined up ashore, see. A couple o' *crackers*, an' if we play our cards right—' He winked. 'Tonight's our last run, see—'

Ludd had been flattered; such camaraderie was overwhelming. This was the Navy all right. All for one and one for all. Bungy Williams had turned from his locker. 'Have yer got a clean collar yer can lend me, Lobby?'

Almost dead ahead, from a horizon lost in greyness, a light blinked, rising and falling over *Virtue*'s bows. Lobby Ludd choked, reached for the Aldis lamp. 'Challenge, sir— Freddie King—'

That's right, he seethed. When it *happened*, the soddin' Yeoman was below, drinking his bleedin' tot.

The Commander grunted. 'Very good. Answer him.' He turned to the officer at his side, similarly duffel-coated. 'I'll give odds it's *Pennyroyal*, and she's had us on her screen for the past hour. Campbell's a fool, chancing his arm before we're visual.' The time of rendezvous and the approximate direction of *Virtue* would be known to *Pennyroyal*, and the little fluorescent blotch on the radar screen, closing steadily, could hardly have been anything else but the expected destroyer. But it might, just might, have been something else. Hayes-Mailer's annoyance was reinforced by envy; *Pennyroyal* had radar and *Virtue* had not. The still invisible corvette, new from Harland & Wolff only the previous year, had been installed with prototype equipment for trials purposes off Northern Ireland and had subsequently been permitted to retain it. 'I must have a word with that young man,' Hayes-Mailer decided. 'He's a bit too damn keen.'

His companion nodded without comment, then moved to a voice-pipe. 'Half-ahead on both, Coxswain. How is she steering?'

Echo-like, from the voice-pipe, came the chang-chang of the telegraphs and then the Coxswain's voice. 'Half-ahead, sir, steering three-five-oh. She's a bit lively, sir, but nothin' *extortionate*.' The First Lieutenant grinned and moved away. 'If *Pennyroyal*'s where she ought to be, sir, we should be under the lee of Bardhsneshorn in half an hour.' Hidden by John Rainbird's duffel-coat a thin gold ring shone newly between two tarnished ones on each cuff, the result of some hurried tailoring in Liverpool. As a lieutenant-commander, he might have expected to be standing on the bridge of his own ship, but recent events had moved too quickly, and *Virtue*'s assignment had been infinitely more urgent than the reappointment of one officer.

The Commander climbed down from his chair, stiffly, yawning. Hayes-Mailer was tall, lean, slightly stoop-shouldered, and showed every day of his forty-two years. 'When we've secured, Number One,' he said, 'reduce dutymen to a minimum and pipe make and mend.' He turned. 'Yeoman—?'

Lobby Ludd groaned. Every bleedin' time—

But the Yeoman had reappeared, without a met. report, breathing rum fumes. 'Sir?'

'Ah, Yeoman. We shall be in company in a few minutes. Make to *Vagrant, Pennyroyal, Trooper* and *Truelove*: "Ships may send boats for mail as soon as I have anchored. Commanding officers will report aboard *Virtue* at sixteen-thirty for briefing. Thanks in advance for bottle of gin each will bring with him. Saccone & Speed in Liverpool bombed." That's all.' He reached into a pocket for a battered cigarette-case. 'By the way, Yeoman — is the Coxswain still wearing his flying-boots?'

They had been steaming northwards across the Firth of Clyde when they had hauled in the floating corpse. It had been that of an RAF flying officer, in a half-inflated life-jacket, but the body had been long in the water, and both face and ungloved hands had been eaten to the bone by fish. There was nothing to be done but the removal of an identity disc, a stitching into canvas — for which the Coxswain volunteered — and a rapid reburial.

The airman, however, had been wearing a pair of fine, fur-lined boots. True, they were sodden, conceded the Coxswain, but that was a matter of small consequence. It would be tragic to bury a pair of fur-lined boots. . . .

When the Coxswain, Bogey Knight, pulled the boots from the corpse, the sea-rotted feet came away with them. It was an added complication, but, undismayed, Bogey flushed out his acquisitions with a hose, placed them in the galley for drying, and on the following day was wearing them.

'Yer jammy bastard, Lobby,' snorted Signalman House, the disgruntled afternoon watchman whom other mess-mates addressed as 'Shit' — a pseudonym that Lobby Ludd did not yet feel sufficiently well acquainted to use. 'A bloody make an' mend, man! Would tha soddin' believe it!' He sniffed, shrugged himself deeper into his duffel-hood. 'Anyway, it's bangers an' mash, an' Chinese wedding-cake.' He eyed the bridge morosely. 'One day,' he promised, 'I'm goin' to bloddy say somethin'!'

* * *

Commander Norman Hayes-Mailer addressed himself to a wardroom that was wreathed with tobacco smoke and closely thronged with officers, including the commanders of the four warships in company.

'Gentlemen. It will be painfully evident that the Admiralty scraped the bottom of a very empty barrel when they mustered this rag-bag of a convoy escort — two over-age destroyers, two trawlers and a corvette, with only one radar installation between the five, to get us through to Murmansk. And the hunting and shooting season has already started.'

He's worth better than this, John Rainbird thought, watching his senior. Hayes-Mailer was a fine seaman, a superb navigator; he had once confided that he had been a midshipman in *Malaya* when the German High Seas Fleet had surrendered in 1918, and had drawn his first cask of pickled tongues — the traditional privilege on assuming command of a destroyer — at the age of twenty-four. Then something had gone wrong. It had been something to do with a collision on the China Station during the twenties. There had been a court of enquiry, but John Rainbird had never followed up the story. Now most of Hayes-Mailer's age-group were senior captains and several were flag officers. At least one sat in Whitehall, manipulating hundreds of warships like pawns on a vast chessboard. Hayes-Mailer, the brightest of his Dartmouth class, commanded a broken-winded destroyer and had the temporary supervision of four other vessels which were among the least important and the most readily expendable in the Navy.

'You'll forgive me, I know, if I quickly review a few facts of which you may already be aware.' He smiled wryly. 'Let's take the worst first. *Tirpitz* has been joined at Trondheim by *Admiral Hipper*, while the two pocket battleships *Lützow* and *Admiral Scheer* are at Narvik. Any one of these is capable of tearing our little lot to scrap iron in a few minutes, using only secondary armament. They are accompanied by a half-dozen large destroyers.'

He paused. 'The Eleventh U-boat Flotilla, of about a dozen boats, is based on Bergen, and the Fifth Luftflotte has more than 300 aircraft deployed between the airfields at Bardufoss — between Narvik and Tromso — and Banak, just east of North Cape.' He toyed momentarily with the sheaf of papers in his hand.

Lieutenant-Commander Campbell, commanding *Pennyroyal*, with long blond hair that irritated Hayes-Mailer for reasons that had nothing to do with long blond hair, reached for his pink gin and said, 'Hot shit,' then laughed. Nobody else did.

Hayes-Mailer frowned, went on. 'The met. forecast says probably bad weather, and that's good. It'll ground enemy aircraft and make U-boat attacks difficult. But in case you don't know, Campbell' — the Commander looked up — 'bad weather north of the Faeroes is *bloody awful* weather.' Campbell grinned, unabashed. He was a Western Approaches man. These Arctic salt-horse sailors thought they had seen it all.

'I don't have to tell you that "V and W" boats weren't built for long periods of bad weather. The trawlers are better sea-boats, but they're still a rough ride. Their major deficiency is a top speed of only eleven knots, and that means we can't shake off enemy submarines that are tracking on the surface. In short, we can't run from anything.

'All right, that's the worst of it. As for the rest —

well, for a beginning we're carrying only four passengers.' Several faces jerked towards him, and he nodded. 'That's right — the four merchantmen now anchored in Seydhisfjord — a nicely balanced quartet, two tankers and two freighters, and all big.'

Roper, of *Vagrant*, interrupted. 'Why the hell weren't they—?'

'Why weren't they with PQ17, which left hereabouts a few days ago? They ought to have been, but they missed it. One ran aground while getting away from Reykjavik and had to be hauled off. Another had storm damage. The third had engine trouble, and the fourth had suspected typhoid on board which turned out to be nothing. Anyway, it was obvious a fortnight ago that they would not sail with PQ17, and so my Lords have dumped them into our laps.'

Hayes-Mailer allowed a few seconds for his words to be digested, then resumed. 'Before anyone asks why they can't be delayed until the next scheduled convoy, I'll tell you. First, the Russians are getting nasty minded. They don't believe our reports of convoy losses; they claim we simply don't send the ships in the first place. Mind you, Russian submarines have already sunk more battleships than the German Navy ever had, but we don't talk about that. However, the PQ17 escort is convoying thirty-three vessels. There ought to have been thirty-seven, which will give our Russian friends a little more fuel for criticism. Also, after the *next* convoy, PQ18 in September, there won't be another to Russia for three months. Priority is being given to North Africa, which will make the Russians even more hopping mad. That's why Whitehall has decided to gamble a few clapped-out scows in getting these four cargoes through.'

The expression on Campbell's face plainly indicated his resentment at hearing his almost new *Pennyroyal* described as a clapped-out scow, but he said nothing. The two trawler officers said nothing because they were considerably the junior of the five commanders. Roper puffed on a monstrous pipe, eyed the glowing bowl closely, then shrugged. 'This is *Boys' Own Paper* stuff. I didn't think that even Whitehall could have come up with anything so bloody stupid. It's the wrong season for playing silly buggers, Norman' — he had known the Commander long enough for the privilege — 'and if we're jumped, nothing — *absolutely nothing* — can save us from being slaughtered. By Christ, we'd better pray for bad weather like we've never prayed before.'

'We-ell—' Hayes-Mailer fumbled for the cigarette-case that looked as if it had been clenched in a watertight door. 'There's another factor — which is why we're discussing business here instead of around a polished table in Reykjavik. We have a few doubts about Icelandic security.' He selected a cigarette as carefully as he might a Havana cigar. 'In April, PQ13 lost five out of thirteen ships. Nearly two months ago — May — PQ16 lost seven out of thirty-four, which wasn't too bad as losses go. But the Germans are on their toes, and they'll pull everything out of the bag for PQ17. Perhaps they've already begun. And the Admiralty had brought out the best china. Just listen. PQ17's close escort consists of six destroyers, two anti-aircraft ships, two submarines and eleven trawlers, minesweepers and corvettes. Four heavy cruisers under Dalrymple-Hamilton are a hundred miles ahead of the convoy — and that's not all. On 29 June Admiral Tovey left Scapa Flow with *Duke of York,*

Victorious, the American battleship *Washington*, three cruisers and a clutch of destroyers to cover the convoy as far as Bear Island. In addition, nine submarines are deployed north-west of North Cape, and we understand that four or five Russian submarines are stationed off the fjords in which the German heavies are anchored.' He paused. 'In any language, gentlemen, that's something.'

There were several low whistles, and again Hayes-Mailer took time to allow his listeners to formulate a mental picture of the vast Naval forces that were being jockeyed into position to the far northward and, by comparison, the insignificance of the little collection of ships off Seydhisfjord. Campbell sat up, suddenly attentive, and the two trawler commanders glanced at each other. This was something beyond the humble world of trawlers.

'That's right,' the Commander nodded. 'Big stuff. It means that, weather conditions permitting, the Germans will have all their attention drawn towards the big parade, and their resources are not unlimited. God forbid that PQ17 should get hammered, but it is unlikely to get through scot free. Hopefully, the Germans will never dream that a few days behind the Lord Mayor's Show there's a dung-cart. But I think we ought to understand that the four ships we're escorting aren't just small fry. They're all above 15,000 tons. In case you don't already know, the two tankers are both American, each loading about three million gallons of aviation spirit; the two freighters are British, carrying tanks, crated aircraft, and ammunition. There's a lot of material in those four bottoms that we can't afford to lose, and it has already been pointed out to me that any of them is more valuable than any of us.

'There's no time to waste if we are to hang on to PQ17's coat-tails. We shall slip at 0430 tomorrow, which will mean a decent night's sleep for most of us. I suggest you close mails at 2000 tonight. I'll ask for a drifter from Seydhisfjord to pick them up — and anything else you want to leave behind, excluding yourselves, of course.' He smiled. 'Now' — he folded his papers neatly — 'my Number One will read you the usual bill of fare. There'll be a copy for you each to take with you, but we'll run through it, just in case there are any queries.'

John Rainbird cleared his throat. 'Gentlemen. The merchant ships will proceed in two divisions of two, astern of *Trooper* and *Truelove* respectively, while *Pennyroyal* will take station ahead and assume radar guard for the convoy. *Virtue* and *Vagrant* will be stationed on the port and starboard quarters respectively of the rearmost merchantmen. Being the fastest escorts, they can overtake the convoy if necessary and no time will be wasted in turning.' He lifted a sheet of paper. 'Here is a sketch for each of you, with bearings and distances, also the convoy route with its alterations of course, and times.

'All components of the escort will maintain continuous asdic watch. Contacts should be reported by light, and by convoy R/T only if light is impracticable. There will be strict W/T silence, the usual exceptions prevailing. All ships will maintain watch on broadcast BN and convoy R/T, and hold transmitters on appropriate ship—shore H/F frequencies. If R/T has to be used, it will be on minimum power.' He drew breath. 'This is all routine procedure, gentlemen; your telegraphists will find nothing unusual in it.

'Speed ten knots unless otherwise ordered. That will allow us an extra onion if we need it — although eleven knots won't make much difference. In the event of a ship being disabled, escorts will not, repeat not, stop for survivors without the permission of the Senior Officer. It is not expected that we shall stream paravanes, or zig-zag, but you have your tables. I am sure it is not necessary to remind you about lights, the disposal of refuse, excessive smoke, the necessity for maintaining station, the need for keeping upperworks free of excessive ice and for keeping machinery active if the temperature is sub-zero. It is assumed that you are all fully fuelled, and in all respects ready for sea.' He sat down. It hadn't exactly been an impressive delivery. He might have thrown in a few fighting platitudes, like Noël Coward always did. He thought of them before and afterwards, never at the time.

They sat silently for several seconds. Roper unscrewed the stem of his pipe and blew down it. One of the trawler officers cleared his nose loudly into his handkerchief and then glanced around apologetically. 'Sir,' he said. 'Casualties. We only carry a Sick Berth Attendant.'

Rainbird looked towards Hayes-Mailer. The Commander nodded. 'If circumstances permit, you can transfer casualties to *Virtue, Vagrant* or *Pennyroyal*, if necessary by jackstay, or alternatively one of these will transfer a surgeon to you. But the rule that applies to survivors applies equally to casualties. I cannot allow a ship to be endangered by reducing speed or stopping. Your SBAs may have to do what they can without our help.' Hayes-Mailer's eyes lingered on the face of his questioner. 'You're Lieutenant Furloe, aren't you? Of *Truelove?*'

'Yes, sir.'

'Any relation to Vice-Admiral George Furloe?'

'Yes, sir. He's my father.'

Rainbird saw the Commander's face tauten very slightly. 'And your father is well?'

'Thank you, yes, sir. Retired, of course, a bit hard of hearing, and needing a stick. He writes bloodthirsty letters to *The Times*, which they never print.'

Hayes-Mailer rose to his feet as if the brief exchange had never occurred. 'Well, gentlemen, if there are no more questions, perhaps you'll take another drink?'

Once again, Roper seemed to be exuding smoke from every pore. 'Congratulations on that half-ring, young Rainbird.' He chuckled. 'As I get older, lieutenant-commanders get younger and younger, like bloody policemen. You must be on top line for a compass platform of your own, eh? Those new "M" Class boats, now — they're something that destroyer sailors always dream about but never get. Six four-point-sevens in twin turrets, eight tubes, four pom-poms — 48,000 shaft horse-power and 36 knots. Two thousand tons of murderous steel!' He chuckled again. 'But, best of all, I hear the wardroom has a lie-down bath. What joy, what bliss!'

'What he means, Number One,' the Commander levelled a finger, 'is that with a lie-down bath he wouldn't have to put his pipe out.'

The address system shrieked. It was 4 a.m.

'D'ye hear there? Morning watchmen and sea-duty men close up. Secure all scuttles and watertight doors.

Ship will assume first state of readiness.'

In messdecks and passageways men lashed hammocks that would not be slept in again for the next two weeks, during which time few men would enjoy an opportunity to undress. They would snatch hours, even minutes, of sleep on lockers and mess-stools, in corners and against bulkheads, insensible to noise, motion, and feet that trod around them. Men who had duties on the upper deck – gun crews, lookouts, signalmen – had donned red-glass goggles ten minutes before leaving the light of the messdecks, so that their eyes would require no period of attunement in the blackness above. The fo'c'sle party and the sub-lieutenant, who only a year before had been a schoolteacher in Basingstoke, were already on deck, shivering against a cutting wind, stamping, swinging their arms, swearing. Communications were being tested, and the galley chimney vomited a sudden plume of sooty smoke that would soon attract the indignant attention of the First Lieutenant. Below, men pulled on seaboots, struggled into duffel-coats, balaclava helmets, mitts, took a last, surreptitious draw on a cigarette in a cupped hand. Others – stokers, telegraphists, artificers, damage-control men – groped their way aft, descended ladders, burrowed like moles into dozens of obscure and cramped steel crannies in which they would remain incarcerated for the next four hours. Underfoot, the decks were vibrating.

Hayes-Mailer turned from the wheelhouse voice-pipe. 'We'll let *Pennyroyal* and the trawlers get clear, Number One, then latch on to the starboard quarter of *Brazos River*. When we've settled down – say 0900 – we'll go to exercise action stations.' He hummed tunelessly for a few seconds, and then, 'If you'd like to go below for coffee, Number One—?'

Rainbird was aware of the Commander's dislike of sharing occupancy of the bridge, to where off-duty officers were tempted to gravitate, to use it as a vantage-point when something of interest was happening. Hayes-Mailer tolerated his watch-keeping personnel, but the platform was too small to accommodate 'goofers', whatever their rank, and on occasions he had said so in a loud voice.

'Thank you, sir.' Rainbird hesitated. 'The fact is, it's my morning watch, sir.'

The Commander glared, grunted. 'Ah — yes, of course.'

On the flag-deck, Lobby Ludd watched *Pennyroyal*, *Trooper* and *Truelove* move slowly to seaward — *Pennyroyal*, with foremast radar scanner revolving, unable to resist flashing, 'Good morning. Nothing like being up early for a brisk stroll, I always say,' which, the Yeoman predicted, would have the same effect on the Commander as a large dose of salts. Idling, *Virtue* and *Vagrant* turned in wide circles, heeling drunkenly as they met a broadside sea, waiting for the merchant ships to emerge from Seydhisfjord. They came at last, darkened, the freighters *Empire Mandate* and *Chessington*, the two long tankers *Brazos River* and *Olympic Madison*, so low in the water that their midship freeboards were only just visible in the half-light. Following them with a glass, they seemed to Lobby Ludd to be completely deserted of life; there was a gun on each stern, but none seemed to be manned.

He turned the telescope towards *Vagrant*, almost a mile inshore. It was odd, he realised, how seldom a sailor saw his own ship in its entirety, as others saw her.

Except for her camouflage, *Vagrant* was identical to *Virtue* — a slim, low-profiled shape with two funnels, the foremost of which was the taller, narrow 'Woodbine funnel' common to all pre-1918 destroyers. 'When I was in the *Veteran*,' Stripey Albright had assured the mess, 'we did thirty-five knots an' no bother. That was in the Med, in '31. Soddin' hard times, mate. Metal polish? No such thing as metal polish. Bleedin' brick dust an' petrol, that's wot.'

'And yer wore pigtails,' said Bungy Williams.

The other destroyer, still circling, had passed temporarily to starboard, with her bows lifting as she dug her screws deep. It was peculiar, Lobby Ludd mused. Soddin' peculiar. There must be a thousand ships in the Navy, but the one he was looking at was *Vagrant*.

L/Sea W. Ludd, 4 Mess, HMS Vagrant, c/o GPO London.

It was soddin' peculiar.

Within an hour his extremities were aching with cold. There was an increasing north-easterly wind, with flurries of snow and sleet that periodically reduced visibility to a half-mile and obscured from view all but *Brazos River*, ahead and to port. His woollen balaclava, pulled up to cover mouth and nose, was wet, and his face itched; the augmented clothing he wore seemed totally inadequate; the cold insinuated determinedly into the tops of boots, climbed cuffs, and his exposed upper face was like icy marble, numbed.

'All right,' Yeoman Shaw said. 'Ludd, you can nip into the BWO for five minutes, 'ave a cup of kye and a smoke. Five minutes. All right? Don't stay there all bleedin' day, nattering to the sparker.'

The Bridge Wireless Office was a tiny compartment, barely larger than a wardrobe, just aft of the compass platform, from which, in more normal times, manoeuvring by W/T was carried out. It now housed a single operator keeping watch on the convoy R/T frequency; other telegraphists and coders were located in the Main W/T Office, below deck.

As Lobby Ludd entered, he was immediately enveloped by intense, exquisite warmth. The air was smokily opaque. 'Shave off,' Bungy Williams snorted. 'Shut that bleedin' door. Was yer born in a field? Ah — wotcher, me ol' Lobby.' He waved expansively towards a large aluminium jug filled with steaming cocoa. ' 'Ave some kye. I've been keeping it 'ot on the 'eater for yer.' He winked. 'A drop o' strongers.'

Strong was an understatement. The cocoa was like liquid mud, clogging the teeth, painfully sweet and scalding — but it was marvellous. Lobby Ludd clenched his hands gratefully around the hot, dirty cup.

On the bulkhead, above a B28 receiver, a loudspeaker was hissing gently. The hiss turned into a thin, metallic voice.

'Bandstand, Bandstand — this is Scipio. Stand by to alter course together, forty degrees to starboard. Stand by — stand by — Execute!'

Bungy Williams' bovine expression had disappeared. He had pulled his headphones over his ears as his pencil wrote simultaneously. Then, with one movement, he tore the top leaf from the signal pad and half-rose towards a voice-pipe. 'BWO to Bridge. Intercept from PQ17.'

Immediately, magically, a small panel in the bulkhead slammed open. A gloved hand, which Lobby Ludd recognised as the Yeoman's, appeared from limbo and plucked the signal from Bungy Williams' fingers. A voice snapped, 'Ludd! I said *not* all bleedin' day. All right?' Bungy Williams, who owed the Yeoman no deference, rammed the panel shut to forbid further entrance of cold air. 'Ignorant bastard,' he sniffed, and began to roll a cigarette. Lobby Ludd had regained nonchalance. 'Was that' — he nodded towards the loudspeaker — 'anything to do with us?'

Bungy Williams ran the tip of his tongue expertly along the slim cylinder in his stained fingers. 'PQ17's convoy R/T,' he explained. ' 'Undred miles ahead. Same frequency. It ain't supposed to carry that distance, but it does sometimes — freakish, like.' He reminisced. 'I remember picking up a bloke, a radio ham, in Saigon, when I was on exercise wave in Scapa Flow. Anyway' — he pinched excess tobacco from the extremities of his cigarette — 'we're only getting PQ17's close escort commander — that's *Keppel*. They're getting shamfered — torpedo-bomber attacks, it looks like.' He frowned at the modest contents of his tobacco tin. 'Did yer bring any tickler up with yer, Lobby? I'm gettin' a bit low. I reckon the bleedin' mice roll their own up 'ere while I'm not lookin'.'

With the unerring perception of a beagle, Bungy Williams had located their quarries as soon as they entered the crowded Liverpool bar. 'That's them,' he confided, speaking from the corner of his mouth. 'Yours is the one with the tiddley ear-rings.' He nudged his partner. 'Looks like she's got legs right up to her arse. You lucky sod.' He pushed his cap to the back of his head. 'I'll go and chat them up while you get the beer,

Lobby. Pints. An' it looks like they're drinking gin. Better make it a couple o' doubles.'

The two women greeted the arrival of large gins with shrill cries of simulated consternation, which Bungy Williams waved aside loftily. It was fortunate in the extreme that Lobby Ludd had drawn the balance of his credit, with a fortnight's pay, only two days earlier in Devonport, and had spent little since. Bungy Williams ordered more gins, Lobby Ludd paid, and the women giggled.

This, Lobby Ludd decided, was really living. Proceedings, for the moment, consisted of a rapid interplay of conversation between Bungy Williams and the women, of repartee and innuendo, punctuated by shrieks of 'You sailors!' and which seemed to be following a pattern that all three recognised. Much of it was beyond Lobby Ludd's comprehension, but several pints of beer had generated a glow of *bonhomie* within him and, anyway, one couldn't expect everything at once. He laughed, knowingly, when the others laughed, and paid for more gin.

Feigning indifference, an appreciable time elapsed before he managed to take stock of the woman with the tiddley ear-rings who, apparently, was his assigned consort. Sober, he would not have been enamoured. She was every day of thirty-five and probably nearer forty, with big breasts under a summer dress which, as Bungy Williams had observed, revealed more of her legs than might have been considered modest. Still, he conceded, compensating, she had passable teeth, well-kept hair and manicured hands. She wore a wedding-ring.

Some sixth sense warned her of his startled glance. She smiled and wrinkled her nose. 'That's right, luv, and

I know all about sailors.' She giggled mechanically. 'Many's the time I've touched a sailor's dickie, just for luck.' The other woman exploded with mirth, interrupting Bungy Williams' *risqué* story about a golden rivet. When a ship was built, he assured them, the very last rivet was of solid gold. That's right — every ship. And the golden rivet was something that newly joined seaman boys were always taken to see. It was unfortunately in an unfrequented, obscure location, and it was necessary for the unsuspecting boy to bend over to see it clearly—

His listeners squealed. 'If someone showed *me* his golden rivet, luv,' Lobby Ludd's companion confided, 'I'd bend over.' Lobby, to mask his confusion, departed to order two pints and two double gins.

When he returned, she had moved her chair noticeably nearer to his. 'I'm Dolores,' she told him, with slight difficulty. She had told him before, but had apparently forgotten. 'And that's Gloria.' She nodded across the table. Bungy Williams and Gloria had also moved closer together, and Lobby Ludd understood vaguely why Bungy's hand had vanished from sight and Gloria's face was flushed.

'My husband,' Dolores resumed, 'is a Royal Marine.' She hiccuped and put a genteel hand over her mouth. 'He was called back.' Her leg was warmly against his, but his uncertainty had dissolved; he was beginning to feel wonderfully confident. He knew exactly what was happening. This was living. He lowered his own hand, casually. Dolores pressed against him. 'Not here, luv.' She rolled her eyes meaningfully. 'It's like Lime Street Station.' But he was exhilarated. Not here. That meant somewhere else. He tried to wink across the table at

Bungy Williams, but Bungy's attention was fully occupied and Gloria was perspiring gently.

At a later time, Lobby Ludd would have only a shadowy recollection of leaving the Liverpool bar. His equilibrium had become increasingly uncertain, Bungy Williams more loquacious and the two women more discordantly responsive. Somewhere off Leeds Street they had queued in a dimly lit fish and chip shop, and Lobby had remembered the Merseyside boys at *St George* who considered that chipped potatoes should be eaten between two slices of bread, and unfailingly adhered to the principle. 'D'ye wanna chib buddie?' he slurred, and was flattered by the merriment that the witticism generated. 'A chib buddie,' he repeated, and tried to think of similarly roguish drolleries to prove that he was just as much a wag as Bungy Williams. The whole pattern of his life had suddenly become rainbow-hued; it had never before been like this, even in Walham Green. Bungy Williams launched into a song about the good ship *Venus*, whose figurehead was a woman in bed and its mast a rampant penis. It was hilarious.

He had not the slightest idea where they were, but it did not seem important. He was aware of a street of darkened houses, and that Bungy Williams and Gloria were no longer in company — undoubtedly by calculated arrangement. Dolores had unlocked a door with a latch-key, hissed him to silence. 'Just a mo', luv,' she whispered. 'The blackout.'

Moments later, however, he was blinking in the glare of electric light. Dolores regarded him coquettishly. She put a finger to her lips. 'Would you like a drop of port, luv?' He nodded, willing for anything, and she vanished, silent on stockinged feet. Lobby glanced around him.

The room's comfortable neatness was mildly intimidating. There was a double bed under a puce eiderdown, a bedside table supporting a lamp and an alarm clock, a mirrored dressing-table and a matching wardrobe. Three painted wild ducks were arrested in wing-spread flight across a wall.

Dolores had reappeared. 'It's South African Ruby,' she confided, and poured two bumper glasses. Lobby Ludd made a suitable noise and sat on the bed. It creaked accusingly.

The South African Ruby was catastrophic. The floor was sliding on its foundations and the three wild ducks were positively moving towards the wardrobe which, in turn, was elliptical in shape. Dolores peeled off her stockings, stood to push her dress over her hips, then shrugged off her bra. Her breasts seemed to explode from their confinement, white and triumphant. Guiltily, he leaned forward to unlace his shoes, and fell on his head.

The immediate sequence of events was confusing. When it was finished, he was under the puce eiderdown, groping at a naked Dolores while she groped at him. 'I knew you were after my tits,' she exulted. Her lips were wet and devouring. 'Bernard always got hard over my tits. Hard as a rock.' Her fingers assessed tentatively. 'Come on, luv!' Lobby Ludd was very anxious to come on. He had been relishing the prospect for several hours, and he agreed that Bernard had every inducement, but the bed was floating gently and oblivion was very near.

'Christ,' Dolores complained plaintively. 'You ain't going to sleep?'

'Shleep?' he managed. 'Corsh not.' His voice was the last thing he heard.

Bungy Williams transferred a major proportion of Lobby Ludd's tobacco to his own tin. 'Whacko, Lobby. I'll remember yer at Christmas.' He regarded the other benignly. 'That was a soddin' good run ashore in Liverpool, weren't it? Shave off!' He raised ecstatic eyes. 'That party I 'ad. Talk about cock-'appy. All bleedin' night! Shave off! I came back on my soddin' knees! Bleedin' marvellous!' He sighed. 'What was your'n like?'

'Bleedin' marvellous!' Lobby Ludd enthused. He shook his head, eyes narrowed. 'Never known anything like it. One more time, and I'd 'ave been flakers!'

'Ludd!' It was the Yeoman's voice. 'I'll flakers yer all right, if yer don't get back on the flag-deck, at the rush. Git them recognition lights changed. Two reds over white.'

He had awakened slowly and very painfully. His head throbbed, his mouth was foul, he shuddered with nausea. The curtains were open, and he winced. He was alone under the puce eiderdown, and from the middle of the floor, a few feet away, a girl was eyeing him sceptically.

She was thirteen or fourteen, a schoolgirl, neither child nor woman, with dark, page-boy hair, a fresh face, and a Merseyside pertness. 'So yer awake, then,' she observed. 'We don't do breakfas'. It's the maid's day orf.'

Lobby Ludd grappled for comprehension. His clothes were folded on a chair and a few notes and coins were neatly piled on the bedside table with his paybook, identity disc and a bus ticket. He remembered, and groaned.

'You look bloody awfu',' she said.

'I *feel* bloody awful.' He frowned. 'Where's Dolores?'

'Dolores?' She stared, then laughed. 'Yer mean me mum? Dolores, was it?' She shrugged. 'She's gone ter werk. When she ain't boozin' or opening 'er legs for sailors an' Americans, she werks in a canteen.' Her voice trembled with contempt. 'If my dad knew, he'd *kill* 'er.' Lobby Ludd nodded sympathetically, avoiding her accusing glare. 'My dad,' she went on, 'is a Royal Marine. He was on the *Repulse*.'

It was only later, grateful to be free of the house, that Lobby Ludd recognised what she had said. *Repulse* had been sunk off Malaya, six months before.

Two

Both Hayes-Mailer and Rainbird had attended the anti-submarine school at Portland and knew a great deal about the German Navy's under-sea craft. A U-boat had been captured intact, and experts had examined every inch of it.

U-boats operating in the North Atlantic could come from any of a number of bases, including Kiel, Bremerhaven, Brest, Lorient and St Nazaire, but those deployed in that vast icy hell that lay between the coast of Norway, Iceland and Spitzbergen were most likely to be those of the Eleventh U-boat Flotilla in Bergen, commanded by Commander Hans Eduard Cohausz.

They were ocean-going submarines of the type-class VIIC, of 750 tons and carrying a crew of four officers and forty-three ratings. At the economical surface speed of 10 knots they had a range of 7900 miles, reducing to 6500 miles at 12 knots. Maximum speed was 17.3 knots on the surface, 7.6 knots submerged, and the maximum range while remaining dived, on batteries, was 80 miles at 4 knots.

The VIIC carried fourteen torpedoes of which five

were ready-loaded — four in the forward tubes and one in the stern tube. Two more were stowed in the casing and the remaining seven beneath the deck of the forward compartment. Aft of the bridge platform were an 88mm gun and quadruple 20mm AA machine-guns.

An encounter between submarine and surface warship was a lethal game of blind man's buff in which both sides had developed considerable skills, among which could be numbered seamanship and sheer technical ability, quick thinking tempered by patience and, equally important, a facility for anticipating an opponent's next move. An experienced commander seldom allowed his enemy to make a mistake and live to tell of it.

Other factors being equal, the submarine began with an advantage because, low on the surface, or at periscope depth, it could sight surface vessels — particularly a large number — before itself being sighted, and could choose its time and method of attack. Within 5000 yards of an alert warship, however, it could be detected by asdic — those relentless echo-impulses from which there was nowhere to hide. It was then that the submarine became the hunted, and its commander needed every ounce of his cunning and determination if he wished to save his vessel.

The Germans quickly learned that lone casual U-boats had little chance of penetrating an asdic-equipped escort of a convoy, and the controlled multiple-submarine formation was introduced — usually referred to as a U-boat pack, although it was unlikely that one submarine would sight another during a deployment that might last several weeks.

The circumstances of a U-boat attack were unpredictable; there were too many possible permutations for a rigid defensive procedure to be laid down, but Hayes-Mailer had clearly outlined his philosophy to his ships' captains.

'We're not looking for a fight; our role is a defensive one. If we can reach Murmansk without loss, we shall have done more than anyone can reasonably expect. Circumstances always permitting, *Pennyroyal, Trooper* and *Truelove* will stick to the merchant ships like brother never stuck to brother. None of these will abandon his station except in extreme emergency. If any detached action is necessary, it will be left to *Virtue* and *Vagrant*.'

Given an early contact, and with ordinary luck, Hayes-Mailer knew two destroyers could adequately handle one U-boat. If they did not achieve a kill, they could compel the submarine to remain deeply submerged until the convoy had got well clear. The question posed would be how long one or both destroyers could afford to remain sitting on a contact with the knowledge that the submarine had almost certainly reported the convoy's position, course and speed to its Norwegian base. Equally disastrous would be a sighting by one of the long-range Focke-Wulf 200 aircraft of Fifth Luftflotte which scoured the northern sea-routes for twenty-four hours a day. Pray God that all German attention would be on PQ17 or, best of all, that the weather would be so atrocious that aircraft would be grounded and submarines too desperately battered by the elements to undertake any sort of offensive action.

The weather, at least, was beginning to play its part. In the wheelhouse the Coxswain rubbed condensation from the glass of the barometer and shook his head in disbelief. 'Bleedin' thing's bust. It's been goin' full astern since soddin' yesterday.' *Virtue* lurched, corkscrewed, rose, smashed her bows into a sea that exploded over her again and again, burying the fo'c'sle deck and surging madly aft. Life-lines had been rigged, but it was impossible for a man to keep his feet and suicidal to try. Gun crews and depth-charge parties had been ordered to shelter; they crouched in the tiller flat and the galley passageway. Sleet and rain drove in sheets over the bridge structure, freezing to ice in seconds, carpeting decks, clogging ventilators, thickening halyards and stays. The smoke from the funnels whirled, torn away to nothing by a wind that screamed through rigging, every aperture, scored to numb rawness every inch of exposed flesh. With bloodshot eyes the officer of the watch peered over a useless screen for momentary glimpses of *Brazos River*, a long, diffuse shape that rolled off the port bow, or of *Vagrant*, far abeam, bucking and plunging like a mad thing. Only the occasional flicker of *Pennyroyal*'s twenty-inch lamp gave evidence of her position. The two trawlers, each of only 750 tons, would be having a bad time, but they had excellent weatherly qualities, and there had been many times when these little ships had been able to remain at sea when bigger ships had run for shelter.

'If it's like this at Epsom, they'll have to scratch the 2.30,' *Pennyroyal*'s lamp chuckled, and the Yeoman cursed. 'The bleedin' clown's got verbal diarrhoea,' and Lobby Ludd agreed. In the few moments it had taken him to read the irrelevant signal he had been icily sodden. On the bridge, John Rainbird snorted. 'Yeoman. Make to the escort: "Signalling will be confined to operational traffic only." ' He was junior to Campbell of

Pennyroyal, but he wore the Commander's cloak of authority. Lobby Ludd hammered out the snub with grim satisfaction. There was something in being a senior officer. . . .

Below, in the forward messes, there was confusion. Messdeck lockers had disgorged their contents, and decks were cluttered with shattered crockery, sodden loaves of bread, sugar, salt, boots and clothing, cans of evaporated milk, scattered playing-cards, the vomition of refuse buckets. Everything that could move did so. Men reeled through passageways and messdeck flats as if negotiating some crazy fairground amusement, except that a careless foot could mean crushed ribs, a broken limb, a crumpled figure at the bottom of a steel ladder and a fractured skull. Incredibly, men slept, hugging the narrow mess-stools and adhering tenaciously to the tops of tables and lockers as if their lives depended upon remaining horizontal.

'This ain't nuthin',' Stripey Albright assured his fellows. 'When I was an OD in the *Renown* in '27 — that was when we took the King ter Australia, he was Duke o' York then—'

'Christ, swing them bloddy lamps,' Signalman House groaned.

'It was soddin' worse than this, mate. There was two French destroyers off Siam that bleedin' *turned over*. All what was left was a few white 'ats floatin', with little red balls on 'em—'

'Balls,' House nodded.

Coder Francis Crowthorne had been attempting to explain the mysteries of meteorology to the less-than-enthralled first dog-watchmen. 'Depressions and anti-cyclones, which are in effect series of closed isobars —

that is, lines of equal pressure — encircling regions where the barometric pressure is respectively lower or higher than the surroundings—'

'We never 'ad them in my day,' Stripey Albright said.

The address system shrieked. *'First dog-watchmen close up. First dog-watchmen close up.'* Men gulped at bitter-sweet tea, not sorry for the interruption. Coder Crowthorne was an 'educated' HO, a reserved, serious young man regarded with a measure of awe by his less qualified associates, yet possessing a curious naïvety that made ridicule difficult. It was impossible to quarrel with Coder Crowthorne. He was accepted, but he could still be a bore.

Intercepting the continuous flow of ciphered signals on the Admiralty broadcasts BN and HD, and with snatches of intelligence gleaned from the R/T transmissions of the distant *Keppel*, it was possible to formulate a progressively moving picture of PQ17's situation. As the sky darkened on 2 July, the officer of the watch, Lieutenant Fender, had requested the Commander to come to the chart-house below the bridge. 'It looks as if PQ17 is taking a pounding, sir.'

Hayes-Mailer had emerged from the tiny recess aft of the wheelhouse which carried the flattering title of captain's sea cabin but was more usually referred to as the 'skipper's caboose'. It housed a camp bed and a voice-pipe to the bridge. The deadlight over the scuttle leaked rusty water and, during the twenty-five years of *Virtue*'s life, no amount of ingenuity had ever prevented a dirty puddle forming against one bulkhead — a fact that the Commander invariably forgot when he sleepily swung his unshod feet to the deck.

Now he slowly thumbed through the deciphered versions of a dozen intercepted radio signals, his feet braced against the chart-table. The chart-house was damp and bitterly cold, and an inch of brine swilled over his sea boots; many of *Virtue*'s bulkhead doors were watertight only in name. Fender, a small man, had an oilskin many sizes too large for him, which he was able, with assistance, to pull over his duffel-coat. His appearance was incongruous and his movements stiffly restricted, but nobody dressed fashionably for an Arctic storm.

The Commander pursed his lips, clung to the table as the ship pitched. 'Our people in company should be getting the same information, but I'll summarise the situation to them by V/S tomorrow forenoon. Meanwhile' — he considered — 'I'll speak to the ship's company at 2100. I'll do it from the Wireless Office; the sparkers have a genius for cultivating the most narcotic fug in the ship. I don't know how they stay conscious.'

The slow voice penetrated every corner of the ship.

'This is the Captain. Some of you will already know that we are ordered to escort the four merchant ships in company to the Kola Inlet in northern Russia. All being well, we should reach Polyarnoe on the fourteenth, or early on the fifteenth.

'Five days ahead of us, on approximately the same route that we are following, is the much larger convoy PQ17. It is heavily escorted, and further screened by the First Cruiser Squadron. At the moment, PQ17 is just east, or north-east, of Jan Mayen. The weather is bad' — he paused to allow for the inevitable snorts of mock disbelief — 'but it is clear that the convoy has run into a U-boat pack. So far, all enemy submarines have been driven off, but earlier this evening PQ17 was subjected to attacks by dive-bombers for an hour and a half. These, too, were beaten off.

'Tomorrow, however — almost certainly — PQ17 must turn eastward, and those of you who have made this trip before will know what that means.' The word 'trip' was a ludicrous one; it reminded him of coach excursions and cheap day tickets, sticky children and picture postcards. 'If the weather moderates, PQ17 may suffer heavy losses.'

Hayes-Mailer had debated whether or not to refer to the threat of *Tirpitz, Lützow* and *Admiral Scheer*, but had decided not to. It was a complication of which his crew was best left unaware; there would be time enough if the nightmarish possibility ever materialised, and it probably would not.

'We ourselves,' he resumed, 'are already well within the enemy's hunting-ground. I can change our course slightly from that of PQ17, but nothing that is likely to make much difference, and in the end we have to pass north of Bear Island.'

Björnöya. Bear Island. It was a name that not even the most flippant of sailors could hear without flinching mentally. When it was spoken, it was with quiet malevolence. Bear Island, a tiny white speck north of North Cape, separated by a narrow strait from the great Polar ice-cap, marked the ultimate northerly turning-point. Here, for three days, the frozen, storm-battered and tired ships were within easy reach of the enemy's airfields and could expect wave after wave of torpedo-bomber attacks while, all the time, the U-boats snapped at their heels. Add to that the sub-zero temperature, a scything wind and blizzards of cutting ice-particles, grinding, heaving pack-ice and a sea so viciously cold that the survival of a man thrown into it was measured in seconds — all this spelled Bear Island. It was baffling to the convoy sailor that, at home, people talked of Dieppe, Tobruk, Malta, Crete — but speak to them of Bear Island and their faces went blank. They had never heard of it.

'I don't think I have to tell you,' Hayes-Mailer said, 'that the success of this operation depends upon every single one of you.' They were hackneyed, mealy mouthed words; he knew it and so did they. A man did not exert his every sinew, goad himself to the utmost limits of endurance, for 'the success of this operation'. He did so because of an animal instinct for survival. He did so because there was nowhere to run, nowhere to hide, because other men might die but he would not, because while his heart still beat and there was breath in his lungs there remained hope. Survival was the only spur.

'I shall try to keep you informed of events,' he promised. 'The weather is likely to remain untidy for the next day or two, and the galley may have difficulty in preparing hot food, but remember that the enemy also has the same weather, so bear that in mind when you get fed up with corned-beef sandwiches.' He decided to end on a jovial note. 'The Germans probably feel the same way about their *ersatz* sausage. And try to get your clothing dry if you can. We don't want to add rheumatism to our other discomforts.'

Rheumatism. He hoped, b'God, that they lived long enough.

When he regained the cluttered wardroom the

faces of several off-watch officers turned to meet him. There was John Rainbird, his quiet, efficient Number One, who was going to make an admirable Captain D after the war, Lieutenant Fender, RNVR, Surgeon-Lieutenant Nicols and Commissioned Engineer Stevens. He poured himself coffee from a coffee-pot that Stevens had been holding between his knees, partly for its warmth and partly to keep it from emptying its contents over the table. 'Who's on watch?'

'Prentice and the Sub, Fairbrother, sir.'

The Commander grunted doubtfully, then wished he had not. Sub-lieutenants had to learn to take responsibility, and *Virtue*'s officer complement would be intolerably stretched if young Fairbrother were not permitted to stand his own trick. Still, the Commander mused, the wartime Arctic was a tough baptism for a Basingstoke schoolteacher.

'Sawbones — any casualties?'

'Nothing of consequence so far, sir — a couple of stitches in a gashed knee, one sprained thumb, and one nicely developed foruncle.'

'Foruncle?'

'A boil, sir. Otherwise — well — we're low on condoms, but I don't expect a run on them in Polyarnoe. The libido of Russian women is remarkable only for its extreme frigidity.'

In the tail of the bridge, Lobby Ludd wedged himself into a recessed angle of screen and bulkhead which afforded a degree of shelter from the wind. It was night, but hardly dark — barely more than a curious dusk-light which, the Yeoman had told him, was about the darkest it ever became in the Arctic during these summer months. The Yeoman had been unusually communicative, in a condescending way, probably because Ludd had been the only person to talk to, and the shared discomforts of cold, wetness, and the ship's motion that made leg muscles ache with fatigue had somehow narrowed the social gap between them. Even the Officer of the Watch, Sub-Lieutenant Fairbrother, had offered him cocoa in a wardroom cup — after himself, of course, but it was a rare privilege. Lobby Ludd was feeling slightly, very slightly, less jaundiced.

He had heard the Commander's words — it would have been almost impossible not to, anywhere in the ship — during which the Yeoman had directed a wry, confiding grimace at him, and Lobby Ludd had acknowledged it with an identical wry, confiding grimace, although he was not quite sure what it meant. With the innocence of the uninformed he had complete faith in the ability of his superiors; the threat of submarines and dive-bombers was not his concern, and the thought of death had never once entered his young head. The heaving sea and frozen spray, his nausea and chilled limbs, these were the only matters of importance.

Brazos River was clearly visible, and very vaguely ahead of her was *Chessington*. He still wondered at their apparent lack of human occupancy; he had detected no movement on their decks and they had flashed no signals. They simply wallowed ponderously into the sea as if controlled by some remote agency. The Yeoman had explained that, on the Murmansk run, mercantile crews were reduced to an absolute minimum. Seamen took no valuables with them, no kit except a razor and a spare singlet. Signals by light had to be made by the radio officer, and he was probably too busily occupied to stand on a freezing bridge-deck flashing frivolous nonsense like *Pennyroyal*. 'I'd like 'arf their bleedin' pay,' the Yeoman conceded, 'but it's no skylark in a tanker — single screw, see, an' a few thousand tons o' petrol under yer. One bleedin' tinfish, an' it's "Good-night, nurse." '

Lobby Ludd turned his attention towards distant *Vagrant*. He had already peered into *Virtue*'s asdic cabinet, below and slightly forward of the bridge but accessible only through the messdeck and galley flat. The tiny, sound-proofed compartment, linked to the bridge by voice-pipe, was an addition to the ship's original design and housed an Admiralty pattern 125 asdic transmitter/receiver and its headphoned operator. It was, Lobby Ludd considered, identical to the asdic cabinet of *Vagrant*, in which — perhaps even at this moment — sat Leading Seaman William Ludd.

He remembered Walham Green more vividly than almost anything, even more than he did the marble-floored quarterdeck of *St George*, the Commodore and the floggings in the small room, more vividly than Devonport Barracks or even recent Liverpool.

There had been the Underground station from which crowds had vomited every Saturday, and he and his grimy fellows, without funds, had idled about the gates of the football ground, debating vociferously the signifi-cance of each roar from the thousands within. His interest in football had been superficial, but the others talked knowingly about centre-forwards and half-backs, scrabbled for discarded programmes when the game was over. There had been the old theatre, through the exit doors of which they persistently attempted to achieve a furtive entrance, and were equally persistently ejected by irate staff. North End Road offered a variety of distractions. There were market stalls, profuse and interesting litter among which could invariably be found an overlooked apple or a battered orange, an eel and pie shop where, for a few coppers, could be enjoyed a succulent mess of stewed eels floating in parsley liquor, or a hot meat pie with a generous wedge of mashed potato.

There were taverns, reeking of beer, from which the drunks reeled on Saturday nights, hot chestnuts in winter and cut-price groceries at Victor Value's, girls in print dresses and Eldorado ice-cream in summer, pawn-shops, the slipper baths, cockles and whelks, rabbits hung from hooks, pigs' trotters, trays of white, woolly tripe, and crowded Woolworth's, where a boy could spend a whole hour, just looking.

In neighbouring South Kensington, he recalled, were the museums, which were places of infallible entertainment on wet days. The Natural History Museum was a vast labyrinth in which numerous games could be vigorously and noisily pursued until Authority intervened, while in the Science Museum there were buttons to press, handles to turn, wheels to motivate and pumps to pump, and not a ha'penny to be paid for the pleasure. Nobody ever entered the Victoria & Albert Museum or the Royal School of Needlework. Further were Kensington Gardens and Knightsbridge, but these were distant and alien places, where elderly ladies with small dogs did not agree that pavements were for sliding upon, a stretch of grass was for brawling, and every pond had to have stones thrown into it.

He had been Charlie Ludd then, of course, and he had been regarded with some deference by his juvenile contemporaries because he lived in a sweetshop. It was difficult for them to imagine a more exquisite domestic environment. The shop, however, was small and shabby, and for widowed Mrs Ludd, Charlie's mother, it provided only a tenuous income. She had learned that the things that sold most readily in Walham Green were those that afforded the most slender profit margins. She stocked Ogden's St Bruno, Woodbines and Weights, Tizer, sherbert dips and liquorice strips, tiger nuts, wine gums and bubble gum, the *Evening News, Star* and *Evening Standard*, and garish American comic papers.

Charlie Ludd remembered very little about his father, who had died during the late twenties. Ludd Senior, who had been dedicated to the task of remaining unemployed, had alighted from a moving bus into the path of another, and in so doing had provided Mrs Ludd with the first financial means of any substance that she had ever known. She invested them in the sweetshop.

Charlie's older brother William, however, remembered their father, and the straitened circumstances of unemployment, very well. At sixteen, himself workless and the resources of the little shop strained to the utmost, he enlisted in the Royal Navy. Nothing, he considered, could be worse than the daily empty searching for work, empty pockets, the shuffling queue for a few shillings of subsistence money, the grinding frustration and draining morale. But he had been wrong.

William Ludd had hated the Navy from his very first day; it was a Navy of low pay, of discipline discredited by pettiness, of outmoded ritual perpetuated in the name of tradition, of peacetime economies, long and barren foreign commissions, and an officer class indifferent to lower-deck conditions and to the supposition that human dignity was the right of even the lowest. Like thousands before him, and thousands after, William Ludd had been disillusioned and embittered.

He had not, however, paraded his bitterness. During periods of leave he had played the carefree homecoming sailor, with stories to tell and money to spend. To the dark little shop in Walham Green his long-separated appearances were like refreshing breaths of clean salt air. He was briskly jovial, flirting with the girls and blatantly generous to the shop's juvenile customers. He was the mainspring of any social gathering, dancing with the oldest ladies or the smallest infants, liberal with cigarettes and beer, and possessing a repertoire of amusing nautical expressions. It was, the younger Charlie decided, a life-style of the most enviable quality. He did not know of his brother's choked throat on the eve of each departure.

The possibility of his own enlistment did not occur to Charlie Ludd until the war began; without it, his envy of his brother would almost certainly have faded with maturity. Now all the old values had suddenly changed. There were youths little older than himself in uniform. The streets, the bars, cinemas, buses and railways all teemed with men in khaki or blue, indefinably superior to those lesser mortals too old, too young, unfit or unwilling to fight on the beaches. The newest Air Force conscript basked in the aura of The Few, the meekest soldier exuded Dunkirk belligerence, while the Navy was, as it had always been, the cosseted trump card of the British Empire.

There was worse. For a sixteen-year-old with awakening interests in the opposite sex, the mediocrity of a civilian identity was chastening. The war had introduced a relaxation of moral standards that was highly satisfying to predatory young males but, there was no doubt, only uniformed young males. The war might last for a long time, Charlie Ludd had reasoned. If he was ever going to 'get something', he would need a uniform.

To enlist at sixteen he required the signed consent of a parent or guardian, but the approval of Mrs Ludd had not been difficult to achieve. She was a woman of modest perception who surrendered to the logic of any viewpoint if it was argued long enough. Within two years, young Charlie Ludd pointed out, he would have to register for conscription anyway, and there was no knowing to which service, or to what war theatre, he might find himself condemned. It would be better, he suggested, to volunteer now — for the Navy, of course. In two years' time, when he would otherwise have been placing a foot on the lowest rung of a naval career, he would have two years of promotion behind him. Furthermore, he could not fail to gain by having an older brother in the same service, could he?

It was, Mrs Ludd agreed, a well-founded proposition. It would be comforting to know that young Charlie had his brother's company and experienced guidance. She would never have thought of it if Charlie hadn't; it just went to show. Cheerfully, Mrs Ludd wrote her signature on a parental-consent document that Charlie just happened to have. 'And don't forget, Charlie,' she said. 'When you get there, tell the officer about William. He might not know.'

Unfortunately, several weeks elapsed before the Admiralty decided that a deteriorating war situation called for young Charlie Ludd's personal intervention, and it was during this time that William appeared unexpectedly and angrily.

'You've joined the *Andrew*?' he exploded. '*Volunteered*? Yer bloody stupid half-wit! Fourteen years yer've signed for — d'yer know that? Why didn't yer volunteer for bloody prison? It'd be better by 'arf! D'yer think the war's going to last for fourteen years? Christ, couldn't yer have waited till they *dragged* yer in?' He turned to Mrs Ludd. 'And you *let* him?'

Mrs Ludd was only mildly repentant. It had seemed a good idea at the time. She had not realised, of course, that it meant *fourteen* years, but the time would soon pass. It always did. Come to think of it, she mused, it was about fourteen years since Ludd Senior had passed over — and look how quickly that time had gone. She had never suspected that William would be so upset. After all, hadn't he had jolly times, seen foreign parts, returned with souvenirs, and told them of hilarious experiences in Malta? Why hadn't he *said*. . . ?

John Rainbird had never decided whether dawn was a less than likely time for an enemy attack because warships' crews were routinely at action stations, and the enemy knew it, or whether the enemy preferred dawn *because* the ships were at action stations and, aware that the Germans knew it, were considering an attack unlikely. Or, if the Germans knew that the British knew that the Germans knew. . . .

Trying to think one step ahead of the enemy was like sitting in a barber's chair between opposing mirrors, and seeing those mirrors within mirrors stretching away to infinity. If a man thought about it long enough, he would probably go mad.

Later, when there had been time to consider, it seemed highly probable that the U-boat that *Virtue* flushed at dawn had not been contemplating an attack, had been as surprised as the British. It might even have been a submarine with torpedoes expended and fuel running low, returning to base and anxious to avoid any encounter with British warships. But the sea had moderated sufficiently for a submarine attack to be possible, it was dawn, and *Virtue* could not have been more completely ready if she had been exercising off Portland Bill.

'*Asdic to bridge. HE — reciprocating engines, green one-one-oh. Asdic to bridge. . . .*'

Hydrophone effect, the operator was reporting — propeller noises heard through his equipment which, not yet transmitting, was acting as a sensitive hydrophone. Somewhere to starboard, and a little astern, an engine was whirring faintly. It required no cautionary sweep with binoculars to ensure that the operator was not unwittingly reporting the engines of a ship in company, or even a reciprocal echo of one. The sea to starboard was a heaving emptiness; whatever it was that the man was hearing came from underneath.

Rainbird flung himself at the voice-pipe. 'Switch on transmitter. Sweep area.' The palm of his hand thrust against the action alarm, which would hammer a deafening warning throughout the ship; all men were already closed up, but the alarm would tell every single one of them, in magazines, engine room, tiller flat, control positions, that this was no longer just an irritating precautionary activity that robbed men of hard-earned sleep. It was real. Behind him Lieutenant Fender, action gunnery officer, was fumbling a headset over his ears, while on the stern, Rainbird knew, Sub-Lieutenant Coope and his depth-charge party would be mustered, waiting, at the rails and throwers. He could see a pom-pom crewman wrenching a tarpaulin cover from his gun.

'Bridge to asdic. Extent of target?' The Commander was on the starboard side of the bridge, frowning at the grey void beyond.

'*Asdic to bridge. Extent of target five degrees, moving from left to right. Bearing green one-two-oh. Repeat. . . .*'

Below, in the asdic cabinet, the operator had been swinging his oscillator in five-degree steps, first from starboard to head, then port to head, repeatedly, slowly, listening, listening. He had almost missed the sinister purr on his starboard sweep, passed it, came back, listened again. He was alone and blind inside this little sound-proofed tomb, but he could hear what nobody could see — the delicate chukker-chukker of electric motors. It was not his task to interpret, only to report, and to continue reporting. There was another, on the bridge above him, who would speculate, calculate, decide. Now, transmitting, the operator closed his eyes in concentration, hearing a new sound — the hollow peenk-peenk of an echo, telling him of a tangible something out there, submerged. He knew what it was, but it was not for him to say so.

He opened his eyes, riveted them on the compass as his fingers tuned. There was a chronometer in the moist palm of his left hand, and he listened for the Doppler betrayal. He grunted.

'*Asdic to bridge. Target bearing green one-two-five. Extent of target three degrees, moving from left to right, range two thousand and opening. Repeat....* '

On the bridge, Hayes-Mailer stared at Rainbird. 'He's heard us, and he's running.' The submarine — and now it could be nothing else — also had hydrophones. The extent of the target had narrowed in seconds, which meant that it was presenting its narrowest profile, either bows or stern, to listening asdic, and a lengthening range indicated the U-boat captain had turned away. But he had been too late.

'Hard to starboard. Half-ahead both.' *Virtue* must not move too fast or her own engine noise would obliterate the asdic's echo-pulses; the U-boat captain was likely to twist and squirm like a hooked salmon and, if he did, the destroyer would need the probing finger of her asdic. 'Yeoman! To the escort first and then the merchantmen — "Am attacking submarine bearing green one-two-five from station, two thousand yards. Escort will remain on course unless otherwise ordered. *Vagrant* will move to cover rear of convoy." ' No wireless signals yet, which could have enemy D/F stations clawing at him, not even R/T. And he'd not pull *Vagrant* away from the convoy unless he had to. One U-boat did not mean only one U-boat. There could be others, watching, delighted to see the destroyers' attention distracted.

'*Asdic to bridge. Target bearing green oh-five-oh. Extent of target five degrees. Range two thousand two hundred. Repeat....* '

Virtue was still turning. In a few more seconds the contact would be precisely ahead, and then the range would begin to narrow as the destroyer bore down on her quarry. The U-boat would be running for life now, plunging downward into the cold blackness. Within her, the crew would be tense, waiting, listening. Her hydrophone operator would hear the distant but increasing noise of propellers, then the condemning fingers of asdic against the steel hull, like handfuls of dry gravel thrown into a tin pail.

Hayes-Mailer spoke loudly and slowly. 'I am going to make a first run with the target fine on the port bow.' At *Virtue*'s comparatively slow speed it was going to take four or five minutes to cover 2000 yards. There was time for calculation. On the destroyer's stern were two pairs of rails that allowed depth-charges to be rolled into the sea behind, and, on each quarter, throwers that flung, broadside, the amatol-packed canisters. Already the ready-use depth-charges were clamped to their throwers and six were poised on the rails. Ninety more waited to be hoisted from the tiller flat below. 'We shall fire a pattern of four from stern and port sides only, then turn to starboard and repeat the pattern with stern and starboard throwers. All charges one-fifty feet.' His eyes narrowed.

Depth-charges were most effective when they exploded just below and abeam of a submarine, for along the keel were the weaker points of the pressure hull — the ballast-tank vents, pump outlets, propeller shaft, rudder and hydroplane glands. The deeper a U-boat sank, so correspondingly did water-pressure on the hull increase, but increasing depth-pressure also reduced the explosive force of a depth-charge. If unable to shake off an attacker quickly, the U-boat commander must balance the hazard of depth-charges against that of extreme depth, which could crush his vessel like a rotten orange.

From the yardarm a string of flags was streaming, and the twenty-inch lamp was churning out the Commander's warning to the escort. There was an encouraging whoop, carried faintly on the wind, from *Vagrant's* siren as she swung to follow astern of *Olympic Madison* and *Brazos River*, and Lobby Ludd, had he not been fully occupied with a tugging halyard, might have been gratified to see crewmen on the nearer tanker scrambling for their gun platform. In *Virtue*, guns were rotating slowly, depressing, the men watching, praying, for a sudden vision of a submarine breaking surface and at point-blank range. It was improbable, but they prayed. Aft, Sub-Lieutenant Coope and his petty officer were waiting; the depth-charges were primed and set.

'*Asdic to bridge. Target dead ahead, range twelve hundred* — '

' — *Nine hundred* — '

Hayes-Mailer, feet braced and with hands gripping the screen, stared ahead at the sea beyond *Virtue's* bows. If he had been lucky, he had pounced on this U-boat before she had had an opportunity to transmit a report on the convoy's position. A submarine could receive radio signals at depths of fifty feet or more, and did so continuously, but to transmit she had to surface, break radio silence and risk both visual and D/F detection. At periscope depth, signals could be transmitted by raising a hydraulically operated mast, but this had a range of only about fifteen miles, or roughly to the limit imposed by the earth's curvature. The ships of the escort were not monitoring enemy radio frequencies, but Hayes-Mailer was almost certain that the U-boat had not surfaced before *Virtue* had stumbled on her. *Pennyroyal's* radar had detected nothing — nor, for that matter, had any other ship's asdic.

'Bridge to asdic. Switch to SRE.'

The operator had expected the order. Now the peenk-peenk of the asdic echo flooded from every loudspeaker in the ship, and in every compartment, every gun position, conversation froze and men stood rigidly. It needed only moments now before the destroyer flung herself forward at full speed, bows lifting and a bone in her teeth. . . .

There had been another moment, just like this, Hayes-Mailer remembered, but the sea's calm, blue surface had twinkled with thousands of golden coins under a hot sun, dazzling the eyes. He had been in immaculate white, tanned of skin, and young — a self-assured lieutenant on the bridge of another destroyer.

The flotilla had been two hours out of Hong Kong when Captain D had ordered them into two divisions, each of three ships in line ahead, the divisions steaming parallel and 2000 yards apart. Speed was increased to twenty-five knots, and they all knew what was coming: a grid-iron. Captain George Furloe was a rapid-manoeuvring enthusiast; he had written a book on the subject and spent a great deal of his time drawing complex diagrams of ships in formation and evolving equally complicated flag signals for the bemused edification of his juniors. 'Efficiency, speed, teamwork and instant decision,' he told them repeatedly. 'I would rather a commander did a wrong thing quickly and with confidence than the right thing slowly and inefficiently.' When George Furloe took his flotilla to sea, everything had to be done in the most intricate manner possible and at hair-raising speed.

A high-speed grid-iron was an unpalatable experience for the nervous, but was usually more spectacular than dangerous, and an excellent piece of pantomime with which to impress the representatives of foreign powers, who could not possibly imagine their own navies using such suicidal tactics. The two parallel columns would turn simultaneously inwards, which meant that each was steaming towards the other at a converging speed of sixty miles per hour. One division, however, had applied fifteen degrees of rudder and the other twenty degrees, so that, all being well, they would pass through each other, albeit with only yards to spare, and emerge to re-form, with their earlier divisional positions reversed.

It needed calm nerves and an unfailing confidence in one's brother commanders, and young Hayes-Mailer had both. Tomorrow, in Kowloon, Captain Furloe would hold his usual post-mortem, scrawling angry chalk-lines on a blackboard, but there would be no criticism of Lieutenant Norman Hayes-Mailer. When Captain D's masthead predictably flared with coloured bunting, he knew exactly what to do, and ordered fifteen degrees of starboard wheel as he gave his shouting Yeoman of Signals an acknowledging wave of his hand. He wished he had worn sun-glasses; the sun, and the glare off the sea, were almost blinding. Behind him, the Sub-Lieutenant made an entry in the deck log.

Of the two ships of the opposing division between which Hayes-Mailer would steer his own, that off his port bow was Captain D's. Both were closing at chilling speed, and the old fool was cutting it damn fine, Hayes-Mailer decided, but he wasn't going to be intimidated. From his own ship's fo'c'sle deck a man was running aft, glancing over his shoulder, and the Sub-Lieutenant yelled. In that agonising, sickening moment, Hayes-Mailer realised that it had gone wrong. He bawled for starboard wheel, for engines full astern, but it was too late. Captain D's siren howled frenziedly, and then the two destroyers met, beam to beam, with a shuddering crash that threw Hayes-Mailer to the deck.

The court martial in Hong Kong had reached a verdict very quickly; there was almost nothing that Hayes-Mailer could offer in defence, and his counsel's final delivery was little more than an apology. When the flotilla commander's signal had been received, Hayes-Mailer had applied fifteen degrees of starboard helm. His coxswain and his own deck log confirmed it. After that, things had happened too quickly for anything to be certain, but it was more than probable that Hayes-Mailer had stopped his turn a few seconds too soon — and a few seconds had been enough. He and other officers had referred to the embarrassment of sun glare, and Captain Furloe had generously conceded that, ideally, he should not have turned his second division, at high speed and under such demanding circumstances, directly eastwards, but neither should manoeuvres always be executed under perfect conditions. Hayes-Mailer had been over-confident, careless. He had not given sufficient attention to course and bearings, and as a result a man was dead, a second maimed, and two destroyers had been ordered into dry dock. It was not considered possible that Captain Furloe's turn, or his subsequent course, had been anything but precise, or that he might have attempted avoiding action earlier than he had. He had written a book on the subject.

When Lieutenant Hayes-Mailer had returned to the courtroom, his sword on the table lay with its blade towards him.

*   *   *

'Asdic to bridge. Target bearing red oh-oh-five. Range three hundred and opening. . . .'

Hayes-Mailer lowered his head to the wheelhouse voice-pipe. 'Full ahead both!' The telegraphs clanged.

'Extent of target ten degrees. . . .'

Virtue's bows climbed, smashed through a hill of grey water and plunged beyond it drunkenly, climbed again, with thickening smoke pouring from her funnels and her screws threshing. The amplified asdic echo was peenk-peenking madly, then turned to a continuous scream that tortured the ears.

'Instantaneous echo!'

Hayes-Mailer straightened. 'Stand by depth-charges!' There was less than a hundred yards to cover, then, 'Fire pattern!'

Immediately, all eyes turned aft, but *Virtue* was already turning sharply to starboard, her speed reduced to half, before the four explosions mushroomed. Below, the asdic operator had swung his oscillator astern.

'Asdic to bridge. Target bearing green one-four-oh . . . one-three-oh . . . green oh-nine-oh. . . .'

The guns were traversing again, this time to starboard. 'Mixture as before, Number One,' the Commander confirmed. 'We'll take the target on the starboard bow this time — pattern of four, both rails and starboard throwers. Set rail-charges to one-fifty feet, throwers to two hundred — just to give our friend something to bite on.'

Lobby Ludd raised himself on the flag locker for a better view, and the Yeoman snorted. 'Ludd! What d'yer think this is? Bertram Mills?' He relented. 'If yer fall in the 'oggin', we ain't stopping ter pull yer out, see.' He pointed to the flattened, frothing area of sea on the starboard beam. 'All right, keep yer eyes on that, boyo, and keep its bearing in yer mind — ninety, eighty, seventy, see? — and if yer see anything break surface — *anything* — then sing out, sharpish.'

For Lobby Ludd the recent rapid series of events was still unreal. He had seen this in a film, last year at the Essoldo, only it had been a Japanese submarine, and John Wayne, clutching a broken arm, had turned the shot-torn PT boat towards the enemy, drawling, 'OK, Lootenant, let's give them monkeys the pay-off from Uncle Sam!' There had been no complications, like a Force Seven freezing wind that cut through his clothes like a knife, numbly aching fingers in icily sodden gloves, an empty stomach that contorted and, worse, a desperate desire to piss. Didn't film heroes ever need to piss? And when Errol Flynn and Maureen O'Hara had been trapped in that cave for nine days — at the Regal — what happened when one of them wanted to crap?

He, Lobby Ludd, had wanted to, when he and Bungy Williams had stood before the First Lieutenant with their caps off, that morning after the night before in Liverpool, having overstayed their leave by three hours. Bungy Williams, first to face their inquisitor, had told his own harrowing story.

'I caught the bus in plenty of time, sir, but right outside the Adelphi 'Otel we was struck by lightning.' He lifted his eyes in horror. 'I 'spect it'll be in orl the papers—'

'Lightning?' The First Lieutenant glanced up at a cloudless azure sky. 'Did you say lightning?'

'Yessir. It was a hollercorst. The roof came in, an' there was bodies everywhere, wimmin screaming, kids on fire, an' the driver burned ter a cinder. Natcherly I did wot I could—'

'Naturally,' the First Lieutenant had nodded. 'You always have the most incredibly bad luck, Williams. Last time, if I remember, the swing bridge got stuck half-way and you were marooned all night. You've also been trapped in a lift, spent five hours changing a car wheel for the Lady Mayoress of Belfast, rescued a small girl from drowning — which explained how you lost your cap, collar and paybook — and we can be absolutely certain that any train you catch will either break down in the middle of Dartmoor or will carry you, unwilling and protesting, to Burnham-on-Crouch.'

'That's right, sir,' Bungy Williams had morosely agreed. 'I do 'ave some bad luck.'

'I just can't wait for the next time,' the First Lieutenant mused. 'Ten days' stoppage of leave and pay.' A few seconds later he looked up from the charge book. 'Ordinary Signalman Ludd? Came aboard yesterday, didn't you? From Boys' Service?' He grunted. 'I suppose you were in the Mersey Tunnel when the roof began to leak, and you had to keep your finger in the hole for three hours, eh?'

'No, sir,' Lobby Ludd confessed. 'I jes' overslept—'

'Hah!' The First Lieutenant's eyes widened. 'Well — that's novel. No' — he held up a hand — 'spare me the details, Ludd.' He considered for several moments, then grimaced. 'All right. It's an achievement to get your name in the charge book within twenty-four hours of joining a ship, but I have a feeling that your nefarious night's activities weren't entirely of your own choosing. You're a bit young for it, Ludd. This time I'm letting you off with a caution. But only this time, you understand? We've both got more important things to think about than this sort of nonsense, and one Williams is enough for any first lieutenant.'

Later, Bungy Williams was incredulous. 'Ten days' stoppage! Shave off. If there's one thing I can't stand, Lobby, it's cocky officers what know it all. What's the good o' *explaining* if they don't soddin' believe yer?'

Virtue attacked for a third, fourth and then a fifth time without apparent success. Tired eyes searched vainly for an eruption of air bubbles or a sudden oil slick, but the wind had risen viciously, and the surrounding sea was a maelstrom of jagged grey and white in which any evidence of damage to the U-boat would be almost impossible to detect and probably scattered in seconds. The ship was rolling and pitching with increasing violence, and several times her screws had lifted clear of the water, to race madly.

Hayes-Mailer's problem was a complex one. The submarine had obviously gone as deep as she dared, and remained unmoving, but he could not guess how long she had been submerged before being detected; it could have been for a few minutes or several hours. Nor could he guess her state of seaworthiness, whether she still carried torpedoes and, if so, how many. The U-boat might be leaking like a sieve, in darkness, with her crew semi-comatose and sucking air through potash-cartridge masks, which absorbed carbon monoxide. She might even be destroyed – a flooded useless hulk. Or she might be unscathed, with sufficient oxygen to keep her submerged for three days. Meanwhile, the convoy had vanished, out of visual touch, and *Virtue* could not remain here indefinitely.

If Hayes-Mailer abandoned the attack to rejoin the convoy, however, he could be leaving a viper in his rear, and the penalty could be disastrous. He eyed the sea, sheeted with freezing spindrift, the snow flying. It would soon be difficult and dangerous to drop charges, perhaps impossible.

He decided. 'One more attack, Number One — port, starboard and stern. Then we'll see. Are the depth-charge crews working with life-lines?'

Even as he gave the order to fire, *Virtue* yawed, then rolled crazily to port. Clutching for a handhold, Hayes-Mailer saw the charges from the throwers ejected sea-wards in a shallow curve, and simultaneously heard the shout. 'Man overboard! Man over— Christ! Two men overboard!'

Rainbird, having just launched the depth-charges with his pump-handle release, had been flung against the empty bridge-chair, but clung to his telephone. 'Two men on the rails, sir — gone over—!' But astern of *Virtue* the heaving sea had erupted. Six massive white geysers climbed skyward, hung for awful seconds, then collapsed in a great welter of spray. *Virtue* shuddered.

'Hard to port! Emergency full ahead!' The Commander's voice cracked. It was going to be too late. Much too late. A ton of high explosive had torn the ocean to shreds over a radius of 200 yards. No puny human frame could have lived through that, even without an overwhelming sea and a temperature considerably below zero.

'Who?'

'Sub-Lieutenant Coope and Able Seaman Foster, sir. The Petty Officer is on his way to the bridge.' *Virtue* had turned back on her original course, and all eyes searched desperately among the white-crested seas that churned on all sides, yet knowing it to be hopeless. 'How the hell did it happen, Arnold?' Hayes-Mailer asked the sodden and dishevelled man who had climbed from below. 'Didn't you rig life-lines?'

'Yessir,' Petty Officer Arnold explained. He was breathing quickly. 'Foster slipped, sir, on the wet deck, and the Sub — Mr Coope — grabbed at him, just as we took that beam sea. It all 'appened in a flash, sir — and then they were gone, both of 'em. They didn't even shout out.' He paused, then, 'It's these rubber boots, sir—'

'Rubber boots!' Hayes-Mailer roared, and the Petty Officer flinched. 'Arnold, how many times have I ordered that men in exposed positions should not wear rubber boots?' For twenty years he and many others had cursed the ignorance of a supply service that provided rubber boots for seamen — rubber boots which were hazardous with the slightest grease or wetness on a steel deck, and which in bad weather were lethal. Yet, he knew, ordinary footwear was an impossible alternative. Only rubber boots, with their thick woollen stockings, allowed men to keep their feet comparatively dry. They would go on wearing them.

'There's no sign of them, sir,' Rainbird reported. 'I don't think—' He hesitated. 'They must have caught the full blast of the rail charges. . . .' It didn't bear thinking about. Every depth-charge spewed hundreds of disembowelled and bloated fish to the surface. . . .

'Asdic to bridge. Contact lost, sir. There's a lot of turbulence—'

The Commander mouthed a rare obscenity. Salt densities, cold and less cold layers, plankton, turbulent sediment, all could screen a submarine from asdic probing. Either the U-boat was a flooded, corpse-filled shell, or its crew could give thanks to their German god for a miraculous survival, because he could not remain much longer.

'Bridge to asdic. Continue searching.' If the U-boat was still alive, it would be lying motionless, with all pumps and motors switched off, the crew not daring to move or speak, beaded with sweat, and the hydrophone operator listening intently for the grim chuckle of asdic, for the noise of depth-charges entering the water — to be followed in seconds by hull-rocking explosions — or the exquisite sound of propellers fading into distance.

But thirty further minutes of criss-crossing the tumultuous target area produced nothing. Hayes-Mailer heaved an angry breath. Two of his men were dead, he had expended twenty-six depth-charges, had lost contact with a U-boat, and now he was miles away from the remainder of his escort.

'Increase speed to eighteen knots, Number One, and give me a course for the convoy, please. Send the morning watchmen below, and see if the galley can organise cocoa or hot soup for all hands, as quickly as possible. Mr Fender, as soon as it is convenient, you will collect the personal effects of the two dead men, and prepare an inventory. Yeoman, ask the W/T Office to send the intercepts file up to me in the chart-house. Depth-charge party to secure, Arnold.' He looked up at the man. 'You will now be in charge.'

Was there anything else? He felt very tired — and this was only the second day. It was hardly believable, yet, that he had lost two men already. He would have to write letters to the next of kin. Young Coope was unmarried, he recalled, with parents in Hampshire, but he could not remember about Able Seaman Foster. He tried to put a face to the name but, annoyingly, could not. Foster? Damn, he ought to know every man in the ship.

'*Bridge Wireless Office to bridge. Fleet Code signal on convoy R/T, to Virtue from Vagrant. Decoded, reads, "Have been struck by torpedo. Convoy continuing at utmost speed on course previously ordered." That's all, sir.*'

Three

Maintaining silence on convoy R/T no longer served any useful purpose. The main body of the convoy had obviously been intercepted, *Vagrant* had been torpedoed, and Hayes-Mailer wanted to speak directly with her commander, Bob Roper. In the Bridge Wireless Office he glanced at the list of callsigns, then took the microphone.

'Mandrake, this is Lurcher. Captain to captain. Over.'

On the bulkhead the loudspeaker hissed, but no answering voice emerged. The eyes of the Commander, the Petty Officer Telegraphist and the watchkeeping operator clashed, expressionless.

'Mandrake, Mandrake, this is Lurcher, Lurcher. How do you hear me? Over.'

The loudspeaker hissed, then spat. 'Lurcher, this is Camshaft. Hearing you strength two. Captain to captain. I have received Mandrake's initial signal to you, but nothing since. Over.'

'Camshaft — that's *Pennyroyal*, sir,' the operator said.

The Commander nodded. Campbell.

'Camshaft, this is Lurcher. Please give me a situation

report. Over.'

'This is Camshaft. In plain language on this frequency—?'

'This is Lurcher. Affirmative.' Right now, speed was more important than secrecy.

'This is Camshaft. Mandrake struck by torpedo port side amidships at oh-nine-three-five and when last seen was stopped. She is no longer within visual range and radar evidence disappeared at oh-nine-five-five. Her last signal by V/S was for Shanghai to proceed at utmost speed in execution of previous orders. This Shanghai is now doing, and zig-zagging. I am in V/S touch with Shanghai and have you on screen. Here follows four groups of code. Stand by. King Peter X-ray, Mike Love Oboe, Jig Fox King, Sugar Tare Dog—'

'Shanghai is the collective callsign for the convoy and escort, sir,' the PO Telegraphist contributed. 'And those four groups—' He was thumbing quickly through a volume of Fleet Code. 'Negative contact. Mean speed eleven knots.'

Hayes-Mailer called to the bridge for maximum speed. *Vagrant* had sunk — there could scarcely be any doubt, and Campbell had almost spelled it out. For a nauseating moment the Commander wondered if the torpedo had been fired by the U-boat that *Virtue* had hunted and lost, but quickly realised that this was impossible. There was another U-boat. It may have waited briefly to ensure that *Vagrant* was finished, and could now be in pursuit of the convoy — but only if the German commander risked surfacing, to achieve the necessary speed.

Campbell, thank God, did not prattle when it came to business. In plain language he had given only those facts of which the U-boat commander would already be aware, but the few quickly coded groups had added considerably more. There had been no radar or asdic contact, which the enemy did not know, and the zig-zagging convoy still maintained a mean speed of eleven knots. Zig-zagging, which meant an alteration of course to port or starboard every seven or eight minutes, would normally have a slowing effect. There was also a collision hazard, while a patient U-boat officer could measure and then predict the zig-zag sequence. For these reasons Hayes-Mailer avoided the stratagem if he could use sustained speed instead.

The two trawlers' best speed was eleven knots. To maintain this and a zig-zag meant that *Trooper* and *Truelove* were holding a straight course while, between them, the four merchant ships repeatedly veered, but at a considerably higher speed than the escort.

'No,' the Commander calculated. 'He won't be tailing the convoy. He can't. If he's wise, he'll settle for *Vagrant* and make himself scarce. If he's a very brave man, he'll be waiting for us to show up. Number One, have you done any sums?'

'Yes, sir.' Rainbird held a scrap of paper in a clumsily gloved hand. 'We shall come up with the convoy in two hours twenty-five minutes, if we maintain this speed, but we'll reach *Vagrant*'s last position in about an hour and a half.' He had said 'if we maintain this speed', which meant 'if you choose not to stop or search for *Vagrant*'s survivors'.

'Thank you.' Hayes-Mailer nodded. He walked to the screen, raised his eyes. Immediately below him was the forward four-inch gun, then the long fo'c'sle streaming with water, the chain cables and the lifting taper of the bows rising and falling, thrusting at the sea. It was a perspective so familiar that it seemed all other environments were merely fleeting aberrations. Roper would have thought that, too, in *Vagrant*. He would have been standing like this when the torpedo had struck.

Virtue was working up to maximum speed. Before modification she would have achieved thirty-five knots, but even twenty-five knots was too fast for this sea, and he was putting the ship at risk. *Virtue* was an elderly lady, and with the immense strain on her hull as she straddled a giant trough, the constant, shuddering concussion, the screws lifting clear and churning crazily, almost anything could happen. But he thought of *Vagrant*.

Destroyers had sustained incredible damage both in action and bad weather, and had lived, but being struck squarely amidships by a torpedo could mean only one thing. Roper, if he had survived the first shattering explosion, would have had time to dispose of his confidential books and charts. He had transmitted a signal to *Virtue* and another to *Pennyroyal*, probably on emergency power, while with every passing minute he knew the convoy and its escort to be disappearing northward. *Virtue* was fifty miles away. The broken ship would be settling, leaning, with the pounding sea pouring into the waist, sodden and freezing men dragging the maimed to Carley floats, the deck lurching and the wind like howling torture. . . .

Better to die quickly, Hayes-Mailer knew, than to linger, half-dead, in that ghastly sea — but they would not cling to life for long, only for minutes. When the torpedo had struck, *Virtue* had been an hour and a half distant. She was still an hour away.

*   *   *

Below, Lobby Ludd had just peeled off his wet clothes and was pouring stewed tea from the mess-kettle when Signalman House appeared. 'Heard the buzz?' he enquired. '*Vagrant*'s been shamfered.'

Lobby Ludd looked up. 'Shamfered?'

'Tinfished. Bleedin' sunk. That's why we're floggin' on. The Yeoman says it'll take an hour to reach 'er — but there won't be anythin' to soddin' reach.'

'Shave off,' Bungy Williams said.

It couldn't be true. 'Are you bullshittin'? Really sunk?'

'Sunk. Finished. *Kaput*,' House nodded, 'with an 'ole in 'er you could drive a bleedin' bus through.'

'Shave off,' Bungy Williams repeated. 'I nearly got drafted to *Vagrant*. Think o' that.' He thought about it, then, 'Christ, where yer goin', Lobby?'

On the flag-deck, Yeoman Shaw stared. 'Ludd? You're bleedin' keen, aren't yer? If you ain't got enough to do I'll soon find you something. If I was an OD, and I'd had the morning watch, I'd 'ave my 'ead down by now, see—'

Lobby Ludd was still struggling with the toggles of his duffel-coat. 'Yeoman — I 'eard about *Vagrant*.'

The Yeoman grunted. 'Well, we don't need your 'elp, Ludd. If we do, I'll 'oist a flag.' Then he looked at the other more closely. 'If you're feelin' sick, boyo, the best thing is ter spew up, and get it over—'

Lobby Ludd felt very close to spewing up. 'My brother,' he choked, 'is on *Vagrant*.'

Both of them rocked on braced feet as the deck tilted. 'Soddin' 'ell,' Shaw gritted. 'I'm sorry, son.' He frowned. 'Yer sure? I mean—'

Lobby Ludd nodded. 'Asdic killick.' He swallowed.

' 'Ave yer 'eard anything?'

Shaw drew in his breath. 'Not much. She took a tinfish, 'midships, and *Pennyroyal* reported she's no longer on radar.' He shrugged. 'O' course, that don't necessarily mean—'

'*Pennyroyal* an' the trawlers knew? One of 'em would 'ave picked up survivors, then? I mean, I've 'eard all this flannel about not stopping for survivors, but if they were bleedin' *there*—?'

'It ain't flannel, son,' the Yeoman apologised. 'A ship can't pick up survivors without stoppin', or going so slow it amounts to the same thing, see. The U-boats know it, an' the bastards wait.' He lifted a hand to the other's shoulder. 'Look, there ain't any point in pretending. I'd say there wasn't much chance, but we'll reach the position in about fifty minutes. Then, well. . . .' He shrugged again.

'And if there is survivors,' Lobby Ludd nodded towards the bridge, 'we'll pick 'em up?'

Shaw frowned, unwilling to voice an opinion. 'I'll tell you what. You go an' sit in the BWO, see. 'Ave a smoke an' some kye, and don't get yerself in a panic. If anything 'appens, I'll sing out. All right?'

Lobby Ludd was uncertain. 'If the Skipper knew— I mean, if—'

'If he knew, son, he couldn't do anything different.' Shaw was immediately sorry he had said it. 'Well, all right. You can tell him, if it'll make you feel you've done something.' He grimaced sympathetically. 'But remember, he's got eight other ships to think about.'

'I know.' Lobby Ludd nodded.

The Commander turned tired eyes from Shaw to Ludd. 'Your brother, Ludd?'

'Yessir. I know there's not much you can do, sir, but if there was a chance—'

Hayes-Mailer stared beyond the bridge rails at a white-crusted sea that clawed at *Virtue*'s flanks. He was silent for so long that Lobby Ludd glanced questioningly at the Yeoman, but the Commander nodded, his lower lip thrust forward.

'The chances of anyone surviving in these conditions are damn small, Ludd. You know that. If it's any consolation, it's a quick and easy way to go — but that's not what you want to hear, is it?' He paused. 'You have my word' — he paused — 'you have my word that if any of *Vagrant*'s survivors are sighted we shall pick them up, whatever the circumstances.' Hayes-Mailer smiled. 'Is that a fair offer?'

Something like a sob came from Lobby Ludd. 'Yessir. Thank yer, sir.'

Regaining the flag deck, Yeoman Shaw squeezed the younger man's shoulder. 'Christ, I was bloody wrong. I'd 'ave sworn blind he'd not do it, not even for *Vagrant*.' He shook his head. 'I'll say one thing, the Skipper's a bloody gentleman. Some officers are pigs, bloody pigs, and there's some that's gentlemen.'

On the bridge, Hayes-Mailer had remained motionless for several moments before turning to John Rainbird, a silent observer of the brief exchange. 'What's our course, Number One?'

'Oh-four-oh, sir. That'll bring us up to *Vagrant*'s last position in about—' He dragged back his glove to look at his watch, but the Commander interrupted.

'Steer oh-two-oh for one hour, please.'

Rainbird lowered his head to the voice-pipe, then hesitated. 'Sir, that'll take us ten or twelve miles west of

Vagrant's position—'

'That's right, Number One. Oh-two-oh, please.'

Rainbird gave the order to the wheelhouse, then straightened. With the constant yawing of *Virtue*'s bows in the sea, the movement to port would be hardly perceptible. He stared ahead, the wind bitterly cold against his face. A full minute passed before Hayes-Mailer spoke again. 'All right, Number One, you're wondering what the hell I'm playing at, is that it?'

'I don't really see, sir, why you had to tell that youngster—'

'No?' The Commander sighed. 'Number One, I never had the slightest intention of stopping this ship to pick up survivors. I have already expressly forbidden all ships of the escort to do so, and they have obeyed. In thirty or forty minutes young Ludd — and half the damn ship's company — will be looking and praying, and if we passed close to *Vagrant*'s position they might — *might* — see something. There could be wreckage, flotsam, perhaps a corpse or two still floating.' He paused. 'There might even be a few survivors, God help them.' He turned pain-narrowed eyes towards the First Lieutenant. 'Number One, we are rejoining the convoy at utmost speed. Nothing else is relevant. *Vagrant* is a back number.'

'Sir,' Rainbird made a final protest. 'We've been with *Vagrant*—'

'For nearly three years?' Hayes-Mailer nodded. 'That's right — *Virtue* and *Vagrant*. It's like saying "knife and fork". They towed us off from Dunkirk, we always beat them at football, and they've still got our 4½-inch wire. I'll tell you something else, Number One. *Vagrant* was my first command — something that a

Naval officer never forgets. It was in *Vagrant*, bless her, that I gave Captain D the shock of his life, off Hong Kong, earned myself a court martial and a reprimand. And do you know who was on the bridge with me on that splendid occasion? It was Sub-Lieutenant Bob Roper.'

He returned his gaze to the sea. 'That's why, if by the remotest chance there are any survivors, I don't want to see them. I don't want young Ludd to see them. Most of all, Number One, I don't want *them* to see *us*.'

'There he is — Jolly Jack 'imself,' William Ludd had scoffed. It had been the only occasion on which their leaves had coincided. 'All dressed up in a tiddley suit an' rolling aroun' like a three-badger. Ain't yer got tattoos and an ear-ring?' But his sarcasm had been short-lived. 'Well, yer've done it, and that's it, Charlie. If things were different, I'd request to have yer in the same ship' — he had been drafted to HMS *Vagrant*, docked in Londonderry — 'but yer don't want a pig-boat of a "V and W", Charlie. If yer lucky, yer'll get a battle-wagon, and swing aroun' the buoy in Scapa while the destroyers do all the sea-time — or, better still, a nice shore signal-station, see, with Wrens an' a NAAFI, an' long weekends up the line. When it's all over, yer can buy yerself out.'

Less than two years remained of his twelve-year engagement although, if the war was still in progress, he must continue to serve for its duration. But he had plans. Things were going to be different after the war. Electrics was the thing. There were going to be thousands of new houses, and people were going to want radios and electric fires, refrigerators, and perhaps even television. He, William, was going to set up a business —

small at first, but it would grow. And, if Charlie could purchase his discharge, they could be partners. Ludd Bros, Radio & Electrical. 'That will be very nice, dear,' Mrs Ludd had approved. 'And electric bulbs. Think of all the electric bulbs when they switch off the black-out.'

It was unlikely, now, that there would be a Ludd Bros in Putney High Street — not that Lobby Ludd had ever warmed to the possibility, until now. With eyes raw and aching, he scanned the great hills of grey water, streaked and capped with white, which dwarfed *Virtue* as she flung herself at them. There were others search-ing, equally intent — Shaw and House from the flag-deck, the forward and after lookouts with their giant binoculars, the huddled, hooded gun-crews, bespec-tacled Coder Crowthorne peering from the shelter of the galley flat, Bungy Williams' face at the scuttle of the BWO, and a dozen others who had left a warm, off-watch sanctuary in the hope of a momentary glimpse of a tossing sea-boat, a raft, or even whirling, scattered debris that would tell where *Vagrant* had died. It would be marvellous, bleedin' marvellous, Lobby Ludd told himself, if there were survivors and William was one of them. It would be like a story. William did not even know that his brother Charlie was aboard *Virtue*. He, Lobby Ludd, would just like to see William's face, that's all, when he was pulled out of the sea. He'd just like to see it.

The Yeoman's hand was on his shoulder. 'Son, it's no use lookin' anymore. We're thirty miles beyond *Vagrant*'s last position, and we'll be up with the convoy any minute.' He hesitated. 'Look, if yer want to be alone for a bit, go in the Skipper's caboose. He won't be

using it, see. I don't know how you felt about him — yer
brother, I mean — but it ain't a disgrace for a man to cry
sometimes, an' it can help, bach.'

Lobby Ludd frowned. 'I don't feel anythin'. Not like
that, anyway. I suppose I ought to.'

The signal from the Admiralty was prefixed 'Immediate', and Hayes-Mailer read it carefully, twice.

'At 1015z/03 U-boat reported to BdU four merchant
ships and four escorts position 68 degs 30 north 13 degs
20 west course 040 speed 10 knots. Claims torpedoed
and sunk destroyer. Presume this to be *Virtue* or
Vagrant but do not break W/T silence to confirm. You
are entering area of fog which should persist until
evening of 4th. Under cover of this alter course due
north to ice limit approximately parallel 72 then continue keeping as far northerly as is consistent with
safety.'

He had been toying with the thought of a brief report
on ship—shore H/F, but now discarded it. The U-boat
had done the job for him and, it was interesting to note,
had reported four, not five, escorts. At Befehlshaber des
Unterseeboote, the U-boat command headquarters, lines
of interception were being pencilled on charts, and in
Kiel Admiral Carls, Naval Group Commander North,
would be debating whether he could afford to detach
any of the submarines of the Eleventh U-boat Flotilla,
already positioned in the path of PQ17, to deal with the
smaller group, five days behind. Carls must be rubbing
his hands with glee, Hayes-Mailer guessed, at this surfeit
of riches. He had ten submarines off Norway, several
hundred torpedo- and dive-bombers, and he had *Tirpitz*,
three other heavy ships and a flotilla of destroyers

waiting in the wings. All he needed was reasonable operational weather.

Fog. It explained why the enemy attacks on PQ17 had not been successful; the enemy had been hampered by fog, which had made air reconnaissance impossible, and the big convoy had, so far, survived unscathed. It was the same fog that *Virtue* was about to encounter.

The change of course, now, would take them deep into the sea of drifting ice and mush, the northern extremity of Denmark Strait, through which *Bismarck* and *Prinz Eugen*, only a year before, had steamed to a rendezvous with *Hood*. It would take them to the edge of the great Greenland ice-pack, an impenetrable barrier which they must follow — north, north-east, then east — trusting that fog, ice and blizzard would conceal them as they crept nearer to Bear Island. It would be a bitter experience for an old destroyer, a corvette and two trawlers with their open bridges and gun positions, their thin plating and inadequate heating. None had been designed to operate 400 miles beyond the Arctic Circle.

'Revert to defence stations,' he ordered. Except for the absence of *Vagrant*, the convoy that steamed ahead of *Virtue* appeared exactly as he had left it — the four big merchantmen wallowing imperturbably, *Pennyroyal* ahead, and the two little trawlers tumbling gamely on the flanks. 'Yeoman. I shall want to send a long P/L signal by light to all ships.' He must reduce speed to conserve the trawlers' fuel, redispose the merchantmen in anticipation of fog; there would be no further zig-zagging. Hayes-Mailer disliked bad weather of any kind — dangerous seas, the sleet and ice that sheeted his decks and clogged his guns — but above all things he detested fog. Only *Pennyroyal* would have the benefit of radar, and she must have the leading station. For the others it would be a matter of groping through clammy, swirling vapour, perhaps a man in the bows straining his eyes for a fog marker towed by the next ahead or, worse, a looming, murky shape to port or starboard, frequent alterations of speed by a few revolutions. But fog was both enemy and ally. If it was frustrating for the British it was even more so for the seeking U-boats and long-ranging Focke-Wulf aircraft, and on balance Hayes-Mailer preferred fog.

'Sawbones.' He had sent for Surgeon-Lieutenant Nicols. 'It's going to be cold — fifty or sixty degrees of frost, which is colder than you have ever imagined.'

'Frostbite,' Nicols nodded. 'It can be nasty if it's not recognised early and treated correctly. It'd be a good idea to warn *Trooper* and *Truelove*, and perhaps the masters of the merchantmen.'

Within an hour the sea was flattening and the ships were moving into the first wreathing eddies of fog, yellowish mist-like tendrils that climbed to decks, fingered the superstructure and misted the binoculars of the men that peered ahead. *Pennyroyal*'s Aldis lamp was interrupted in mid-sentence as the blurring curtain closed astern of her. 'As the actress said to the bishop—'

Signalman House groaned. 'Now we'll never bleedin' know — but if he uses his soddin' twenty-inch ter give us the punch-line, I'll piss meself.'

It was a further two hours before the convoy had been redisposed to the Commander's satisfaction, and he had been obliged to manoeuvre *Virtue* alongside *Brazos River* and *Olympic Madison* to pass his instructions by loud-hailer and to warn them not to use convoy R/T except in an emergency. The Americans seemed pointedly unwilling to read a flashing light, and the PO Telegraphist had complained that both had attempted a radio liaison with *Virtue*, using transmitters that seemed unnecessarily high-powered. A figure on the bridge-wing of each tanker had acknowledged Hayes-Mailer's shouted orders with a cursory wave of a hand, and then disappeared.

On the messdecks, the voice of Vera Lynn poured from every SRE loudspeaker, 'Yours till the stars lose their gloree. . .' and Bungy Williams was explaining the frequent appearance of 'red lead' — tinned tomatoes — at breakfast. 'The Med Fleet captured an Italian tanker loaded wi' twenty thousand tons o' red lead in bulk, see, and Churchill sez if the Navy captured it they can bleedin' eat it.'

The war news was bad. On the Russian front, Sevastopol had fallen to the Germans, who were preparing for a massive summer offensive to take them to Stalingrad. Two weeks before, Tobruk had been overrun, and there seemed that nothing would stop Rommel reaching Cairo and the Suez Canal. In the Far East, the Japanese were everywhere successful, although the BBC had been cautiously optimistic about a sea battle near Midway. Malta was fighting for her life, and in recent months the Navy had lost *Ark Royal*, *Barham*, *Prince of Wales* and *Repulse*, while *Queen Elizabeth* and *Valiant* had been immobilised by Italian frogmen at Alexandria.

To the men in the fragile little ships that crept through the Arctic fog these events were far distant and unreal. Tobruk was on another planet, and few had heard of Midway Island. Each twenty-four hours was a monotonous sequence of watchkeeping — afternoon

watch, second dog-watch, middle watch, forenoon — of
stumbling below, aching with cold, to snatch a meal,
mildly surprised that it was breakfast and not supper,
for the clock meant nothing, and of a few fleeting hours
of sleep, too painfully brief, and awakening, numb with
tiredness, to drag clothing over stiff limbs. They wrote
letters, hoarded their chocolate ration for that always-
anticipated home leave, sponged themselves down from
a bucket and washed their clothes in a small, greasy
bathroom where drains regurgitated foul-smelling waste.
During the long, cold watch-hours the older men
thought of warm beds and their wives' bodies — but
never spoke of them — evenings before the fire, children, lazy Sunday mornings. The unmarried men
thought of girls' bodies — and seldom stopped talking
about them — Hammersmith Palais and hilarious Saturday nights. Their midday tot of rum was a palliative,
jealously regarded, a brief few seconds of luxury, providing for many the only significant moment in a drab,
fatiguing day.

'When I was an OD,' Stripey Albright complained,
'we never 'ad any split-arsed Wrens—'

'Ah, but yer 'ad Suffragettes,' Bungy Williams
pointed out, 'chainin' themselves ter railings for yer. I
bet they was 'ot stuff, Stripey, burstin' their stays wi'
bleedin' suppressed passion. An' think o' them sexy 'igh
button boots. Shave off.'

'Betty Grable, then,' offered Signalman House. 'Wot
about Betty Grable?'

'Don't ask Stripey about 'er,' Bungy Williams advised.
'Ask 'im about Clara Bow.'

When Hayes-Mailer reached the wardroom he sensed

immediately that something had changed. Conversation was forced, and nobody seemed anxious to meet his eyes. He knew the reason — it was his deliberate abandonment of *Vagrant* — and they did not understand it. The First Lieutenant would not have mentioned it, but the change of course away from *Vagrant*'s position was plainly written in the deck log, with the time, and Fender or Fairbrother would have read it, referred to the chart, calculated, and arrived at the only possible conclusion.

'When we reach the ice,' Hayes-Mailer said, 'we shall continue to steam parallel to it, and we can bring both trawlers to the starboard of the merchantmen. There can be no enemy approach from westward.' They listened, but did not look at him. They had known *Vagrant*'s officers almost as intimately as they knew each other, and they were shocked. But they did not, like him, have to be God. It was easy to be righteously critical when the responsibility was someone else's.

'We are no longer intercepting *Keppel*'s transmissions, but we are aware that PQ17 has reached a position north-east of Bear Island, and today will be turning eastward. This means that the heavy covering force under Admiral Tovey will withdraw westward, and Dalrymple-Hamilton's cruiser squadron, also, will not proceed beyond twenty-five degrees east. Today, then, begins the period of greatest danger for PQ17, but with continued bad weather, and a lot of luck, they may get through without loss.'

There was much, however, of which Hayes-Mailer — and, indeed, Admirals Tovey and Dalrymple-Hamilton — knew nothing, or were only incompletely aware. The Admiralty's practice of condensing, and thus often omitting, information in broadcast reports had resulted in misunderstandings before, and would do so again.

With both Baltic and Black Sea blockaded by the Germans, the only remaining routes for British and American war materials for Russia were overland from the Persian Gulf or by sea convoy around North Cape. The first was long and laborious, the second almost suicidal during mid-summer, and Admiral Sir John Tovey, C-in-C Home Fleet, had repeatedly protested at the cost in British ships and lives. Russia's struggle, however, had captured public imagination; ministerial propaganda had turned the Russians into heroes and Stalin into a jovial Uncle Joe, and regard for him fell not far short of that for Winston Churchill. It was a regard encouraged by Communist sympathisers and trade unionists with a powerful factory-floor following. An unhappily large proportion of the British industrial population was more concerned with the welfare of Soviet 'brothers' and their own inflated wage-packets than the lives of British seamen. The convoys to Russia would continue.

PQ17's thirty-three merchant ships, of which twenty-two were American and two Russian, heavily escorted and screened, were eastward bound at the same time as the returning convoy PQ13 was steaming westward. PQ13 had lost five of her thirteen ships during her outward voyage. Both convoys now had powerful elements of the Home Fleet providing distant cover, including two battleships and an aircraft carrier, an independent squadron of heavy cruisers, and a scattering of twelve British submarines and one

French — *Minerve*. This massive deployment was not, however, intended to combat enemy air or under-sea attacks but to meet the possibility of the German battle fleet emerging from Narvik and Trondheim.

The Admiralty's plan was that, should the German heavy ships attack the convoy while it was still west of Bear Island, the British battleships could engage them outside the range of enemy aircraft. Alternatively, the German battle fleet could be drawn westward, away from PQ17. Rear-Admiral Dalrymple-Hamilton's squadron of four heavy cruisers — two British and two American — had been ordered not to proceed further eastward than longitude 25, that of North Cape. Dalrymple-Hamilton had commanded the battleship *Rodney* with distinction against *Bismarck* a year before — an action brought to a successful conclusion by Admiral Sir John Tovey but not inspired by the interference of the First Sea Lord, Admiral of the Fleet Sir Dudley Pound. In early July 1942, Tovey was still C-in-C Home Fleet, in *Duke of York*, and Pound was still at the Admiralty.

On 2 July, five days out and sixty miles east of Jan Mayen Island, PQ17 was sighted and reported by U-255, and shortly after by U-408. Befehlshaber des Unterseeboote ordered the wolf-pack to shadow and attack, and the first dive-bombers took off from their Norwegian bases.

Later that same day the battleship *Tirpitz*, of 52,600 tons, and the heavy cruiser *Admiral Hipper* moved from their Trondheim berths, and the two pocket battleships *Lützow* and *Admiral Scheer*, each of 12,000 tons, left Narvik. All intended to rendezvous, together with a dozen destroyers, in Alten fjord, nearer to North Cape.

Lützow, formerly *Deutschland*, scraped her bottom in the fog before reaching the open sea, and returned to Narvik, while three destroyers were similarly damaged in a fjord in the Lofotens. All the other warships, however, reached Alten fjord on 3 July.

Intelligence of this northern movement of the German battle force had reached the Admiralty in London, but as the report could not be confirmed by reconnaissance it was not relayed to the units at sea, and PQ17, its escort and screening ships were left in ignorance of the threatening new development.

Hayes-Mailer did not frequent the wardroom often, or for lengthy periods. It was, he conceded, a location in which officers appreciated being free of the continuous presence of a commanding officer while, conversely, it was better that a commander should avoid familiarity that might lead to lack of respect. He routinely took a single midday drink in the wardroom, circumstances permitting, and usually had his meals there because it was sensible to do so. Otherwise, except for briefing sessions, he regarded himself as a guest in the wardroom and treated it accordingly.

The loss of Sub-Lieutenant Coope had presented *Virtue* with a manning problem. The ship had a bare minimum of officers when briefly docking in Liverpool — the Commander, three lieutenants and three sub-lieutenants, plus the engineer and surgeon, who did no deck watches. Hayes-Mailer had expected to lose John Rainbird in exchange for another seasoned lieutenant and at least one more sub-lieutenant, but the ship's turn-round had happened too quickly.

On passage, the Commander required two officers on

the bridge, usually a lieutenant and a sub, and kept himself available to be called in any moment of event, doubt or hazard, which meant that, over all, he spent more time on the bridge, or in the chart-house, than any of his juniors. Now, with only three experienced deck officers — Lieutenant-Commander Rainbird and Lieutenants Fender and Prentice — and two sub-lieutenants only a few weeks out of *King Alfred* train-ing, he had considered borrowing a man from *Penny-royal*, but quickly dismissed the thought. *Virtue* would have to make do, and he, the Commander, would get even less sleep than before.

And *Vagrant*. The loss of the sister destroyer had been shattering and still almost unbelievable. One moment there had been a living, disciplined ship and 120 men — officers and seamen, stokers, telegraphists, artificers, all with faiths and loves, with families, mothers, wives — and the next moment there had been nothing, as if ship and men had never existed. The suddenness, the finality of it, was incomprehensible. There would be wives and mothers, too — still unknow-ing — who would not believe it. The words 'missing presumed dead' would keep alive that tiny smouldering hope for weeks, for months. Some of them, even now, would be writing letters to a loved one who was already dead and from whom letters might continue to come. Certainty, however brutal, was surely better than a lingering prayer for a miracle.

In the wardroom his decision to turn away from *Vagrant* would be a subject for debate. Fender, he could be certain, would be critical, arguing that the Com-mander could at least have investigated *Vagrant*'s posi-tion, even if he chose not to stop. It was the righteous point of view. Before the war, Fender had been a pharmaceuticals sales manager, trained to present marketing platitudes as if they were scientific facts, and the two young sub-lieutenants would find him convincing.

Rainbird probably agreed with Fender, but would keep his opinions to himself, even dampen the other's more irresponsible comments, but Prentice would support the Commander's action. Prentice had abandoned an apprenticeship with the Union Castle Line to enter the Navy, and after Hayes-Mailer and Rainbird was the most experienced deck officer. He considered himself a professional sailor, and emphasised it by showing a lack of enthusiasm for anything that Fender said or did.

The Surgeon-Lieutenant and the Commissioned Engineer would have their opinions, but would keep them tightly to themselves. Only a year before Michael Nicols had been a registrar in a Nottingham hospital. Since then he had spent a few months in RNH Haslar, and still referred to below decks as downstairs, a deck as a floor and a bulkhead as a wall. He was the wardroom butt for good-humoured banter, enjoyed being so, and Hayes-Mailer suspected that the young doctor persisted in playing the landlubber just for the amusement of it.

Commissioned Engineer Stevens was the oldest officer in the ship, a man who had crossed the almost impossible chasm between a peacetime lower deck and wardroom. Hayes-Mailer had joined his first ship in 1918, but Stevens, if pressed, could talk about Tyrwhitt's Harwich Force, the Battle of the Bight and Heligoland, and ships like *Broke* and *Swift*. Stevens, small, with thin white hair, was a lonely man who might have been happier in an ERAs' mess; he concerned himself with the engine room and almost nothing else.

Perhaps, Hayes-Mailer sighed, he should have done what almost every other commander would have — steamed at utmost speed to the succour of a sister ship. But few other commanders had a record marred by a severe reprimand for carelessness. A few weeks earlier a suave flag officer who had never commanded a destroyer in his life had been condescending. 'That little business in Hong Kong, Hayes-Mailer — well — I think it's time we forgot that, don't you? There's a new flotilla working up. "Hunt" Class escorts, type two. I should think about the end of August. . . ?'

Yes, he could have taken *Virtue* to *Vagrant*'s position. That had been his first, instinctive intention. The possibility of survivors was not as remote as he had suggested to others or convinced himself. Then, if there had been men in the sea, he would have had to stop; to ignore survivors when there was no obvious enemy threat would have made him a pariah in the eyes of his fellows. But there was no pretence about the danger involved. The U-boat, incapable of overhauling the convoy, might well have been waiting for a rescuing ship to appear, and the loss of *Virtue* would not only have been inexcusable in itself but would have so depleted the escort that the convoy must have turned back to Iceland. If Hayes-Mailer had survived, no plea of extenuating circumstances would have altered the fact that he had placed his ship in hazard and, whatever the outcome, there would be no new flotilla of destroyers in August. . . .

'Roll on the *Nelson*, the *Rodney, Renown*,' Signalman House sang miserably, 'this two-funnelled bastard is gettin' me down.' He regarded his herrings. 'An' roll on my bloddy twelve. Soddin' herrins-in again? If the galley lost their bloddy tin-opener, we'd *starve*.'

'Bleedin' flannel,' Bungy Williams sniffed. 'I bet yer wish yer could join up for ever, like Stripey there. Yer don't get herrins-in every day at 'ome, I know—'

'Yer bloddy reet, I don't. An' I don't get train smash every breakfas', an' baby's head an' muzzle velocity fer supper. Come ter think of it, I don't get bloddy sparkers using my dhobeying bucket ter peel spuds in, either.'

'When I first went ter sea,' Stripey Albright said, 'we didn't 'ave breakfast, only biscuits.'

'I know,' Bungy Williams sympathised. 'An' salt pork wi' bleedin' weevils. That Captain Bligh was a bastard. Yer should 'ave complained, Stripey.'

Lobby Ludd also eyed his mess of herrings in tomato sauce with scant enthusiasm. Herrings, in any form, brought back memories of a quarterdeck and a marble basin swimming with goldfish, a small, bare room with a high window, and a voice that counted slowly. Three . . . four . . . five . . .

His messdeck fellows had left him alone, not referring to *Vagrant* in his hearing. He would not have minded if they had. They glanced at him uncomfortably, glanced away, talked of irrelevant things, and even, by some telepathic agreement, argued hotly and artificially. When conversation flagged, someone would hurriedly spur it on, as if silence were somehow unwholesome.

He wished they would talk about *Vagrant*, so that perhaps he would experience some grief. He ought to feel grief, but he didn't. None of it seemed real. Why didn't they talk about *Vagrant*, instead of herrins-in?

'Since I've been in the bloddy Andrew,' Signalman

House complained, 'I've never 'ad tripe. 'Oo gets all the tripe? I suppose it goes to the soddin' Air Force.'

'Why don't yer write ter the *Daily Mirror*?' Bungy Williams asked. 'Cassandra — he's the bloke. Arsk 'im why the Navy's deprived o' tripe. Arsk 'im.'

Lobby Ludd pushed his herrings aside. We can't have that sot of thing, Ludd. Twelve cuts.

Four

He was Boy 2nd Class C. Ludd, JX245613, of Benbow Division, HMS *St George*, and a nozzer — the lowest recognised status in the Royal Navy. And that, he quickly discovered, meant hardly any recognition at all. His walking days, an instructor had bawled at him, were over. Henceforth he would neither walk nor run, but fly. Given the choice — the only one he was ever to be allowed — of training as a seaman, a signalman or a telegraphist, he had chosen the signals branch, although for no important reason; he was only vaguely aware of the differences. Nobody had offered more than the flimsiest explanation, and nobody seemed sufficiently approachable to ask.

Blue serge in winter, white ducks in summer, always gaiters and boots. Four truckle beds to each single-roomed chalet, concrete-floored and bereft of any other furnishing, intended in peacetime for one economising holidaymaker — tolerable quarters in warm weather but bleakly chill when January blew cold from nearby Douglas Bay. Bathrooms and doorless lavatories could be a 200-yards trot in rain or snow, with cold water at the end of it and the lashing tongue of an instructor for a boy who slowed to a walk. So firmly implanted was the addiction to continuous running that many boys would continue jog-trotting when halted.

There were few idle moments in an intense regimen of practical seamanship, signalling by masthead flags, by semaphore, by flashing, by morse buzzer, and running from one location to another. If momentarily there was no occupation, then an occupation was extemporised. Sport, always compulsory, and under physical-training instructors, included boxing in which opponents were matched by height, not weight, obstacle racing, pugnacious hockey and soccer, but not rugby, a sport reserved for those of a higher social level. A period of each day was spent in the classroom, where Naval schoolmasters taught arithmetic, geography, Naval history and English to boys who, on enlistment, had considered schooldays behind them and were consequently reluctant pupils. Classroom qualifications, however, were necessary for advancement, and they submitted.

In quantity, food was probably adequate for an adult of normal pursuits, but for healthy, physically active youths it was never sufficient, and hunger was a constant companion; food parcels from home — searched for forbidden items by the Regulating Office — were jealously shared and ravenously consumed. In quality, also, the basic ingredients were probably sound, but preparation and cooking by a civilian contractor were atrocious, so that there were times when even the most hungry must push his plate aside. Albeit, before every meal, a bosun's pipe would shrill, the duty officer would shout, 'For what we are about to receive, thank God!' a thousand boys responded, 'Amen!'

Of all offences, smoking, or the possession of smoking materials, constituted the most indefensible. There was a small shop which sold confectionary, for which Boy Ludd had no taste, but not cigarettes, for which he had. Cigarettes, smuggled in from thrice-fortnightly 'shore' periods, were resold at sixpence each — half a week's pay for a Boy 2nd Class. They were usually flattened by being secreted between sock and foot, in a cap lining, or taped in the crotch — stratagems that did not always foil the chief petty officers searching all returning liberty boys. At such a premium, cigarette butts were carefully conserved and repeatedly reconstituted, while matches, equally prohibited, were sliced along their length into several divisions. A skilled match-slicer could divide a single match into five or six valid components.

When a match was unobtainable, a flame could be achieved by removing a light bulb and short-circuiting the live terminals with a wedge of tin foil smeared with boot-blacking. There would be a flash, and the blacking would flare for seconds. It was, however, a hazardous undertaking. The electrical circuit of an entire block of buildings could be fused and a square foot of ceiling blackened, which meant desperate cosmetic action with pipe-clay — held ready for such an emergency — in the few minutes before retribution inevitably arrived. If successfully concluded, the irate, scouring instructors would find only boys solicitously reading their seamanship manuals and righteously indignant at the sudden and unaccountable loss of electric light.

Some time elapsed before Boy Ludd was apprehended in the act of smoking, although this was not remarkable. Whatever differences of background, scholarship or philosophy there existed between the boys, there was a common bond of resentment towards the chief petty officer instructors, and none of these could advance far into the boys' chalet lines without the warning cry of 'Lobs!' preceding him, at the sound of which all cigarette fragments would be quickly pinched out and secreted. Only by deliberately waiting, hidden, in some suspected rendezvous — the lavatories, or an enshrubbed corner of the playing-fields — could an instructor be confident of capturing a red-handed victim.

Boy Ludd had experienced periods of punishment 8*a* and 10*a*, and had spent many hours trotting a wide circle on the parade-ground with a Lee-Enfield rifle held above his head — the penalty for a forbidding list of minor offences of which it was almost impossible to remain innocent long. He had taken great care to avoid being caught in the act of smoking, which meant a flogging. Charlie Ludd would achieve his first flogging for a totally unexpected reason.

Supper at 6.30 p.m. was a meal to justify serious attention; more than twelve hours would subsequently elapse before the hungry boys would eat again, but the near-raw herring occupying each supper-plate exuded a highly suspect smell, and had been pushed aside by all except the most insensitive. There had been protesting murmurs, but the instructors prowling between the tables had called for silence, and an indifferent duty officer had stamped from the mess-hall. This, a rebellious Boy Ludd told his fellows, was beyond toleration. The catering contractor was a profiteering scoundrel who not only provided prison fare in short measure but probably maintained a massive pig-farm on the wasted food that resulted. Nobody in authority appeared to realise this, and it was time something was done. He would go to the top. He would write a letter of complaint to the Commander.

Charlie Ludd did not pause to consider that there might be others with similar convictions but a different remedy. A score or more boys had each taken his herring and deposited it among the goldfish on the quarterdeck.

The hallowed quarterdeck of HMS *St George* had earlier been the entrance foyer of Cunningham's Holiday Camp. It was a spacious, marble-floored area, largely under glass, and adjoined by administrative offices. In its centre, a legacy of happier days, was a sizeable marble basin in which swam a number of fat goldfish. When the last of several hundred boys had trotted across the quarterdeck before the critical eyes of the Master-at-Arms, the goldfish had been joined by twenty-six herrings. The Master-at-Arms was enraged.

Unaware, Charlie Ludd wrote his letter, lacking no encouragement from his fellows, who all agreed that it was a very fine letter and could not possibly be ignored by the Commander. The Commander found it in his 'IN' tray, and he did not ignore it. The food, wrote Charlie Ludd, was unfit for human consumption, and something ought to be done about it. He, Ludd, had one or two ideas which the Commander might like to hear. Herrings, for a start—

Herrings. A few feet from the Commander's office door the quarterdeck reeked of rancid fish. The marble basin had been drained and scoured, the fragmented remains of twenty-six herrings and several dead goldfish had been removed, and the Master-at-Arms was explosively ill-humoured.

When Charlie Ludd was summoned to report, at the double, to the Commander on the quarterdeck, he went with the congratulatory shouts of his comrades and with a sense of extreme satisfaction. On the quarterdeck he was met with a vaguely familiar and unpleasant smell, a simmering Master-at-Arms, and a Commander who coldly informed him that the matter was sufficiently grave to be referred to the Commodore. It was mildly disconcerting. A confrontation with the Commodore usually meant only one thing, and it was an uncomfortable thought. Still, Charlie Ludd decided, it was too late now.

Before the Commodore's table he was given no opportunity to outline his complaints about food. Oddly, food was hardly mentioned, and his one attempt to broach the subject was stifled by a roar of 'Keep silence!' from the Master-at-Arms. The ageing, white-haired Commodore read through the letter several times, glancing up at Ludd. 'Twenty-six 'errings, sir,' the Master-at-Arms confirmed. 'I counted 'em, before they fell to pieces in the water. And four dead goldfish.'

'There never was such an unholy mess, sir,' the Commander contributed. 'It took the whole forenoon to get the thing clean. And the smell.' He shook his head. 'I think this sort of thing has to be stamped on.'

The Commodore nodded wearily. 'It's a well-written letter,' he conceded, with faint surprise. 'Very explicit.' He looked up. 'But we can't have this sort of thing, Ludd. There are approved procedures for voicing complaints and grievances, but yours is not one of them. I will not tolerate demonstrations.'

He considered carefully, then, 'Twelve cuts.'

The Master-at-Arms smiled grimly.

Dressed in clean white ducks, Boy Ludd waited on the quarterdeck for his escort to march him off — the duty officer, the Master-at-Arms and two regulating petty officers. One of the latter carried under one arm a bundle of heavy canes.

He had been given a brief examination in the Sick Bay, but had not expected any reprieve from that direction. He was fit, the surgeon had confirmed, and he should return, after punishment, if he bled.

He marched between them, from the quarterdeck and through the long, covered way to the parade-ground, past the galley, the cinema and the laundry, and then climbed stairs he had never seen before. They halted in an empty room, bare-walled, bare-floored, with a single, high window through which he could not see.

The duty officer tested the weight of several canes. 'This one,' he decided. It was taken by the burlier of the two RPOs. Charlie Ludd, with knees half-bent, found his head clamped firmly between the thighs of the second RPO, and he gripped the man's calves. This, he told himself, is what comes of standin' up for yer rights.

'Twelve cuts, sir,' the Master-at-Arms said.

The officer nodded. 'Carry on, please.'

The RPO braced himself, lifted the cane high and slowly, then brought it forward with every ounce of his strength. An involuntary shout came from Charlie Ludd, and he heaved, pain-racked and shocked. He felt his legs sag and his senses haze, but the RPO's thighs clamped viciously tighter, compelling him upright. Jesus Christ, he choked, and that was only the first. It was inconceivable that he could endure twelve.

'One cut delivered, sir,' the Master-at-Arms reported.

'Very good,' the officer responded agreeably. 'Carry on with the punishment, please.'

'Two . . . three . . . four. . . .' Through a scalding mist of nausea, Charlie Ludd could hear the Master-at-Arms counting the strokes that smashed into his flesh, each an explosion of indescribable agony that was beyond human toleration and yet must be followed by another, and another. '. . . Eight . . . nine. . . .' *Soddin' Christ!* How impossibly distant was twelve? He would never reach twelve.

But he did. 'Twelve,' the Master-at-Arms said. 'Twelve cuts delivered, sir.'

The duty officer did not look at Charlie Ludd, who, released, had fallen to hands and knees, with eyes clenched and mouth loose. Over him, the RPO massaged his own calves, gouged by the boy's nails. 'Punishment concluded,' the officer confirmed, and left the room. The RPO swore softly, and Charlie Ludd raised himself dazedly on legs that were like water.

'Right, Ludd,' the Master-at-Arms cautioned. 'Now yer know what happens to troublemakers. I'm going to be *watchin' you* from now on. I don't like your sort. You just put one foot wrong, see, and yer'll wish yer've never been born.' He sniffed. 'Get yerself to the Sick Bay, at the double, and don't spend all day about it. I said *at the double!*'

His fellows' laughter died when he eased off his trousers, and several winced, sucking in their breath. A heavy, black bruise spread entirely across his lower buttocks, furrowed by the cane blows and speckled with pin-heads of congealed blood. He touched the area gingerly with his finger-tips. 'It was a bastard,' he said. 'A proper bastard.' They eyed him respectfully, not doubting. 'If I'd been prepared,' he explained, 'I'd 'ave known what to expect, see? But I wasn't prepared.' They nodded gravely. 'Next time,' he promised, 'I'll bleedin' know.'

One of them fumbled hurriedly in a cap-lining, produced an inch of crumpled cigarette. ' 'Ave a drag, Charlie.' It was a generous gesture. 'I was savin' it fer after Rounds.' They watched him paternally as he puffed smoke with slow deliberation. 'That bleedin' Master-at-Arms,' he pronounced, but was unable to think of a sufficiently scurrilous expletive. 'If I ever meet 'im when I'm on soddin' leave—' He snorted.

But on leave he had forgotten the Master-at-Arms, the flogging, the daily pettiness, the bullying instructors and perfunctory officers. For fourteen wonderful days he was his own master, to rise when he chose, walk where he wished, even to walk. He could stroll the entire length of the North End Road with his cap on the back of his head, his cuffs upturned, a cigarette nonchalantly between his lips, and that far-away look in his eyes that became a man who had seen distant horizons and done many things. He did not talk of his experiences, and modestly shrugged aside questions from his admirers. There were things a man did not talk about, and they understood.

He was Jack ashore. Total strangers and soldiers and airmen who had been no closer to the enemy than Catterick and Bury St Edmunds offered him beer, and considered themselves privileged when he accepted. Old men patted his shoulder approvingly and tipsy old ladies kissed him. Mrs Ludd fussed possessively, darned his socks and ironed his collars with exquisite care.

And there was Eileen Wilkins, who earlier had tossed her head disbelievingly. 'You? Joining the Navy? I'll believe *that* when I see it.' Eileen Wilkins was superior, a year older, an inch taller, and a product of the Fulham Borough Polytechnic, which was more conveniently located than Girton. She resided with her parents in Parsons Green, subtly more genteel than Walham Green, frequented Putney, which was better still, and had a telephone, the undeniable hallmark of the élite.

Charlie Ludd had coveted Eileen Wilkins for several years, since he had first observed interesting differences in the opposite sex, but they had moved in different circles which seldom overlapped. She had usually been escorted by older youths with long scarves and blazers, who talked of the summer vac. or the rugger finals at Rosslyn Park, and his few exploratory advances had been cooly parried. Eileen Wilkins had the ability to gaze at an unwanted suitor as if he simply wasn't there. She was blonde, shapely, and very confident.

Now, he met her as she emerged from the Town Hall at the conclusion of her weekly first-aid lecture. It was an encounter that was not as accidental as his look of surprise suggested.

'Well!' His eyes widened. 'If it ain't Eileen Wilkins! Now there's a coincidence. I was only thinking o' you the other day. Can't think why—' He pondered. 'Ah, yes. I was talking to our Commander Wilkins on the quarterdeck—' He extracted a cigarette from a packet, offhandedly. 'And I jes' wondered—' His match flared in a cupped hand. 'You ain't related to a Commander Wilkins?'

She was momentarily disconcerted. 'No — that is, I

don't think so. . . .'

'No? Commander Robert Wilkins. We was jes' talking about this and that, y'know.' He glanced at the dimly lit entrance of the Town Hall. 'Jes' finished evening classes? Where's yer schoolboy friends?'

'First aid,' she corrected. She had regained her composure. 'Well, I must—'

'First aid,' he nodded approvingly. 'Yes, that can be very useful. 'Ave yer done shrapnel wounds yet? Nasty thing, shrapnel.' He narrowed his eyes reminiscently. 'I could tell yer—' But he shook his head modestly, then brightened. 'Well, I'm walkin' your way. I'll carry yer splints for yer.'

She would have protested, but he was already walking beside her. It was mildly disquieting but, she conceded, she had no reason to be alarmed. She was, after all, almost eighteen, and there was nothing improper in sharing the company of a man in uniform. In the darkness they were unlikely to be recognised by anyone who knew her. Freda Harris, at the Polytechnic, was always talking about her dates with itinerant servicemen — not that she, Eileen Wilkins, considered her meeting with Charlie Ludd to be anything like a date, but she *might* mention it casually to Freda Harris tomorrow, adding that he was serving with Commander Wilkins, a relation. Commander Robert Wilkins.

'Yer've got to watch these lights,' Charlie Ludd said as they crossed the road, and took her arm. 'D'yer know there's no black-out in Gibraltar?' He had read it in a newspaper. 'No black-out. Lights everywhere, like Piccadilly Circus.' She expressed polite surprise. 'Yer'd never think there was a war on, in Gib,' he went on, 'but, o' course, there ain't much point. The Germans know exactly where Gib is, without any lights.'

'Don't they know where London is?' she enquired. 'Why do they know where Gibraltar is, but not London?'

'Ah, that's different.' He couldn't think why; the newspaper had not explained. He changed the subject quickly. 'What say we walk across the Common fer a bit o' fresh air? When yer've been at sea' — he chuckled apologetically — 'yer get used ter fresh air.'

Eileen Wilkins was apprehensive. It was unlikely that the air was significantly fresher on a few hundred yards of urban common than in any other part of Fulham, but that was not her immediate concern. 'Oh, I don't think so. It's horribly dark—'

'Dark? That ain't real dark,' he scoffed. 'Not like the Atlantic. That's dark, all right. In the Navy, yer've got to 'ave six-six vision, *and* pedal a bike while yer 'anging by yer 'ands.' She could not see the relevance, but made a further protest. 'It's not a nice place. There've been several girls accosted—'

'Huh!' He snorted belligerently. 'Jes' let anyone try, that's all. I'd jes' like to see anyone try. I could tell yer a thing or two. . . .' But he refrained.

The Common was very dark indeed, defeating even Charlie Ludd's six-six vision, and he could not seem to locate even one of the several criss-crossing pathways. ' 'Evvy cloud, seven-eights strato-cumulus, that's what it is,' he decided. 'This is the sort o' thing the U-boats like.' Unfortunately Eileen Wilkins could not see the grim set of his jaw in the darkness. 'Imagine yerself on the bridge of a corvette. . . .'

She was too busily imagining other things. 'If we simply walked in one direction for more than thirty seconds,' she suggested, 'we'll reach somewhere we'll recognise. I think the New Kings Road is over there.' She pointed.

'No,' Charlie Ludd disagreed. 'That's where we've jes' come from. It's a scientific phenomenon, losing yer bearin's in the dark, an' the Navy's been studying it fer years. Now, if I 'ad a compass. . . .'

They had stumbled into an immense black obstacle. Eileen Wilkins gave a little shriek of relief. 'This is the static water-tank at the back of the flats. Now I *know* where we are.'

'Per'aps it is, and per'aps it ain't,' Charlie Ludd cautioned. 'Yer must remember they move these things around, ter fool the bombers. That's why the Navy don't 'ave their ships' names on their caps—'

'They don't move static water-tanks!' she retorted. 'Anyway, it was here at seven o'clock. Why should the Germans want to bomb a static water-tank?'

'That's the 'ole point,' he explained. 'They don't. They want ter bomb where there *ain't* a static water-tank.'

'I don't believe it,' she accused. 'I don't believe—' But she was closely confined between Charlie Ludd and the static water-tank, and was uncomfortably aware that his hands had lifted her skirt. 'I'm not that sort of girl,' she said firmly.

'Yer going ter be,' he said, 'any minute now. Yer ain't brought me all over the Common fer nothin', 'ave yer?'

This, she realised, was what Freda Harris hinted at. There was no harm, Freda always said, so long as you didn't let them go too far. What was too far? After all, she was nearly eighteen, the same as Freda, and Freda had rolled her eyes deliciously.

'If yer'd jes' relax a bit,' Charlie Ludd suggested. 'That's better. Yer might as well be comfortable.' Was this far enough? she wondered. Freda had said that, if you weren't careful, things got out of control.

'My hand ain't cold, is it?' he enquired solicitously. ' 'Ang on a sec. The trouble with these Navy trousers, they ain't got flies.' She could not guess what he meant, but then she did, and she was horrified.

'It's always the same, the first time,' he consoled her. 'If yer don't like it, jes' say so, an' I'll take it out, see? Jes' bend yer knees a bit, an' yer'll find it's made ter measure. Better than first aid.'

Aghast, Eileen Wilkins wrenched her skirt down. 'You weren't really going to—' The truth was shuddering. '*Sexual intercourse*—?'

'Not exactly,' he explained. 'I jes' thought we might try it fer size, see. Did yer ever read *No Orchids fer Miss Blandish*? She didn't like it at first, but afterwards she couldn't get enough—'

'I am *not* Miss Blandish.' She stiffened. 'I do *not* have vulgar relationships with sailors in the black-out. You'll find that sort in Hammersmith Broadway. If you *don't* mind, I'm going home, and if you *don't* mind I'll go by myself. My father is a Special Constable, and if he *knew*—'

'Yer'd better pull yer bloomers up,' Charlie Ludd advised wearily, 'or yer'll tread on the elastic.'

Five

All day on 4 July the eight ships steamed steadily northward through swirling, yellow-whitish fog that hid from them the vast wastes of the Greenland ice-pack which they knew lay somewhere to port. The sea's swell was thickly sluggish, black, floating with flat ice fragments that the ships' bows brushed aside, surfaced with a wispy, cold steam born of the dying remnants of the Gulf Stream and the bitter Arctic wind. Ahead, *Pennyroyal* was groping her way by radar, and Hayes-Mailer had relaxed restrictions on convoy R/T so that warnings of the larger floes could be relayed. Occasionally the fog would thin, and they would sight all the ships for a few minutes, blurred like an old sepia-tinted photograph, before the haze congealed again, to leave each in claustral isolation. There was no sky, no horizon, no beginning and no end. It was an eerie unknown world where men could not live, where the cold seared the lungs and froze extremities until blood circulation stopped, when the touch of exposed metal could tear the skin like a burn.

That same morning, north of Bear Island, the same

114

fog that had provided cover for convoy PQ17 lifted, and from a break in the low heavy cloud a German torpedo-bomber pounced on a 7000-ton American freighter, laden with tanks. Having achieved a hit, the aircraft disappeared, and the convoy thrust on, waiting for the full weight of an enemy air onslaught. The hours passed. The sea was calm and there was little wind.

At 0615 Admiral Tovey's force of *Duke of York*, *Washington* and *Victorious* turned away, westward. Submarines and aircraft were not their concern, and there was no news of any movement by *Tirpitz*.

'This is the Captain. I promised that I would keep you in touch with events as far as possible, and that is why I am talking to you now. Most of you will know that we have changed course to a more northerly route than that originally intended, and what happens during the next few days will depend very much on the experience of PQ17, which is ahead of us' — Hayes-Mailer paused — 'because what happens to PQ17 is very likely to happen to us.'

A sheaf of signals rustled in his fingers. 'The information we have is taken from intercepted wireless signals. It's rather sketchy, and my interpretation may not be entirely accurate, but it would seem that PQ17 was attacked by a single aircraft at dawn. The American ship *Christopher Newport* was badly damaged, and she was sunk by a U-boat later in the day.

'There were no further air attacks until 1800, when enemy aircraft were driven off, but two hours later another attack by twenty-five dive-bombers resulted in the sinking of three more ships.'

There was really no need, he had decided, to mention

Tirpitz, Lützow, Hipper and *Scheer*. The enemy heavy ships were locked in Narvik and Trondheim, and it must now be impossible for them to make any contribution to the German attack on PQ17. Still, their absence was comforting.

'There is no evidence that any elements of the German battle fleet have left their anchorages in Norwegian fjords. Our own heavy ships have therefore turned back to Scapa Flow, and the cruiser screen, also, has been ordered to withdraw westward. Convoy PQ17 has another twenty-four hours during which it will be within reach of enemy aircraft — and, of course, submarines — but there is a powerful close escort, and we have every confidence that Murmansk will be reached without further loss.

'With regard to ourselves, there is no doubt that our situation is one of considerable danger, and that danger will increase as we move eastward. I believe our change of course, and this fog, will have thrown the enemy off the scent. They will have their hands full with PQ17; their submarine and air crews will be tired, and many will have expended torpedoes or be short of fuel. Even so, I know that every single one of you will remain vigilant and, if we are brought to action, you will do your utmost to ensure that this ship gives a good account of herself. There is no going back now; we can only go on.'

He braced himself for his final words. 'Yesterday two of our ship's company died — Sub-Lieutenant Coope and Able Seaman Foster. Even more tragic, our sister ship *Vagrant* was torpedoed, and we sighted no survivors.' His voice remained steady. 'I am aware that at least one crew-member of this ship had a brother in

Vagrant; many more of us had friends of long standing. I do not intend to talk to you about the fortunes of war, only to remind you that Sub-Lieutenant Coope, Able Seaman Foster, and the entire company of *Vagrant* died at their battle stations in the true traditions of the Navy in which we serve.' The words were sour on his tongue. 'I have every confidence that, when the time comes, this ship's company will also display the same devotion to their duties.'

On the messdeck there was a new and mildly disturbing topic of conversation.

'German battle fleet?' Bungy Williams speculated. 'The Ol' Man wouldn't have mentioned that jes' for a skylark. He must 'ave thought there was a *chance* of 'em coming out.' He considered. ' "There's no evidence that any elements o' the German battle fleet 'ave left their anchorages." Well, there was no bleedin' evidence that the *Bismarck* 'ad left 'er anchorage, was there? Or the *Graf Spee*?' He looked for Coder Crowthorne. 'You oughter know, Brains Trust. What's the German battle fleet?'

Coder Crowthorne removed his glasses to polish them, and blinked. 'In Norwegian waters there's *Tirpitz*, *Lützow*, *Scheer*, and the cruiser *Hipper*, and in German harbours the *Scharnhorst*, *Gneisenau* and *Prinz Eugen*. The *Tirpitz* is the same class as the *Bismarck*.'

'Shave off,' said Bungy Williams. 'That lot could make us look bleedin' sick. After the *Bismarck*, nobody's going to tell me that German battle-wagons are made o' plywood an' run on margarine, or German sailors have low morals, and can't see in the soddin' dark. If the *Bismarck* shamfered the *Hood*, what

117

wouldn't the bleedin' *Tirpitz* do to us?'

'We sunk the *Bismarck* in the end, didn't we?' Lobby Ludd suggested. We, he had said. He had been in *St George*, and he remembered clearly that day in late May, last year, when a ramrod gunnery training officer had strode into the mess-hall. The bosun's pipe had squealed and the officer had shouted, 'For what we are about to receive, thank God!' Then, 'SILENCE!' A thousand boys had frozen, and the officer thrust forward an angry chin. 'We have sunk the *Bismarck*!' Seconds later the mess-hall exploded into roaring cheers. They had shouted themselves hoarse, stamped feet, climbed on tables, and even the instructors had grinned. They had sunk *Bismarck*, and *Hood* had been avenged.

'An' we could sink the *Tirpitz*,' Bungy Williams nodded. 'We could creep up behind 'er while she weren't lookin', and pull 'er bleedin' plugs out.'

'Fer Chris' sake!' Signalman House had his ear close to the SRE loudspeaker. 'Why don't you sods talk a bit louder? Then I won't 'ear bugger-all. I sent up a bloddy request, see — "Two-way Family Favourites" — an' wi' all this soddin' cackle —'

'A request?' Bungy Williams stared, incredulous. 'Shave off. Did you 'ear that? "An' our nex' number is fer Signalman Shit House, of HMS *Virtue*, somewhere at sea." Shave off. What did yer ask for, Shit?'

Signalman House coloured. ' "The Lights of 'Ome".'

' "The Lights of 'Ome"?' Bungy Williams guffawed. 'Now that's bleedin' touchin', I must say. I never knew you 'ad lights in your 'ome, Shit.' Signalman House bridled, and Bungy Williams held up a conciliatory hand. 'All right. I'll tell yer what. For 'alf yer tot, I'll sing yer any request yer like, *an'* do yer a bleedin' tap dance.'

Hayes-Mailer had gone to his sea-cabin, so numb with
fatigue that he swayed. He had not, he realised, had four
hours of uninterrupted sleep since leaving Liverpool; he
needed a shave and he felt dirty, but at this moment he
desired nothing but to lay himself down and surrender
to oblivion. He peeled off duffel-coat and sea-boots, but
there were footsteps on the steel deck beyond the door,
and then a knock. It was the Petty Officer Telegraphist,
grave of face.

'Sorry to disturb you, sir. There's a couple of deciphered intercepts that I thought you might like to
see — before anyone else. What I mean is—'

The Commander knew what the man meant. Although all incoming signals were assumed to be addressed to a ship's commander, in practice they went first to
the officer of the watch, and it was unusual for the
wireless office to bypass the man on the bridge. There
were, however, occasional signals that a commander
might wish to read and fully assess before their contents
became common knowledge. 'These are the only copies,
sir,' the Petty Officer said in a conspiratorial voice, as if
there might be eavesdroppers.

'Thank you, Sparks,' Hayes-Mailer nodded. 'All right.
Leave them with me.'

'Yessir,' the other whispered, and withdrew, dis-
appointed that he could not remain for a few moments,
a confidant. Hayes-Mailer pressed his eyes tightly shut,
compelling himself to concentrate. Then he looked at
the signals.

He could not, immediately, interpret what he read. It
was impossible. He went back to the beginning and read

again. It was still impossible. He reached for his sea-boots.

On the bridge, Lieutenant Fender slid himself hastily from the tall chair at the Commander's appearance, and Sub-Lieutenant Waddell smothered a cigarette in his coat pocket. 'Hello, sir,' Fender said. 'I thought you had turned in.' His voice was almost reproachful. It was the middle watch, very cold, but far from completely dark. Only the fog still swirled. *Virtue* steamed astern of, and equidistant from, the two big tankers, both just visible. 'Nothing much to report, sir,' Fender went on. '*Olympic Madison* is a bit erratic, but she can't do much harm on that side. *Pennyroyal* came through about ten minutes ago to say she calculates we're thirty to forty miles eastward of the real ice and, so far as radar was concerned, there was nothing nasty in the woodshed.'

The Commander grunted, then turned. 'Is there any coffee left in that thermos, Sub?' It was bitterly cold. Waddell jumped. 'Yessir, but I'm afraid we haven't any clean cups.'

'Never mind a clean cup.' He climbed stiffly into the tall chair vacated by Fender, peered over a screen made almost useless by condensation. The exhaled breath of all three was like white smoke. 'Who has the morning? The First Lieutenant? All right, now listen — and you can pass this on to him. Last night the Admiralty ordered Dalrymple-Hamilton's cruisers to retire westward at utmost speed.'

Fender was only mildly surprised. 'At utmost speed, sir. Isn't that a bit dramatic?'

'Bloody dramatic, Fender,' Hayes-Mailer gritted. 'Because twelve minutes later he received another signal. PQ17 has been ordered to scatter.' He swung his chair in

120

a half-circle, to face them.

There was no sound except the hum of the engine fans, the almost inaudible whine of a generator, and a distant whispering chuckle as the ship's bows scythed through the fog-shrouded, endless sea of ice rubble. Hayes-Mailer could see the shrugged figure of the port-side look-out, the trunk of the foremast with its drapery of halyards, aerials and insulators, the black cowling of the forward funnel. It was snowing again, the small white flakes whirling like confetti out of the fog; the cold was intense.

Fender's jaw had dropped. 'Scatter?' He wiped away the clot of ice that had formed below his nostrils. '*Scatter*, sir? Doesn't that mean—?' Waddell, not yet comprehending, glanced from one man to the other.

Hayes-Mailer nodded. 'Only one thing. Enemy surface ships.'

Now Waddell understood. '*Tirpitz!*' he blurted.

'You've got it first time, Sub,' the Commander said, 'but don't drop that coffee, and keep your eyes on those tankers ahead. I don't suppose they'll be watching us.'

'But *Tirpitz* was in Trondheim, sir,' Fender protested, '800 miles from PQ17. And the Admiralty tell us *now*?' Then another thought struck him. 'If PQ17 scatters, with or without *Tirpitz*, it'll be massacred, won't it?'

'*BWO to bridge. From Pennyroyal, sir. Have you seen Admiralty's contribution to the Fourth of July? How about that for a stinkeroo?*' The telegraphist's voice was apologetic. '*That's what he said, sir.*'

Hayes-Mailer frowned, leaned forward. 'Thank you. Tell *Pennyroyal*, "Both Admiralty's signals received." Then call all ships of the convoy and escort. I shall speak to commanders and masters during dawn action stations. That's all.'

The Sub-Lieutenant stood at the screen, conscientiously watching the blurred shapes of the ships ahead and gauging two cables, which was four times the sprint track at Hampden Grammar. He tried to visualise a hundred-yards track and then multiply it by four, but it was difficult when, behind him, his two seniors were discussing *Tirpitz*.

Fender felt his stomach twist with panic, and he fought to control it, to speak calmly, to speak at all. 'She'll not be alone, sir, will she — *Tirpitz*? I mean—' Christ! With eight 15-inch and twelve 5.9-inch guns, fifty-six smaller guns, six torpedo tubes and four aircraft, there was no ship in the Royal Navy that could stand alone against her. Her sister *Bismarck* had fought four capital ships and several heavy cruisers, destroyers, and the aircraft from two carriers before being overwhelmed by sheer weight of metal. Now, a reincarnation of *Bismarck* was loose in the Arctic, and convoy PQ17 was scattering like sheep from a blood-hungry tiger. But there were other predators waiting — the U-boats and dive-bombers — and they waited for just this moment of helpless ships running blindly. . . .

'She'll have company,' Hayes-Mailer affirmed. 'Raeder wouldn't risk his ace without king-queen-jack to support it.' And, he might have added, a jealous Admiralty, fighting a theoretical war two thousand miles away, had suppressed vital information until it was too late for the commander-in-chief to close with the enemy. 'Anyway,' he went on coolly, 'if we keep going in this direction, we'll be the first to know.'

'The first—?' The meaning of the Commander's words

came to Fender like a blow in the face. An old destroyer, a corvette and two trawlers, mustering five absurd little four-inch guns between them, were steaming deliberately towards *Tirpitz*. His stomach cringed again. Was this really happening to Lieutenant Geoffrey Fender, RNVR London Division? He was supposed to be *Virtue*'s gunnery officer, but in *President* and Whale Island they'd said nothing about engaging a super-battleship with four-inch pea-shooters. He wouldn't know how. Christ, what the hell was he doing here?

The Old Man couldn't be serious. Fender gave a knowing chuckle for the benefit of the Sub-Lieutenant, hammered his gloved palms together to provoke the circulation. 'You'll be taking avoiding action, sir?' He hoped his voice was casual. 'Returning to Reykjavik?' That was why the Commander was going to speak to the convoy's captains at dawn.

'Coffee from a thermos flask,' Hayes-Mailer said, 'always tastes of cork.' He glanced at Fender, surprised. 'Avoiding action? Good God, no. What for? We've only got half a story. Besides, the ocean's a big place — plenty of room for us and *Tirpitz*, if she's really at sea. What do you say, Sub? What did they teach you at *King Alfred*?'

Only a few hours earlier, in the wardroom, Fender, Waddell and the Commissioned Engineer had listened to Hayes-Mailer's voice over the SRE and, when he had referred to *Vagrant*, Fender had snorted impatiently. 'Jesus, that's the sort of comment that tears the guts out of anyone's respect for a commanding officer.' The Commissioned Engineer had placed down a tattered magazine, risen quietly to his feet and left the wardroom. Waddell had looked uncomfortable. 'We-ell . . . ,'

Fender had gone on, regretting his words and wanting to justify them. 'We didn't sight any survivors because we didn't look for the poor bastards. We were too busy saving our own bloody skins.'

Waddell turned from the screen. His eyebrows and lashes were white with ice, and his breath had progressively frozen below his nostrils to cake his upper lip with a sugar-icing moustache. Within his duffel-hood his face was that of a grotesque old man. 'Well, we did enemy ship recognition, sir, but they all looked the same to me.' He grinned. 'I don't recall that they told us much about the German Navy at all. Sub-lieutenants are expected to be seen and not heard, and confine themselves to the fo'c'sle working party, painting ship and inspecting libertymen.' He paused, then added cheekily, 'And watching the next ahead.'

Hayes-Mailer chuckled. 'It doesn't change much, Sub, the higher you go. There's always someone with one more ring than yourself. You can command a ship, a flotilla, even a fleet, but your orders still come from a senior who's not interested in your opinions or personal emotions, whether they involve painting the ship's side, picking up survivors, or taking a convoy through to Murmansk — which, until we receive orders to the contrary, we are going to do. You can't fight a war by only obeying those orders that happen to coincide with your own philosophy.'

He's not talking to Waddell, Fender recognised. He's talking at me.

There had been no information of the German battle fleet, however, for thirty-six hours, and Sir Dudley Pound, in the Admiralty, had only assumed that *Tirpitz* was at sea and intent on attacking PQ17. Against the consensus of advice from his staff, Pound had ordered the convoy to disperse while, in fact, *Tirpitz*, *Scheer* and *Hipper*, with eight accompanying destroyers, were anchored in Alten fjord, 400 miles from the convoy. By dawn, however, PQ17 had scattered across the Barents Sea.

Dalrymple-Hamilton, with his four cruisers, had already exceeded his instructions by remaining in the proximity of the convoy as far east as longitude 30. Uninformed of the whereabouts of the enemy surface force, but with orders that left him no choice of action, he took the six destroyers of the escort, under Commander J. E. Broome in *Keppel*, under his command, so that he could at least deliver a torpedo attack against the overwhelmingly stronger enemy he expected to meet at any moment.

'It ain't good looks what matter,' Bungy Williams told the mess, 'it's technique, see. F'instance' — he surveyed his listeners — 'if Brains, there' — he indicated Coder Crowthorne — 'or Stripey, walked into the Palais de Dance, what would 'appen?' Nobody ventured to speculate, so he told them. 'Nothin'.'

He paused for effect. 'Nothin'. Sod-all. But why? you are askin'. Because they don't 'ave *technique*, see. When I walk into the Palais de Dance there's an electrifyin' silence. Ain't that right, Lobby?'

Lobby Ludd was flattered. He made an agreeable noise and shrugged in a knowing, man-about-town manner. He had never been to the Palais de Dance, only the Civil Defence social evening in the Town Hall.

'Natcherly, yer've got ter be able ter tango,' Bungy

Williams resumed. 'Cheek-ter-cheek stuff, see. None of yer bleedin' fox-trots. Then yer give 'em the ol' flannel.' He embraced an imaginary dancing partner. 'Slow, slow, quick-quick, slow. "Do yer come 'ere often, darlin'? My life, that perfume. Californian Poppy, ain't it? Ah, yes, I can tell yer've 'ad professional tuition — the way yer move. As soon as I saw yer dancin' with that pongo, I sez, 'Shave off, she's 'ad professional tuition. Sticks out a mile.' If I'd known we was goin' ter meet, I'd 'ave brought yer some nylons. I've got so many I don't know what ter do with 'em. Fifteen denier. That's if yer wear nylons, o' course. Yer do? Shave off. Now there's a thing. I'll tell yer what. 'Ow about tomorrow night? You was goin' ter wash yer 'air? Yer 'air don't need washin', darlin'. Shall we say the Gaumont at nineteen 'undred? All right, seven o'clock, then. Afterwards, steak, eggs an' chips, none of yer whale-meat casserole. . . ." '

'Main W/T to bridge. Distress call on 500 k/cs. Zaafara attacked by dive-bombers and sinking. . . .'

'It's started, sir,' the First Lieutenant said grimly. 'It's going to be sheer bloody murder.'

And as the day wore on the sheer bloody murder continued, 600 miles away, as *Virtue* and her fellows listened helplessly and with deepening dejection. PQ17, now accompanied by only a handful of small escort vessels, fought for survival.

'Mayday, Mayday, Mayday. . . .'

The crew of the rescue ship *Zaafara* had been picked up by *Zamalek*, but then *Carlton* was torpedoed by U-334. Later during the day six merchant ships were sunk by aircraft and six by submarines, including *River*

Afton, carrying the convoy's commodore. The previous day, the American destroyer *Wainwright* had celebrated the Fourth of July by shooting down one of the four enemy aircraft destroyed. Today, the fifth, it was *Daniel Morgan*'s turn to fight desperately against wave after wave of dive-bombers and to shoot down two. She would continue to fight for twenty-eight hours before being sunk, and then her crew would suffer four torturous days in lifeboats, in snow blizzards and subzero cold, eventually to reach the bitter coast of Novaya Zemlya.

The cause of the Admiralty's alarm — *Tirpitz*, with *Scheer, Hipper* and the destroyers — was still in Alten fjord. The battle fleet's commander, Admiral Schniewind, also had an apprehensive chain of command above him, and was experiencing less than adequate cooperation from the Luftwaffe. He had earlier been embarrassed by fog; now the German air-crews were so busily engaged in attacking the helpless British merchantmen that they neglected to transmit information. Somewhere at sea were *Duke of York, Washington* and *Victorious*, and Hitler himself had forbidden *Tirpitz* to put to sea if an enemy aircraft carrier was within flying range. Schniewind, however, was now aware that Tovey's heavy squadron had turned away eastward at 0615 on 4 July, and an air patrol from the Lofoten Islands had seen no British warships between longitudes 14 and 26. It must be the moment for *Tirpitz*.

Lobby Ludd's earlier nausea had gone, he had adapted to the ship's repetitive routine, and was now a fully accepted member of the mess. The loss of his brother in such close proximity had earned him an odd measure of

127

maturity in the eyes of his fellows; their wariness had dissolved and they could refer to *Vagrant* without embarrassment. Yeoman Shaw was friendly, and had even suggested that his subordinate might request a recommendation for advancement to full signalman. Life was not so bad, Lobby Ludd decided. His duties were monotonous and wearying, but with the resilience of youth he could sleep on a locker or mess-stool with the closing of his eyes, awaken with an expletive. Obscenity was an integument of every expression, until obscenities became so commonplace that a sentence without one was a rarity. Men complained continually, but habitually rather than with conviction, and forgot their complaints in seconds. If it was not the poor food it was the lack of mail or the taste of the rum, the injustice of cleaning duties, of dawn action stations, the quality of the potatoes or the staleness of the bread. There was a crude but jealously preserved protocol, established over centuries of shipboard confinement, which even the most cynical did not abuse, because men must live together, cheek by jowl for weeks, and without concord their existence would be insufferable. They played cards noisily — usually pontoon, solo whist or cribbage — or 'uckers', a complex version of ludo, told highly coloured stories of runs ashore, sexual adventures, or boasted of their intended life-style when the war ended.

The ship was rife with rumours — the obsessive 'buzz', sometimes based on a half-truth but often complete figments of a wishful imagination and embroidered with every telling. On their return from Russia, said one, there would be three weeks' leave for all hands. *Virtue* was going to America, insisted another, for a dockyard refit; to Jamaica, because someone had heard the First Lieutenant remark that he had not tasted a fresh pineapple for years. No, it would be Capetown; there were gallons of pale blue paint in the paint locker. 'That's the place — Capetown,' Stripey Albright assured them. 'There was so many wimmin chasing us matelots, Gawdalmighty, it was worse'n bleedin' Navy Week before the war. You blokes don't remember Navy Week. Thousan's of people an' kids crawlin' everywhere — up the bridge, down the engine room, sprogs bein' sick, old ladies fallin' down, and all the ODs waiting at the bottom o' ladders ter see up the parties' legs. . . .'

The Civil Defence social evening at the Town Hall had hardly fired the enthusiasm of Walham Green. A piano, a guitar and an accordion laboured bravely through 'White Cliffs of Dover' while the floor remained deserted, and then, inspired by Charlie Ludd's entrance, plunged into 'The Sailor with the Navy Blue Eyes'. Two dozen people were scattered around the perimeter of the floor or stood at the refreshment table drinking bottled beer and gazing distantly in the direction of the sandwiches — spam, spam and cress, dried egg, or dried egg and cress. From the walls, tired slogans exhorted the public to join the AFS, grow more vegetables, refrain from careless talk, and to attend a post-natal clinic on Tuesdays and Fridays. A large WVS lady sold Charlie Ludd a raffle ticket, for what potential reward he did not enquire, and then he saw Eileen Wilkins, as he knew he would.

She saw him simultaneously, and flushed. 'Well, well!' Charlie Ludd was surprised. 'Jes fancy! We seem ter be bumpin' into each other everywhere. Did yer get 'ome all right last night?' Then he grinned obliquely at her companion. 'Ain't yer goin' ter introduce us?'

Eileen Wilkins swallowed uncomfortably, but her companion simpered. 'I'm Freda — and I know who you are. You're Charlie Ludd.' Freda had eyes that told him she knew all about it. 'I'm with Eileen at the Poly. You're a fast worker, I must say!' Charlie Ludd made a mental note that a further acquaintanceship with Freda might be interesting. 'I 'ave ter be,' he confided gallantly. 'I've only got till Saturday.' He glanced around. 'It ain't exactly Carroll Gibbons' Dance Night, is it? There must be a good film at the Essoldo.'

Freda Harris had suddenly gasped. 'Eileen!' She whispered urgently. 'Don't look now, but do you know who's just come in? Owen Melville of the Borough Engineer's Department! *You* know.' She raised a furtive hand to pat her hair and then became fixedly interested in the ceiling.

'Friend o' your'n?' Charlie Ludd enquired politely.

'No — that is — well — we know him,' Eileen Wilkins managed. 'At least, Freda knows him.' She glanced around for the ladies' cloakroom, but could not see it.

Owen Melville approached briskly. He was a young man with highly polished hair and shoes, a stiff white collar and a confident dealing-with-the-public manner. 'Good evening, ladies,' he smiled, then glanced at Charlie Ludd.

Eileen Wilkins had reddened even more deeply. 'This is Charles Ludd, Owen. Charles' — she drew a deep breath — 'this is Mr Owen Melville.'

'Owen,' the other offered. 'Owen Melville.' His handshake was confidently masculine. 'The Navy, eh? Good show. We're always glad to see you lads. Home on leave?'

'Well,' Charlie Ludd said, 'yer didn't see my submarine tied up outside, did yer?'

Melville laughed, adjusted the knot of his tie. 'And how are things out there on the briny, Charles?' He did not wait for an answer. 'As a matter of fact, I'm on duty myself this evening. We like to encourage these Civil Defence affairs.' He lowered his voice. 'Borough Engineer's Department, y'know.'

'Ah, yes,' Charlie Ludd nodded. 'Something ter do with drain 'oles, ain't it? We've got 'em on ships, only we call 'em bilges. Nasty job, but I s'pose someone's got ter do it. I 'spect yer see some 'orrible things down there — dead babies, rats—?'

'If you'll excuse Freda and me for a few minutes,' Eileen Wilkins decided, and Charlie fumbled in a pocket. 'Yer'll need a penny,' he offered. 'There's usually a free one, but yer can never tell who used it last. Ain't that right, Owen?'

The young man frowned at his wristwatch. 'I was hoping to catch the Town Clerk,' he murmured, then looked up. 'Perhaps I can get you a drink, Charles? A light ale?'

'I don't mind,' Charlie Ludd conceded. 'Rum. Navy size, o' course.' He had never tasted rum in his life and had no desire to; fortunately there appeared to be only crates of bottled beer behind the refreshment table.

But Owen Melville returned with a glass containing a generous measure of rum. 'Nelson's blood, eh, Charles? You're in luck, old chap. They keep the spirits under the counter, but I do have a bit of pull with the catering staff.' He chuckled.

'Whack-oh,' Charlie Ludd approved. It smelled terrible and it tasted like petrol. 'O' course,' he said, 'this civvy stuff ain't the same as the real thing.' He hoped it wasn't, b'Christ. Melville shuddered. 'I don't know how you can drink it neat.'

'It takes years,' Charlie Ludd agreed. It probably did.

'If I'd thought,' Melville said, 'I'd have come in uniform myself. I'm in the Home Guard, y'know. Some people might laugh at the Home Guard, but we've got a keen bunch here in Fulham, and we could show the regulars a thing or two.'

' 'Specially now yer've got air-guns,' Charlie Ludd nodded, but Eileen Wilkins and Freda Harris had reappeared. 'Ah, here we are,' Charlie greeted them. 'When yer bustin' ter go, it's murder, ain't it?'

'I really think we might show a good example,' Melville suggested. 'Someone ought to start. Shall we dance?'

'Yer a cheeky boy, Owen, but I'll give yer the last waltz,' Charlie offered. Melville drew a deep breath and bowed in the direction of Eileen Wilkins. 'May I have the pleasure, Miss Wilkins?' Charlie Ludd was left with Freda.

'I dance the South American way,' he told her, 'which yer might find a bit tricky. Jes' try an' foller. Yer'll soon pick it up.'

Charlie Ludd's South American way was to clamp his abdomen firmly to his partner's and propel her remorselessly backward in approximate accord with the music. 'If you get any closer, Charlie,' Freda warned him in a whisper, 'you'll be arrested for rape. And you'll rupture yourself. Why don't you save it for later? We've got all night.' Charlie Ludd was delighted. 'Blimey, is that what they teach yer at the Poly? Or is it all part o' first aid?'

'Animal genetics,' she said. 'Bulls and stallions, rams — and cocks.'

'Yer don't say!' He considered. 'Eileen ain't passed the birds an' bees part yet.'

'A bit frigid, was she?' Freda shrugged. 'Blondes often are. Besides, she *was* a virgin.' She shook her head. 'A blonde virgin — that's the worst combination. Brunettes respond quicker, especially if they've had a little experience.'

'Is that so?' Charlie Ludd grinned. 'Yer know, I'd call you a brunette.' He glanced around. 'It's gettin' a bit warm in 'ere, ain't it? I reckon we oughter—'

'It's not warm, Charlie. It's you.' She winked. 'Tie a knot in it, or you'll never last out. By the way, did you bring anything? Durex, I mean?'

Charlie Ludd gulped. 'No, I didn't think—'

'Well, never mind,' Freda decided. 'You won't need one tonight.'

This, Charlie Ludd decided, was going to be a piece of cake. Of course, he always knew that a uniform made all the difference, but he had never anticipated it being as easy as this. They'd never believe it in *St George*. Mind, it probably wasn't entirely the uniform; he had always suspected that he possessed a certain personal magnetism, but undoubtedly the uniform helped. And he had twelve years of this ahead of him. The prospect was almost intoxicating. Well, whenever he needed a respite, he could always wear civvies.

The Civil Defence social evening seemed endless. Serious-faced couples rotated dutifully as the band toiled through waltz and quick-step, boomps-a-daisy and hokey-cokey. The air became smokier and the sale of bottled beer grew brisker, the sandwiches curled, the dancers perspired, and visits to the cloakrooms became more frequent. Freda Harris resigned herself to Charlie Ludd's unvarying South American way, and Charlie complimented her on the manner in which she had 'picked it up'. The National Anthem came as a relief to both of them.

Eileen Wilkins and Owen Melville seemed to have already departed, which was a good thing; Charlie Ludd didn't want complications. There was nothing like a clear field. 'Well,' he said, 'I'll walk yer 'ome.' Or somewhere.

'Not walk,' she corrected. 'The train first. I live in Wimbledon. Are you sure you want to, Charlie?' She squeezed his arm. 'I mean, it's a long way.'

It was a long way indeed, but the reward was tantalising. If Charlie Ludd was any judge, Freda Harris couldn't wait to get her knickers down. 'I wouldn't dream,' he assured her, 'of letting yer go 'ome by yerself on a dark night like this. Yer meet all kinds.'

Thirty minutes later, alighting from the train at Wimbledon Park, Freda made a disquieting discovery. 'Charlie, if you don't go now, you'll miss the last train back, and it's miles. You'll never get a cab.'

It was very annoying. Charlie Ludd experienced a moment of uncertainty, then shrugged it aside. He had come too far to abandon the prize now. She had better be worth it, that was all. He sniffed. 'It's only five stations.'

Fifteen minutes of further walking brought them to a darkened street of neat houses and gardens. 'I must say you've behaved like a gentleman, Charlie.' Freda had a hand on a garden gate. 'Most men have one-track minds, and all they think about is sex. I'm glad you're not like that.'

Charlie Ludd was perplexed. He managed a laugh. 'Well, as a matter o' fact, I ain't any different.' He glanced around. 'Ain't yer got somewhere — a shed, or something? It looks like rain.'

She gasped. 'Charlie, you didn't think—?' She shook her head. 'I couldn't, not the first time I met someone. I can't think what gave you that impression. Was it something I said?'

'Didn't yer tell me ter tie a knot in it?' Charlie Ludd insisted. 'Didn't yer ask me if I 'ad a Durex?'

'And I *said* you wouldn't need one,' she said. 'If you want to kiss me, I don't mind.' She had placed the chest-high, wrought-iron gate between them. 'But no feeling around. And, if you come to the dance next Wednesday, Charlie, I *might*—'

'I won't be 'ere next Wednesday,' Charlie gritted. 'Look, yer've got me all 'otted up—'

She shrugged. 'I'm sure I didn't do anything. If you're feeling randy, that's your fault — and you've got all the way to Walham Green to walk it off. If it's still the same when you get home, pour cold water over it. It always works.'

Charlie Ludd was shocked. 'That's animal genetics, is it? D'yer think I'm a bleedin' Cocker Spaniel?' His indignation swelled. 'D'yer know what they call your sort?'

She nodded. 'I'm a prick-teaser,' she said, and he was even more shocked; but the next moment she had gone. He stared miserably at the dark sky. 'Brunettes respond quicker,' he snorted disgustedly. He had several miles to tramp, and it was beginning to rain.

135

*   *   *

'A bit o' ground bait always 'elps,' Bungy Williams told
them. 'Nylons, a bar o' nutty or, best of all, some
dhobeying soap for 'er mother or some tickler for the
ol' man. There's nothin' like being invited up 'omers.
Sooner or later the ol' folks will go ter bed, and then yer
can 'ave yer nibble on the settee. She daren't make no
fuss, see, and it's better than 'aving yer arse in the wet
rhododendrons. It's like takin' cake from a baby. Ain't
that right, Lobby?'

By late afternoon on 5 July there was still no news of
Tirpitz. She might be anywhere in the thousands of
square miles of Arctic seas ahead. The fog was thinning
rapidly, and *Pennyroyal* was still making negative radar
reports, but a few blotches on her screen could be
Tovey's heavy squadron, Dalrymple-Hamilton's cruisers,
or the German battle fleet. *Tirpitz* had radar; the
contact could be mutual, and the enemy could bear
down on *Virtue* and her companions at thirty knots.
There was no place to hide, and to run would be futile.
It would all be over very quickly, and the British ships
would be smashed into the icy sea from a range far
beyond that of their own pitiful armament. Even a
suicidal gesture by the old destroyer was no longer
possible. *Virtue* had been stripped of her torpedo tubes.

During the forenoon the hands had been engaged in
the bitter task of clearing the ice that progressively
accumulated on decks and upperworks, clogged guns
and machinery, nullified aerials and lights, and steadily
and ominously increased the ship's top-weight until her
stability was threatened. In the warships men worked
wearily with brooms, paint-chippers and hammers,

136

strewed salt and sand. Capstans and deck-winches were kept in motion, all guns rotated, raised and lowered continuously, to prevent lubricant and hydraulic oils from freezing solid. On the decks of the merchant ships, also, steam-hoses were being used to clear frozen boat-hoists, ladders and doors. It was mildly satisfying to know that the American sailors had been compelled to abandon their warm quarters for the primitive task of clearing ice. The British had always resentfully envied the alleged American addiction to labour-saving devices, their washing-machines and potato-peeling machines, refrigerators, ice cream, soft-drink vending machines. There was no labour-saving device for clearing ice; it had to be done on an open deck with blue-cold hands and rawly aching feet, and in seconds the steam would condense and freeze, and there would be more ice, more congealing, flour-like snow. . . .

At 1140 that forenoon, as the doomed ships of PQ17 fought despairingly against dive-bombers and U-boats, and westward of them the heavier British ships searched for an enemy surface force which was not at sea, while *Virtue* shepherded her charges north-eastward through thickening ice-rubble, her crew ignorant of what the next hour might bring, Admiral Schniewind, in *Tirpitz*, had received orders to launch his battle fleet from Alten fjord. The coast, literally, was clear, and there was no British warship within 400 miles. *Tirpitz, Scheer* and *Hipper* raised anchor and by 1300 had cleared the entrance of the fjord and turned north-eastward at an economical twenty knots, screened by their destroyers.

Three hours later *Tirpitz* was sighted by a Russian submarine, K-21, which fired torpedoes. The Russian Commander, Lieutenant Lunin, believed that he had made two hits, and would later be made a Hero of the Soviet Union, but *Tirpitz* was unaware of the attack or even of the presence of the submarine. Of greater relevance, however, at 1700, K-21 transmitted an enemy report in English, betraying the position and course of the German battleships and destroyers. It was the first proof, received by the Admiralty, that *Tirpitz* was at sea and shaping course to intercept PQ17.

During the same evening the British submarine P-54 also sighted *Tirpitz*, but her speed of 11¼ knots on the surface and 9 knots submerged was too slow for her to press home an attack.

The Russian wireless transmission and the appearance of P-54, however, had warned the Germans that the *Tirpitz* operation had been compromised. Indeed, Admiral Tovey's heavy squadron had wheeled about and was racing back towards North Cape. Tovey could not hope to bring *Tirpitz* to action — he was 450 miles away — but his approach might well dissuade the enemy from proceeding. He was right. From Hitler, through Admiral Raeder, the order to withdraw reached Schniewind. *Tirpitz*'s part in operation 'Rösselsprung' — the Knight's move in chess — was no longer necessary. PQ17 was already being cut to pieces, and the battle fleet should return to harbour. Reluctantly, at 2151 on 5 July, Schniewind turned his ships, and at 1130 on the following day anchored in Kaa fjord. *Tirpitz* had not fired a shot, but the Admiralty had already condemned PQ17 to massacre by issuing long-range orders but no supporting information to allow commanders at sea to assess the situation and act accordingly.

The urgent voice of *Pennyroyal*'s operator had just burst

from the loudspeaker in the Bridge Wireless Office when Lobby Ludd saw the aircraft. In that infinitesimal moment of time during which the human brain is capable of debating a wide range of possibilities, he questioned whether he should believe his eyes, decided that he could, wondered why he, apparently, was the only person to have seen anything, experienced shock, and then decided to do something about it. 'Aircraft bearing green oh-seven-oh!' His hands were cupped around his mouth, his heart pounded, and his voice was pitifully inadequate. 'Aircraft bearing green—!'

The action alarm-bell exploded, hammering deafeningly. '*BWO to bridge. From Pennyroyal. Aircraft bearing green oh-six-oh, five miles. Repeat. . . .*'

'BWO. Make to all ships. "Emergency enemy aircraft. Stand by to alter course together forty degrees to starboard. Stand by. . . ." '

There was a confusion of noise, of feet pounding on steel decks and ladders, the crash of doors, the ear-paining yammer of the alarm-bell, men shouting orders at others only yards away, obscenities.

'A single Focke-Wulf 200, sir — about four miles, say six thousand feet and climbing—'

'*Enemy aircraft. Enemy aircraft. Starboard oh-eight-oh — oh-nine-oh. Angle of sight oh-three-oh. All short-range weapons load — load — load. Commence tracking—*'

'*Number one pom-pom on target and tracking—*'

'*Number two pom-pom on target and tracking—*'

Jesus Christ, reflected Lobby Ludd — after all this, there'd better be a bleedin' aircraft.

On the bridge, all binoculars were turned to starboard. High to the east the German pilot had pulled his big four-engined machine into a steep climb, banking, almost as if he were recoiling in surprise, and the sudden surge of his engines was clearly audible. They could see the underside of both wings, watched as the aircraft turned in a wide circle, safely beyond reach of their guns. 'He's not going to attack,' Hayes-Mailer decided. 'He's got what he wanted, blast his luck.' He spoke calmly, but he was very angry. The fog, the change of course, had been for nothing. It was incredible, but in the whole of this vast, empty ocean they had been stumbled upon by a single enemy aircraft whose pilot, at this moment, was probably laughing at his good fortune. In a few minutes the convoy's position and course would have been plotted and would be crackling in morse code to Bardufoss or Banak — and there was nothing the British could do about it.

Lobby Ludd had a proprietory interest in the Focke-Wulf. Wasn't anyone going to shoot at the bleedin' thing? What was the good of him sighting an enemy aircraft if everyone just looked at it? From 500 yards away there was a prolonged spatter of machine-gun fire. It was *Olympic Madison*. 'Silly bastards,' the Yeoman sniffed. 'That's jes' what yer might expect from a bunch o' trigger-'appy Yanks — trying ter knock down a Focke-Wulf at five miles with a streak o' piss.'

Lobby Ludd agreed. 'Silly bastards.' He nodded.

The Commander lowered his head to a voice-pipe. 'BWO. Cancel that alteration of course. Then make to *Pennyroyal*: "In future I shall expect you to report the approach of an enemy aircraft before my own look-outs." That's all.' Behind him, a glance from Rainbird froze Fender's half-grin. Campbell of *Pennyroyal* was being given a rap on the knuckles over convoy R/T, which was chastening to any ship's commander and would be particularly so to the confident Campbell. There were a number of reasons, none of them *Pennyroyal*'s fault, why the Focke-Wulf had not been detected earlier, but Hayes-Mailer needed an outlet for his annoyance. That single aircraft might have been a dozen, he seethed, aware how unlikely was the possibility.

'She's gone, sir,' Fender said, unnecessarily.

Still, given more warning, he might have swung the entire convoy around to a reciprocal course, to give the impression that it was proceeding towards Iceland instead of Russia. No, that would not have fooled the Germans for more than a few minutes. They had the earlier U-boat report, now they had this one, and it would be absolutely certain that this odd group of ships was heading for North Cape; there was nowhere else to go.

Rainbird and Fender were pointedly not looking at him, but he sensed exactly what they were thinking.

'I doubt whether there will be U-boats deployed this far westward,' he considered, 'but we are about two hours' flying time from the Norwegian coast. It's my guess that Fifth Luftflotte will be giving all their attention to PQ17 today, perhaps until noon tomorrow, by which time, anyway, we can expect U-boat interception. In the meantime they won't let us out of their sight a second time. We'll be seeing that Focke-Wulf again.'

Hayes-Mailer stared beyond the bridge screen, ahead, still angry. Then he turned.

'Yeoman! Send to *Truelove*: "Your erratic station-keeping suggests you have steering defect. Either report defect or maintain tighter station." ' He was being bloody-minded and he knew it. 'And, Yeoman, who was the rating who sighted the enemy aircraft?'

'Ludd, sir. Ordinary Signalman Ludd.'

'Ludd?' He remembered, and nodded. 'He did well. Has he shaken down? About his brother, I mean.'

'Yessir, I think so. He don't talk much.' Yeoman Shaw gazed towards *Truelove*. 'O' course, he don't know about our change o' course away from *Vagrant*, sir — after what you said to him.' Shaw's face was innocent.

' 'Ere comes 'Awk-eye,' greeted Bungy Williams. 'Wotcher, Lobby.' He proffered his tot. 'Go on — fill yer boots.' He frowned anxiously. 'Sippers, not bleedin' gulpers. I thought we was goin' ter get a stick o' bombs right down the after funnel. Shave off. That would 'ave shaken up ol' Steamboat Stevens. Yer'll be gettin' a Red Ink on yer conduct sheet, mate.'

Signalman House offered his own rum. ' 'Ave arf,' he said morosely, but not to be outdone in generosity. Bungy Williams was incredulous. 'Well, I'll write 'ome! D'yer see that?' He looked around. 'Shit's pushin' the boat out! I always said we're gettin' bromide in our bleedin' tea. Shave off.' There was a popular conviction that servicemen's tea was laced with bromide to dampen sexual excitement. 'Stick ter kye, Shit. It's full o' vitamins an' it's good fer growin' boys.'

'It goes ter bloddy show,' Signalman House went on. 'With all them seamen look-outs scratchin' their arses, it was a soddin' good thing we was awake on the flag-deck. I was arf a mind ter bloddy say somethin'.'

Lobby Ludd nodded in grave agreement. 'And did yer see *Olympic Madison*?' He had nursed the Yeoman's words for just such an exchange. 'Trying ter knock down a Focke-Wulf at five miles with a streak of piss?' He snorted. 'Bleedin' trigger-'appy Yanks!'

'O' course,' Stripey Albright contributed, 'you blokes don't remember the Spanish Civil War. I was in the Med then, in the *Warspite*—'

'Was that the one with the sails or the paddle-wheels?' Bungy Williams enquired.

'You can larf,' Stripey warned the mess. 'It was the bleedin' peacetime Navy that 'eld the Empire together, I can tell yer. Where would Gibraltar be now, if it weren't for the bleedin' peacetime Navy? Tell me that.'

Bungy Williams pondered. 'I reckon it'd be in the same soddin' place,' he decided. 'Shave off. It'd take more'n Pickfords ter move it.'

'Malta was the place in peacetime,' Stripey Albright reminisced. 'Gawdalmighty. Yer'd start orf in the Gut — the Bing Crosby, the Wheel o' Fortune, the Cleopatra and the Galvanized Donkey — pints o' bleedin' Blue Label and wimmin flashin' their parts, five bob short time an' git up them stairs, chicken an' chips, then more Blue Labels till they comes out yer bleedin' ears. Then stagger over ter Sliema ter see the tit show, an' a bottle or two o' jungle juice. Yer could go on drinkin' Blue Labels all bleedin' night, and if yer weren't picked up by the patrol, or got in a fight, or spewed up, yer'd crash down in Murphy's doss-'ouse.'

Bungy Williams shook his head. 'Soddin' 'ell. The war must 'ave come as a 'oliday fer the bleedin' peacetime Navy.'

Six

During dawn action stations on 5 July, Hayes-Mailer had summarised the situation over convoy R/T for the benefit of the ships in company. It was possible, he told them, that *Tirpitz* was at sea. If she were, however, there was no evidence that she presented a threat to themselves. Since the loss of *Vagrant* there had been no contact with the enemy, and it was more than likely that the Germans now had no knowledge of the whereabouts of *Virtue* and her fellows. German U-boats and aircraft would be wholly committed to seeking out and attacking the ships of PQ17 — an operation that could occupy them for several days. There was a limit to the performance of both aircraft and submarines, physical and material. They must replenish fuel and ammunition; their crews, also, needed respite. It was probable that by the time *Virtue* reached Bear Island the enemy would have already shot his bolt, and the smaller convoy would achieve Murmansk unscathed, perhaps even unseen.

Within a few hours, however, that situation had changed. The German battle fleet was known to be at sea, PQ17 was in the process of being annihilated, *Virtue* and her convoy had been sighted, the fog had dispersed and the weather was calm. Now the enemy held all the cards. At 1600 the Focke-Wulf reappeared, this time with ample warning from *Pennyroyal*. As before, Hayes-Mailer prepared the convoy for a rapid alteration of course, to turn into a torpedo attack which, if made, would come from abeam or, if bombs were dropped, to confuse enemy accuracy.

But the Focke-Wulf was alone and had no intention of venturing within range. It circled leisurely just below cloud base, droning tauntingly, followed around the horizon by the high-angle three-inch guns, pom-poms and Oerlikons, the officers and lookouts with binoculars, gun-crews with stinging eyes half-closed against the bitter wind. It was difficult to believe that, in the cabin of that circling aircraft, so near, a navigator was calculating and a radio operator tapped a morse key, heavily muffled gunners fingered the triggers of their guns, and the pilot watched, each of them intent on the destruction of the eight distant toy ships that seemed barely to move in the white-flecked sea below.

Following thirty minutes of slow circling, the Focke-Wulf climbed into the cloud and disappeared, flying due south, *Pennyroyal* reported, until out of radar range thirty miles away. Precisely four hours later an identical Focke-Wulf materialised, having been detected by *Pennyroyal* approaching from the north-east. The procedure was the same; the aircraft circled for thirty minutes, then made off to the southward.

The pattern was emerging. 'They haven't been sent just to look at us,' the Commander decided. 'The Luftflotte probably haven't got that many spare aircraft to play with. It's my guess they're the routine long-range patrol — say from Banak out to Jan Mayen, southward to the Faroes, the Shetlands, then back up the Norwegian coast, or something like that. The pilots have been briefed to locate us during each flight, confirm our position, course and approximate speed, and then proceed. They're keeping us nicely pigeon-holed until they're good and ready.' He speculated. 'Every four hours,' he repeated, 'until they're ready.' It was like being condemned to death — waiting for the eight o'clock footsteps beyond the cell door, and knowing that the end was decided and inevitable.

There was nothing much to say. 'If we altered course, sir,' the First Lieutenant mused, 'at the trawlers' maximum speed, in four hours we'd only cover fifty miles. That means that if we turned back on a reciprocal course we'd be about a hundred miles south of where they'd expect to find us. It wouldn't be enough. With better speed, of course, we *might* just regain the fog — if it hasn't already dispersed behind us.'

The master of *Brazos River* had reached a similar conclusion. His voice crackled over convoy R/T.

'If this outfit stays on this course, Commander, we're dead ducks. It was a damn fool idea in the beginning, but now it's a blow-out. I don't want to teach you your business, but if we can't go on, then we've gotta go back. OK? Now, listen. According to the register, the four merchant ships and your corvette are all capable of better than seventeen knots. I guess my chief engineer will squeeze eighteen. It's only those goddam trawlers that are holding us back. OK. I suggest we high-tail it back toward that fog-bank, every ship independently at her best speed. Maybe some of us won't make it — but, if we continue on our present course, none of us will.'

Hayes-Mailer took *Virtue* abeam of *Brazos River*, edging the destroyer to within yards of the big tanker, and then addressed her by loud-hailer.

'Thank you, Captain. At all costs I wish to avoid scattering the convoy. You will know what that meant to PQ17, ahead of us. If the enemy discovers that we are no longer north-bound, the very first possibility they will wish to eliminate will be the reciprocal course, back to Iceland. They will plug that gap immediately and, fog or no fog, we cannot wander around like Flying Dutchmen indefinitely. However, I agree with you about the inadvisability of proceeding on our present course. I am considering an alternative. In view of the slight possibility that convoy R/T is being monitored by the enemy, please make all tactical communication by loud-hailer or light.'

The American master agreed reluctantly. 'OK, Commander, I guess you know what you're doing, but you'd better come up with something fast. One thing's for sure — those five-and-dime guns of yours aren't going to worry the Krauts none, and it looks like your Admiralty guys have left us to the wolves like they did PQ17.'

Virtue dropped astern. 'Our American cousin isn't feeling very stars-and-stripey today,' Prentice commented.

'Neither would you be,' Rainbird said, 'if you were sitting over a few thousand tons of high-octane fuel in mid-Arctic on 6 July 1942.' An alternative? he wondered. What alternative?

'Number One,' the Commander ordered. 'I'd like the latest met. report, some coffee and you in the charthouse in fifteen minutes. I'm going to have a hot shower and shave while I'm thinking.'

When he reached the chart-house, Hayes-Mailer looked fresher than he had for several days. He nodded at Rainbird, took the weather report that filled five sheets of foolscap signal-pad, lowered himself to his elbows over the chart-table and clicked on the light switch. 'All right,' he said, 'let's see.'

For a long time he read, referred to the chart, read again, grunted, once raising his head to stare at Rainbird as if the other's blank face offered some solution. At last he rose, drew a deep breath.

'Number One, that Yankee skipper is right. We can't remain on this course, even approximately. The enemy has calculated, correctly, that we're following the ice north and then north-east, and they can pinpoint us at any moment. When the Focke-Wulf Condor appears next time, we want him to report that we are still plodding along at ten knots in the same direction.

'That will give us four hours. Immediately the Focke-Wulf has disappeared, *Trooper* and *Truelove* will turn 180 degrees and steam at maximum speed, south-west, for Iceland. The remainder — ourselves, *Pennyroyal* and the four merchantmen — will turn due east. If Campbell can flog eighteen knots out of *Pennyroyal* — and he probably can — we shall be ninety miles eastward, with the probability of fog ahead, when the enemy discovers we're not where we ought to be. All right, Number One' — he looked at Rainbird enquiringly — 'put yourself in that pilot's place and tell me exactly what you'd do.'

Rainbird considered. 'Having approached from the north-east — the convoy's projected course — I'd be reasonably certain that it was not to northerly. Well, I'd check my navigation, perhaps ask for D/F bearings if that's possible. And I'd know the convoy couldn't be to westward. When I was satisfied that I was in the right place, but the convoy wasn't, I'd report the fact to base.' He paused. 'I'd stooge around in a wide circle, but not for too long; I'd have to watch my fuel. Then I'd turn southward, flying zig-zag legs — say fifteen minutes to south-east, fifteen minutes to south-west.' He paused again. 'And then, probably, I'd sight *Truelove* and *Trooper*, and I'd know I'd been done.'

'But you didn't consider searching to eastward?' the Commander asked.

Rainbird frowned. 'No, sir, you're right. The possibility of the convoy heading towards the Norwegian coast, directly toward German aircraft and submarine bases, and even *Tirpitz*, wouldn't occur to me — until I saw *Trooper* and *Truelove*, alone. Then I might kick myself.'

'And then?'

'Well, I'd report the trawlers' position and course, but I couldn't attack. I'd be carrying long-range fuel-tanks instead of bombs, and the trawlers have eight Oerlikon guns between them. So I'd leave them alone. Besides, there'd still be a chance that the remainder of the convoy was even further south, having left the trawlers behind. I'd let headquarters worry about the trawlers.'

Hayes-Mailer nodded slowly. 'And where does that leave *Virtue* and the convoy?'

'Steaming at a rate of knots toward the Norwegian coast, in fact' — he moved forward to look at the chart — 'straight at North Cape to rendezvous with *Tirpitz*, *Scheer*, *Hipper*, eight destroyers, a dozen U-boats and 300 bombers. As soon as Naval Group

Command North learns that we've been lost, they'll have search aircraft in the air—'

'But not searching the area where half the German Navy has been running amok. With luck we'll have fog, and I'm counting on most of the enemy force deployed against PQ17 having returned to base.' He fumbled for his battered cigarette-case, carefully selected a cigarette.

The First Lieutenant was silent, then, 'Well, sir, we might pull it off just because it's crazy — and we'll need to tip-toe through the tulips.' He leaned over the chart thoughtfully. 'If we can be confident of fog or poor visibility, that'll stymie air reconnaissance. The Germans will be relying on second-rate coastal radar, and that leaves the U-boats, which, as you say, could be withdrawing.' He shrugged. 'There's one thing. With a bit of luck, *Trooper* and *Truelove* should reach Seydhisfjord before the Luftflotte overtakes them. They'll have the fog that we want.'

'No, they won't,' Hayes-Mailer said. 'Behind us the weather's bright and clear as far as the Shetlands.'

Rainbird frowned, looked down at the chart again for a few seconds and then back at the Commander. 'In that case, sir,' he decided, 'they might not reach Seydhisfjord.' They would be like a pair of puppies, with nowhere to hide, running from a pack of wolves.

'They might not, Number One. It depends upon what value the enemy places on two trawlers, and whether they're prepared to divert aircraft to attack them when there are fatter targets somewhere in the area. The fact remains that we can't afford the luxury of two eleven-knot trawlers, and they may as well run for it now. Their lack of speed outweighs their value as fighting units.' He lit his cigarette. 'We're hedging our bets.

150

Trooper and *Truelove* will either get clear, or they'll draw the enemy's attention which would otherwise be given to us.'

Heads we don't win, tails we lose, Rainbird considered.

The Focke-Wulf approached on time from the northeast, climbed, and circled slowly, while the men watching from below thought wistfully of the fighter aircraft that were crated in the holds of *Chessington* and *Empire Mandate* — just one of which, in a few seconds, could tear this detested intruder out of the sky. There had always been an undercurrent of resentment towards the RAF which, on the face of things, appropriated the major share of available aircraft but seemed to be fighting a different war to the Navy. 'It's too bloody cold up here for the Brylcreem Boys,' Yeoman Shaw sniffed, 'and they'd be late back for the soddin' NAAFI.' Lobby Ludd agreed. It gave yer the shits.

Apparently satisfied, the Focke-Wulf swung away, southward, and ten minutes later *Pennyroyal* reported that she had lost radar contact. 'Yeoman,' Hayes-Mailer ordered, 'make to *Trooper* and *Truelove*, please: "Proceed in execution of previous orders. Good luck." ' The two trawlers, already briefed, heeled as they turned to starboard. Far ahead, a signal lamp was blinking from *Pennyroyal*. A final, farewell quip from Campbell to the departing ships, the Commander guessed, but the corvette's directional Aldis was unreadable in *Virtue*. 'Hoist change of course and speed, please. We'll execute as soon as all ships have acknowledged.' The flags were already bent on the halyard. They climbed to the masthead, a flare of colour fluttering against the grey

151

sky. The trawlers were clear, with *Trooper* following astern of *Truelove* as both steadied for the course. Young Furloe, on *Truelove*'s little bridge, must be feeling very lonely, Rainbird thought. Furloe, son of Vice-Admiral George Furloe, sometime Captain D, China Station. Rainbird glanced at Hayes-Mailer speculatively, but the Commander was not looking at the trawlers.

'All ships acknowledged, sir.'

'Very good. Execute, please.'

Discernibly, *Virtue*'s fo'c'sle lifted as her speed increased and, astern, the froth of her wake was beginning to tumble. At the blunt bows of *Brazos River* was a curling white feather. An alteration of course of eight points, or ninety degrees, was simple enough for an agile destroyer, but the mercantile masters had little experience of manoêuvring in formation, few had engine-room revolution-telegraphs, and their engineers were unaccustomed to frequent changes of speed by a few revolutions. Hayes-Mailer watched anxiously as the wallowing length of *Olympic Madison* swung to within forty yards of *Chessington*'s stern. A collision at this time would be disastrous. By God, it was cold. The snow was whirling again; the trawlers had already disappeared. And it was going to get colder. Gun-crews, look-outs and signalmen stood with hunched shoulders, their peaked faces turned from the icy wind. These men, Hayes-Mailer thought angrily, should be wearing well-padded Arctic clothing instead of the duffel-coats which were the Navy's only concession to men in exposed positions, supplemented by the gloves, sweaters and balaclava helmets knitted by wives and mothers, towels around necks and football stockings under boots.

152

' 'Midships. Steady.'

'Steady, sir. Course oh-nine-oh.'

Due east, directly towards North Cape, where PQ17 was fighting for survival.

Fourteen of PQ17's ships had been sunk on 5 July, two on the following day — one by aircraft and the other by a U-boat — making a total, so far, of twenty. *Tirpitz* and her squadron were anchored in Kaa fjord, forbidden to participate, but the British did not know this. The remnants of the convoy struggled to reach the desolate coast of Novaya Zemlya or the Mahtoohkin Strait, with submarines and Junkers 88 bombers still hounding them. Two ships were sunk on the seventh and one on the eighth. USS *Hoosier* and the Panamanian *El Capitan* were destroyed when within fifty miles of the White Sea and safety. Of the 200,000 tons of war materials carried by the convoy, only 70,000 tons reached their destination.

In Moscow, Stalin was sceptical. There had never been thirty-three merchant ships in the first place, he asserted. There had certainly not been more than fifteen.

Stripey Albright produced a small photograph from his ditty box. 'There's a picture o' me,' he said, 'taken when I was an OD — outside the Guild'all in Pompey. Yer see them stone lions on the steps? Well, every time a virgin walks past, they stand up an' roar.'

Bungy Williams peered over his shoulder. 'Shave off. 'Oo's that with yer — that Scotch pongo in the kilt?'

'That ain't a Scotch pongo,' Stripey retorted. 'It's my party—'

'Yer don't say?' Bungy marvelled. He peered again. 'So it is. Well, fer pissin' down the sink!'

'As a matter o' fact, she was an usherette at the Plaza,' Stripey claimed. 'That's where I met 'er.'

'In the dark,' Bungy nodded. 'Stands ter reason.'

'It was all right, see,' the other insisted. 'When she was on the tickets, I got in fer nothin'.'

'Shave off. And, after yer'd seen *Bride o' Frankenstein* sixteen times, what did yer do on 'er day orf? Take 'er ter the bleedin' pictures?'

Boy Ludd had been in *St George* for several months when his mother recalled that, many years before, she and Ludd Senior had visited the Isle of Man. At the time of their marriage Ludd Senior had been employed as a porter at Euston and, in a gallant mood that was seldom to be repeated, he resolved on a honeymoon in Douglas; he and his bride could travel free, and it seemed sensible to exploit this fringe benefit by travelling as far as possible.

The young Mrs Ludd, who was three months pregnant, remembered the occasion very well. On the sea crossing from Fleetwood she had been miserably sick, experienced morning sickness for the next seven days, and was sick again on 'the return journey. Although Manx beer, as Ludd Senior declared, tasted like boiled liquorice, and probably· had the same effect on his bowels, he spent most of his honeymoon drinking it, and sleeping with a newspaper over his face, while Mrs Ludd gazed at the sea, dreading the inevitable moment when she must cross it again.

There were consolations. Their lodgings, five minutes from the promenade, were modest but pleasant, managed by a buxom Mrs Kelly, whose husband was a jobbing plumber. Mrs Kelly kept a good table; good plain cooking couldn't be beat, she claimed, and she didn't care what anyone said. She was generous with potatoes, slightly less so with boiled beef or cod, and always added a dessert of rice pudding, tapioca or prunes. There were some, she confided darkly, who exploited guests unmercifully, but nobody could say to Mrs Kelly's face that they rose hungry from her table. The Ludds' bedroom smelled vaguely of camphor, the bed on which Ludd Senior exercised his conjugal rights was lumpily uncomfortable, and a resigned Mrs Ludd followed with her eyes the sinuous course of a crack that crossed the ceiling from corner to corner as her husband panted over her. The bedroom window refused to open and, despite Mr Kelly's professional calling, the adjacent lavatory cistern gurgled without pause throughout the night hours while Ludd Senior snored. For all these minor shortcomings, however, it was a week's holiday that Mrs Ludd would recall with nostalgic fondness. She would never experience another with which to compare it.

It seemed unlikely to Charlie Ludd that, after twenty-five years, Mr and Mrs Kelly would still be in residence or, if they were, that they would remember the guests of so long ago and feel that they owed him a welcome. He could generate little enthusiasm over his mother's suggestion that he should call at the address she sent him. However, Douglas in wartime offered few entertainments for one with stringently limited resources. On thrice-fortnightly afternoons of liberty the boys of *St George* could walk an almost deserted sea-front, gaze at the interned aliens behind their tall wire fences, who gazed back, or examine the contents of shop windows with the certain knowledge that they were unable to buy anything and, even if they could, it would be confiscated. The cinema was beyond their means, but there was a Salvation Army canteen that offered three half-slices of bread and jam for a penny, which had to be balanced against an early return to the establishment for a slice of bread and margarine and a small rock cake for nothing. Against the jetty would probably be moored one of the ferry steamers, a few drifters, and the small patrol-launch *Radiant*. There was the long walk over Douglas Head, but a walk in any direction was purposeless and meant only a long walk back. Almost any location that did not cost money was out of bounds. They were required to walk without loitering, with caps straight and gas-masks slung, coats buttoned and collars turned down, forbidden to congregate in groups, to shout or whistle, to travel by bus, board a vessel or consort with older servicemen. On balance, Charlie Ludd decided, he might as well investigate the Kellys' address. It could be no more futile walking there as anywhere else.

Liberty inspection by the Officer of the Day was exacting, with a few unfortunates dimissed for minor discrepancies in dress, or hair inadequately shorn. The usual warnings were read aloud and, there being no slovenly drill movement to justify the cancellation of shore leave for all, the boys were marched to the main gate, anxious to put several minutes between themselves and the establishment.

Charlie Ludd found the house with its hanging baskets of lobelia, a small gnome who had lost his fishing-rod, and a sign proclaiming 'Marine Vista'. The only vista apparent to Charlie Ludd was the precisely similar house opposite, which had a privet-hedge and a miniature windmill. Again he debated the wisdom of his undertaking. He had two sizeable cigarette-stubs that could be safely enjoyed in one of the promenade shelters, or he could afford three half-slices of bread and jam or a penny cup of tea, but not both. To choose either would mean no postage stamp for his weekly letter to Mrs Ludd. Alternatively, he could join the usual coterie of boys who repaired directly to the town aquarium to enjoy the warm radiators in the tropical-fish section, or he could sing hymns with the Christian Endeavour, and be given a colourful postcard that suggested that all little children should be sent to Him. It was an excruciating choice, but finally he rang the bell of Marine Vista. There was nothing to lose.

To his surprise, Mr and Mrs Kelly were still very much in residence. Mrs Kelly, white-haired but still buxom, ushered him into a kitchen where her aged husband sat in his slippers below a caged budgerigar and spilled cigarette ash over his waistcoat. Ludd, did he say? Old Mrs Kelly's eyes were vague. Well, it was a long time ago. It must have been just after the war — the first war. But would he like a cup of tea? Charlie Ludd would. And could he manage some cake? Charlie Ludd could. Yes, Mrs Kelly recalled, there had been a honeymoon couple once, from London. Mr Kelly agreed. He remembered clearly. Did Charlie smoke? Charlie Ludd did. He was not convinced that the Kellys remembered anything, but it seemed unimportant. The massive slice of cake was superb, and he had hardly licked the crumbs from his fingers when his empty plate was filled again. It was the year they had the Cenotaph, Mr Kelly decided

157

with an air of finality, and offered him another cigarette. Mrs Kelly watched the second slice of cake disappear. She had some jelly trifle. . . .

'I like to see food put away,' Mrs Kelly approved, and Charlie Ludd was very willing to oblige. 'I don't suppose they give you much up there.' The training establishment of *St George* was a phenomenon of which local people were wary. It had never been explained; there were bugle calls and whistles, glimpses of trotting boys and gaitered instructors, stories of penal discipline. There were few opportunities for fraternisation; the Navy did not encourage it and the boys' shore-leave periods were too brief for social relationships to be easily promoted. 'Up there' was a closed environment that smacked of some kind of Borstal, and its youthful population was regarded with a degree of sympathy but equally with reserve. If boys had to be segregated and disciplined like that, then there was probably more in it than met the eye.

Charlie Ludd, however, did not seem to be particularly criminal, only hungry. She gave him a very large portion of jelly trifle, decided that there was nothing very substantial about jelly, and sliced some cold ham. 'If I'd known you were coming,' she apologised, 'I'd have done something special.' Charlie Ludd assured her politely that the fare was excellent and agreed that he would like tomatoes with his cold ham and — yes — perhaps some bread and butter. More tea? Well, if there was some in the pot.

And he may as well finish off the cake, Mrs Kelly suggested; it would only go stale otherwise. In that case, Charlie Ludd conceded, he may as well. Finally and gloriously sated, he relaxed in an armchair and smoked one of Mr Kelly's cigarettes.

'You must come again,' Mrs Kelly offered, 'mustn't he, dear?' The war had treated the Isle of Man lightly. There were shortages and inconveniences, but there had been no daily sirens, no bombings, no nights in shelters, no children evacuated. True, there were fewer visitors, the beaches were empty, the promenade kiosks were closed, there were compounds for aliens and there were more uniforms than usual, but the war was distant, its progress followed through newspapers and radio. Mrs Kelly had knitted socks and scarves, and contributed parcels for soldiers, but had never known to whom they had gone, which was mildly frustrating. Now, at least, she had a well-scrubbed and polite young man who ate her home-made cake with the appreciation of one who had eaten nothing for a week. 'Yes,' she insisted, 'when you come again, I'll do something special.' Mr Kelly spilled more ash over his waistcoat. 'It was the year they had the Cenotaph,' he affirmed. 'It couldn't have been before, because we only did bed and breakfast. So it must have been the year they had the Cenotaph.'

'*Virtue, Trooper, Truelove* from Admiralty repeated *Pennyroyal*: Operational Priority: Enemy aircraft transmission at 1215/06 reports two Military Class trawlers position 69.20N 10.10E course 220. This is incompatible with your position estimated from earlier course and speed and suggests trawlers have been detached. If correct and in view of trawlers' compromised position *Trooper* or *Truelove* to transmit clarification immediately.'

The Petty Officer Telegraphist gave his opinion. 'If *Trooper* or *Truelove* reply on ship—shore H/F, sir, the

Admiralty might retransmit their report on broadcast. Or they might not. We can't tell unless we monitor H/F for, say, the next twelve hours. That'll mean putting every telegraphist on watch, including myself, without relief. Or we can order *Pennyroyal* to assume guard on broadcast—'

'No.' The Commander shook his head. 'Thank you, Sparks.' If Furloe in *Truelove* had any sense, he would delay any transmission for several hours, and then be very discreet in the wording of his signal. If Hayes-Mailer could choose, Furloe would maintain W/T silence; there was nothing he could tell the Admiralty that would help the situation. However, a lieutenant could hardly be expected to ignore an OP order from the Admiralty.

He handed the paper to Rainbird. 'The Admiralty has discovered that it has mislaid a convoy.' He smiled grimly. 'This convoy. There must be quite a flap on in the Ops Room. What with PQ17 being knocked for six, *Tirpitz* on the loose, and half the Home Fleet steaming around in ever-diminishing circles, they now have the enemy reporting *Trooper* and *Truelove* chugging along in the wrong direction. What has happened to a destroyer, a corvette, two tankers and two freighters?'

Rainbird was thoughtful. 'It didn't take the enemy long to latch on to *Trooper* and *Truelove*, sir — and they're still well within enemy flying range. They could be in trouble.'

'But they aren't yet,' the Commander said. 'The enemy has found the trawlers but they've lost the convoy. That's a point to us. And I can't believe they will put a squadron of bombers into the air for a 1500-mile round flight for two trawlers when those aircraft could be concentrating on us. Two trawlers aren't going to worry the enemy, but those four merchant ships could mean a lot of dead Germans if they reach Murmansk.'

Three hours passed without incident – three hours during which the two trawlers must be creeping toward the safey of an Icelandic fjord and, with luck, RAF air cover. Above *Virtue* the clouds were low, unbroken and sullen, and visibility, in the constant twilight that scarcely changed throughout the day and night cycle, was about eight miles except when reduced by falling snow. The ship pushed through a long, slow swell, elbowing aside the white ice mush that streamed past her flank, tumbled in the wake of her screws and then closed again astern of her. Ahead, *Pennyroyal* was clinging to eighteen knots – a knot better than her designed speed – but, Hayes-Mailer calculated, Campbell would tear his engines to ruin before he asked to ease down. It was not *Pennyroyal*'s engines that caused the Commander's concern so much as her viciously increased fuel consumption. And all ships were making a lot of smoke.

Better a reduction now, to save something for later. He turned for the Yeoman, but the man was already at his shoulder. 'Operational Priority from Admiralty, sir.' Hayes-Mailer took the signal, turned his back against the wind.

'*Virtue* from Admiralty repeated *Pennyroyal*: Operational Priority: U-boat callsign U-L reported to Bergen two Military Class trawlers torpedoed and sunk 69.15N 10.15E at 1625/06. No report received from *Trooper* or *Truelove* Admty's 061436z refers. Knowledge of your present position and course uncertain.'

161

Hayes-Mailer swore quietly and obscenely.

Lobby Ludd and Signalman House were peeling potatoes, slicing them into a galley dish.

'Lancashire 'ot-pot made wi' bloddy corned dog,' House lamented. 'Has tha' heard owt like it?' He snorted. 'If yon bloke Fray Bentos was bloddy heer, ah'd ram corned beef fritters up 'ee's arse wi' the toe o' my soddin' sea-boot.'

'Yer bloody lucky,' Stripey Albright commented. 'In my day we never 'ad fritters—'

'That's right,' Bungy Williams agreed. 'In Stripey's day they 'ad beef on the 'oof. They 'ad ter kill a bullock on the soddin' fo'c'sle every stand-easy — an' save the blood fer the Master-at-Arms. Ain't that right, Stripey?'

'That ain't far out,' Stripey nodded. 'When I was in the *Veteran* — that was in '31 — we didn't 'ave refrigerators, see. We sent a "blood boat" ashore every couple o' days fer meat. An' no bloody motor-cutters, neither. We *rowed*. If we was at sea fer a week, we was on salt 'orse, mate.' He snorted disdainfully. 'An' bread? We 'ad biscuits that near broke yer bloody teeth.'

'I always wondered about yer teeth,' Bungy Williams sympathised. 'But I didn't want ter be personal.'

When Charlie Ludd presented himself at Marine Vista on his next shore leave it was plain that Mrs Kelly had 'done something special'. There was cheese-and-onion pie, sardines, tinned fruit and evaporated milk, bloater-paste sandwiches, sponge cake, ginger cake, and Bridie Kelly.

Bridie Kelly was fifteen, Irish, red-haired and blue-eyed, very shy, and with a protuberant young bosom that drew Charlie Ludd's gaze immediately. Bridie came from Dublin, Mrs Kelly explained, and Mr Kelly amplified this by adding that she was one of the Dublin Kellys. It would be nice, Mrs Kelly thought, if Charlie had company of his own age. Charlie speculated on the age of consent, glanced again at Bridie's breasts, and decided that, if she was big enough, she was old enough. The only question was opportunity.

Bridie offered little encouragement. She sat with eyes demurely lowered and delicately nibbled a bloater-paste sandwich. In his armchair, Mr Kelly spilled cigarette ash over his waistcoat and told his wife that she ought to have had kippers. Had Charlie ever had Manx kippers? Charlie Ludd confessed that he had not, but the sardines were fine. Mrs Kelly protested that they only had kippers on Sundays. 'You *know* we only have kippers on Sundays,' she accused Mr Kelly, who then pointed out that they had kippers on Sundays when nobody came to tea, but if someone came to tea on a Wednesday, then there was no reason why they shouldn't have kippers on a Wednesday. Mrs Kelly was defeated by this logic. 'If Charlie wants kippers, he can *have* kippers,' she volunteered. Charlie Ludd, having committed himself to cheese-and-onion pie, tore his attention away from Bridie Kelly's breasts to suggest that kippers were a pleasure he would be prepared to forgo until some other occasion; at the moment he was excellently provided for.

'On Sunday, then,' Mrs Kelly determined. 'Do they let you out on Sunday?' Charlie Ludd agreed that he was let out on Sunday, although it was the least favoured day for shore leave. Wartime Douglas offered few distractions for the impoverished on weekdays; it offered none on Sundays. Even the aquarium was closed.

Mrs Kelly had an idea. 'You must let Bridie take you for a nice walk on Sunday afternoon. Mustn't he, Bridie?' Bridie blushed, startled. 'I have to go to church,' she pleaded; but Mrs Kelly shook her head. 'Not on Sunday afternoon, Bridie,' she corrected. 'A nice walk over Douglas Head, and back for tea.'

'And we'll have kippers,' Mr Kelly said.

'I said, we don't have to have kippers only on Sundays,' Mrs Kelly refuted. 'If Charlie wants kippers on Wednesday he can have kippers on Wednesday.' She returned to her earlier topic. 'I'd come with you myself, but I'm not one for walking these days.'

'Perhaps if we didn't walk too far,' Bridie ventured, 'you could come.' Charlie Ludd took a slice of sponge cake, unconcernedly.

'No, dear,' confided Mrs Kelly. 'The truth is, I usually have a nice doze on Sundays. I don't like to miss my little doze.' Charlie was relieved, and smiled resignedly at Bridie. For fifteen, he considered, she had as fine a pair as he'd ever seen. And red hair, too. Mrs Kelly beamed at them both. 'You have your nice walk, and I'll do kippers.'

On Sunday, Bridie was waiting apprehensively for him at Marine Vista, dressed in a pale blue costume, a hat and patent-leather shoes, and carrying a prayer book in a white-gloved hand. They had all of three hours, Mrs Kelly assured them, so there was no need for hurry, and it was going to be a warm afternoon. Did Bridie want to leave her hat and gloves? Bridie declined. She always wore a hat and gloves on Sunday, she said. It wouldn't seem like Sunday otherwise. Charlie Ludd smiled understandingly, and she blushed.

Together they walked solemnly along the sea-front, past the harbour and up the climbing road towards Douglas Head. Conversation was strained and, on Bridie's part, limited to coy monosyllables. Charlie Ludd tried a light-hearted story about that morning's church service in the gymnasium of *St George*, and the lesson read by the Commodore. Bridie responded at last. 'You're not Catholic?' she enquired, and gripped her prayer book more tightly.

Charlie Ludd considered. 'Not entirely a Catholic,' he decided. 'Only in parts.' He explained. 'I've got "C of E" in my paybook, see, but if the Catholic padre's got something on — like a film and biscuits — then I'm Catholic.'

Bridie frowned. 'Are you confirmed?' she challenged. 'Do you attend Holy Communion?'

'Not any more.' Charlie Ludd shook his head. 'I tried it, but it ain't worth all the trouble. Yer don't get a chance of a good swaller before 'ee whips it away, an' them little wafer things ain't fit fer sparrers.'

Bridie was pensive, but they had reached the broad green brow of Douglas Head, scattered with grazing sheep among tangled banks of yellow-flowering furze. 'It's nice up 'ere,' Charlie Ludd approved. 'Shall we sit in the shade fer a bit?' She wore a blouse that buttoned down the front, he noted.

She followed him doubtfully over the grass. 'I don't think we should sit down,' she protested. 'It's not very clean.' Several sheep eyed them impassively, chewing.

In a secluded, shrub-surrounded hollow, hidden from all gaze save that of the sheep, Charlie Ludd gallantly spread his Sunday-clean handkerchief. 'There yer are,' he offered. ' 'Ow's that?' He tossed his cap to the grass. Bridie drew a deep breath and lowered herself primly, sitting precisely on the white square. 'You can't see the sea from here,' she warned, but Charlie Ludd did not seem to care. He sat himself beside her, intimately close.

'I knew this was going to happen.' Bridie stared into distance, flushed but stiffly unmoving as Charlie fumbled with the buttons of her blouse. 'I knew from the beginning.' She had not removed either hat or gloves, and still clutched her prayer book.

Charlie Ludd's expectations were fully satisfied. 'Beauties,' he affirmed. 'A pair o' real beauties. I'd never 'ave believed it. I wish I 'ad a camera.' Bridie swallowed. 'Don't crease my blouse, please. It's Limerick lace, and I keep it for church.' She sat upright with eyes resignedly closed, and did not resist Charlie's hand when it moved between her legs. 'Are you sure there's nobody watching?' she whispered. 'I couldn't bear it if someone was watching.' Charlie Ludd gave a cursory glance in several directions. 'Only the sheep,' he assured her. This was going to be so easy, it was hardly believable. His fingers met soft pubic hair. He had wondered about red-heads; now he would know for certain. 'If yer'd jes' lay back a bit,' he suggested, 'it'll be all over before yer can ask fer more.' He grappled with his own obstinate buttons. 'Why don't yer take yer 'at off? And yer won't need the prayer book.' He lowered his trouser flap. 'There's thirty-six different ways, but we'll start wi' the easy ones till yer get the 'ang of it.'

Bridie's eyes widened, and she turned them modestly away. 'No,' she said firmly. 'Not in my best clothes. They'll get all crumpled. And not on a Sunday. Besides, you're not a Catholic.' She glanced speculatively at the phenomenon that Charlie Ludd's unbuttoned trousers had revealed. 'If you were a Catholic—'

Charlie Ludd snorted. 'O' course I'm Catholic. I oughter know.' He would have sworn to being Hindu if necessary. 'I was only jokin' before. If yer like, I'll go ter Confession after, so yer'll 'ave nothin' ter worry about.'

Bridie considered. 'But not lying down. Can't you do it standing up?'

He sighed. 'Standin' up, walkin', jumpin', or ridin' a bike,' he agreed. 'An' I can whistle at the same time.' He climbed to his feet. 'Well, if yer standin' comfort'bly, we'll begin.' Bridie rose, pushed her knickers over her knees and looked around anxiously. 'Don't stand on my shoes,' she instructed. 'And you won't do anything on my skirt, will you?'

'Blimey,' he grunted, and parted her thighs. This was it, at last. It was going to be marveilous. And it was only half-past two. He could have it in soak for two hours.

But Bridie had suddenly tensed. 'No, I can't. I've changed my mind. I can't do it while we're being watched.'

'Watched?' Charlie Ludd peered around. 'There ain't a soul in sight. 'Oo's watchin'?'

'The sheep,' she explained. 'They're staring at us. I couldn't bear to do it while they're staring at us all the time—'

'Gorblimey,' he gritted. 'I'll chase 'em away.' His lowered trousers hampered an immediate foray, but he waved his arms and shouted. The sheep regarded him benignly and continued chewing. 'If yer shut yer eyes,' he suggested, 'yer won't see 'em. Besides, sheep do it all the time. 'Ow do yer think they 'ave lambs?'

Bridie stared at him for several seconds, incredulity filling her eyes. Then she shook her head firmly. 'But people can't have babies unless they're married,' she ruled. 'Everybody knows that.' She smoothed her skirt carefully. 'Grass stains are awful things to clean. Can you see any grass stains?'

Charlie Ludd's inspiration was draining. 'If I went ter a nudist camp,' he calculated, 'it'd be pissin' wi' rain, and they'd all be wearin' raincoats.' He reached for his cap wearily.

It was not Campbell of *Pennyroyal* who complained about the speed, but the freighter *Chessington*.

'Regret unable to maintain pressure for eighteen knots. Earlier engine defect corrected in Reykjavik has recurred. Must reduce to twelve knots to avoid complete breakdown and can risk better speed only in extreme emergency.'

'These bastard merchantmen,' Fender snorted at Waddell. 'Why the hell's she at sea with defective engines? Because her damn-bloody owners won't spend money on a proper refit, that's why. Christ, if we'd known, we needn't have lost *Trooper* and *Truelove*. They could still be here.' He choked. 'When those fat bastards in Leadenhall Street publish their annual report on profits, they ought to print eighty names under "sundry expenses". . . .'

Seven

He had ignored the possibility, because of its remoteness, that the trawlers might be intercepted by a U-boat. Even at only eleven knots a 175-foot trawler was an elusive target for a submarine, presumably submerged, capable of a 7½-knots maximum. It was more than likely that two U-boats had been involved. A few days before, in the same area, *Virtue* had attacked an enemy submarine and *Vagrant* had been sunk by another, but any such speculation was academic. *Trooper* and *Truelove* had been destroyed, eighty more men were almost certainly dead, and he, Hayes-Mailer, had ordered it. In four days he had lost three warships and 207 lives, and there were probably not half that number shared between the four merchantmen he escorted — one of whom had now reduced them all to twelve knots. Fender was right. If *Chessington*'s master had been a Naval officer he would face a court of enquiry, possibly a court martial, for taking a vessel with suspect engines on a hazardous passage and, in so doing, endangering the other ships in company. The merchant skipper had gambled on the convoy being confined to ten or eleven knots, and had said nothing, had not even warned the Commander of a possible engine failure when *Trooper* and *Truelove* had turned for Iceland.

'What are possibilities of repairing defect?' he had flashed to *Chessington*. The merchantman had replied, 'Regret no possibility. Require dockyard facilities.' For a fleeting, angry moment he had been tempted to abandon her, but knew he could not. The speed-reduction signal fluttered listlessly from *Virtue*'s mast-head, and *Pennyroyal*'s light twinkled. 'That was exciting while it lasted. Have lost all paint from funnel and Chief ERA has ulcers.' Above them the clouds were low, lead-coloured, but there was no sign of fog. With every hour that passed the cold seemed more intensely, painfully penetrating. For the short time that the ships had thrashed at speed through the ice mush there had been a perceptible change in the men's mood. They had grinned with cracked lips, exchanged apprehensive chaff, climbed ladders with an urgent elasticity that had not been there before. Now, with speed again reduced, the mood had gone. They had shrugged themselves deep into their duffel-hoods, stared with red-rimmed, dis-interested eyes at the endless, unchanging emptiness of sea and sky, each alone with his thoughts. Speech was an effort, and when exchanged was brief and morose; on the messdecks there was an undercurrent of ill-humour that could flare into hostility for the most trivial reason. They cursed *Chessington*, who had thrown away the convoy's most vital means of survival, for which *Trooper* and *Truelove* had been sacrificed — its speed.

What the hell were they all doing here? Alan Prentice was debating. A hastily gathered convoy, inadequately escorted, and probably pushed into the unknown as a sop to the cynical Russians and their vociferous fellow-travellers in Britain, who demanded high industrial wages, made cigarette lighters from cartridge cases as music played while they worked, slept in warm beds and complained about the rations that others had died in bringing to them. He, Prentice, had been a fool to transfer to the Navy. He could still be with Union Castle now, with a Mate's ticket, a useful war bonus, and probably comfortably trooping between Southampton and the Cape. Instead, he was standing on the icy open bridge of an old destroyer that had apparently been written off as expendable by the Admiralty, escorting four merchantmen who should never have been despatched and had never been given a real chance of achieving their destination. Well, Prentice mused, he could blame nobody but himself; nobody had compelled him. He had wanted a fighting service, not a mercantile one, and he had got what he wanted.

Geoffrey Fender had choked back the feeling of horror he had experienced at the threat of *Tirpitz*, and his uneasiness was hidden behind a façade of sarcasm and satire that was becoming annoying to his wardroom fellows. Fender had served almost a year in *Virtue*, operating out of Londonderry, and sported the tarnished cap-badge and shabby raincoat which would not have been tolerated in a larger vessel but were as much the hallmark of the small-ships officer as the loosened top button of the fighter pilot. Earlier service in a battleship in Scapa Flow and, earlier still, his annual periods of peacetime training, had not fully prepared him for the rigours of destroyer life in the Arctic, and in this he was far from unique. He had come through several submarine hunts and aircraft attacks with no emotion other than nervous excitement, but the possibility of a surface action against superior enemy warships, during which he would be responsible for the performance of *Virtue*'s guns, twisted his belly into knots every time he thought about it.

And he had always considered that the Commander disapproved of him since their first meeting. Fender had joined *Virtue* in Belfast — a tired, rust-streaked old ship still in dockyard hands. There was nobody else aboard except two sub-lieutenants — the last of the previous ship's company and anxious to hand over the vessel to anyone who claimed it — and a small Care and Maintenance party of seamen and stokers. Fender, with two new gold rings on his cuff and straight from the pomp and polish of a battleship, had been pleased to assume responsibility until an unknown Commander Hayes-Mailer arrived. He mustered the disgruntled seamen at 0800, when the ship's colours were hoisted, and then, reminded by the dockyard superintendent that the ship was not yet in commission, quickly hauled them down again.

That same evening, in the lounge of the Grand Central Hotel, Fender had fortuitously stumbled into the two sub-lieutenants, who were enjoying a final evening's recreation before leaving for Devonport. They were accompanied by two young ladies of debatable character and did not greet Fender's appearance with particular warmth. Anxious to impress, however, Fender insisted that all four should return with him to *Virtue*'s wardroom. It was almost Christmas, and he had the key of the duty-free stowage. The old ship, after all, owed the two young men a few gins, and the ladies' company for an hour or two would be most welcome.

In the wardroom of *Duke of York* Fender had been very small fry, but in *Virtue* he could be expansive with impunity. Gin followed gin and the gathering grew progressively less inhibited. The two younger officers had been anxious to depart for a more intimate exchange with their ladies as soon as they could do so without offending their senior, but Fender kept glasses generously filled and the ladies gave no indication of disapproval. The younger men shrugged at each other, resigned.

Repartee was becoming *risqué* when the two ladies confessed that they were nightclub dancers. What sort of dancers? Well, they danced with fans or balloons. Fender, growing noisily fuddled, was delighted. In that case, he wagged an erratic finger, they must pay for their entertainment by dancing on the wardroom-table. He was the senior officer, and those were his orders. He placed a randomly selected record on the radiogram.

The ladies demurred coyly. Their dance routine entailed disrobing, but only with fans or balloons. If Lieutenant Fender could provide fans or balloons they would oblige, but not otherwise. After all, they were artistic dancers, not strip-teasers. There was a difference.

Fender considered, and then had an inspiration. In the duty-free spirits locker he had noticed a cardboard carton containing one gross of Durex rubber condoms. When he produced them triumphantly, unsteady on his feet, the ladies shrieked.

Inflating the condoms was a riotous procedure. Many of them burst, and the three men needed several intermediate gins to sustain their energy while the ladies continued to shriek. Each would inflate ten, Fender ordered, which meant thirty balloons. The most modest of dancers could happily disrobe behind a barrage of thirty balloons — although, he winked, there was no guarantee that all would remain intact for the entire duration of the dance. Balloons were notoriously unreliable, and the whole thing was going to be a hoot.

It was. The ladies were lifted, protesting, to the table, the radiogram erupted into music of no consequence, and the makeshift balloons were launched into motion. Behind them the ladies squirmed provocatively with hands fluttering, removed their easily unbuttoned dresses, stockings and bras, tossing them languidly aside. The officers cheered and gulped happily at their gin. The ladies turned their backs, waved arms, then adroitly peeled down their knickers and wriggled white buttocks. The officers roared their approval.

There was an annoying interruption. The door of the wardroom had opened quietly and a man had entered. He was tall, spare, tan-faced, wore a well-tailored grey suit and held a soft hat in one hand. He had stood silently for several seconds, watching, before Fender became aware of him. Fender belched. 'Who the hell are you?' he slurred. 'Who the hell let you aboard?' Some bloody dockyard clerk, he guessed, with no damn business on a warship.

The man did not answer immediately, but turned an expressionless gaze from the ladies on the table, who had suddenly ceased their posturing, to the clutter of glasses and bottles and the carpet strewn with fragments of condom rubber and underclothes. Then his eyes rested sombrely on Fender. 'My name is Hayes-Mailer,' he said. 'Commander Hayes-Mailer. I'm the captain of this ship.' He paused. 'Who are you?'

Fender clambered desperately to his feet, groping at a

tie that had become unknotted. 'Fender, sir —
Lieutenant Fender — just joined. These' — he waved
a hand — 'are Sub-Lieutenants Caswell and Butcher,
of the last ship's company.' He tried to remember
the ladies' names, but could not. He shuddered. 'Welcome aboard, sir. . . .'

The Commander's cold eyes turned slowly towards
the two younger men, who, in the space of a few
seconds, had become very sober. 'I know you will wish
to escort these ladies ashore immediately,' he suggested,
'and I am sure you can telephone for a cab at the
dockyard gate.' The ladies were dressing with incredible
speed. 'And, Fender, when you have personally cleaned
up the wardroom, please come to my cabin and explain
why you have broached duty-free stores in harbour, and
expended medical supplies, without my permission.'

If *Virtue* had delayed her sailing from Liverpool for
twenty-four hours, John Rainbird had told himself
several times, he would not have been aboard. An
obliging Wren writer in the Rear-Admiral's office had
even told him his relief's name — a Canadian lieutenant
travelling up from London, which meant another RNVR
man. At the mention of a Canadian, he had seen
Hayes-Mailer frown very slightly. *Virtue* had enjoyed
the luxury of a regular Navy lieutenant for its Number
One since commissioning, and Rainbird's name in the
half-yearly promotions list, which accorded him his
half-ring, had caught them both by surprise. There had
been a celebration in the wardroom, with everyone
expecting that he would soon be gone, hopefully to a
command of his own, but equally likely to the un-
inspiring routine of a capital ship or, worst of all, a

shore establishment. *Virtue*'s sailing orders had intervened. It was extremely unlikely that Hayes-Mailer could have delayed the ship's departure but, Rainbird suspected, he had not been displeased at a turn of events that meant the Canadian kicking his heels in Liverpool for a few weeks.

He had never achieved a close relationship with Hayes-Mailer. Both men were bachelors — unusually, all *Virtue*'s officers except Stevens, the Commissioned Engineer, were unmarried. Both the Commander and Rainbird were 'salt horses' — officers who chose to remain purely seamen rather than apply themselves to gunnery, communications or other specialist fields in which advancement was often more favourable. He admired Hayes-Mailer's professional ability, his unstinting devotion to his task and his uncanny knack of always being on the bridge in moments of difficulty or hazard. He had all the qualities that Rainbird would wish to possess, but he was insular, almost unapproachable, courteous but never confiding, good-humoured but never familiar. Rainbird realised that he knew almost nothing about the Commander, did not understand him and probably did not like him. Would he, Rainbird, be another Hayes-Mailer in ten years' time?

Gazing over the screen from his chair, his eyes narrowed against the flurry of fine snow and his gloved hands around a mug of scalding cocoa, Hayes-Mailer was balancing the odds. He was not the unemotional machine that others considered him; he had cultivated an air of imperturbability during his long years of slow promotion, to mask the resentment that often rankled within him — a resentment that had first flared when he stood before a polished table in Hong Kong, a long time ago, and knew that another had broken him to protect his own reputation.

Responsibility was a damnable thing, Hayes-Mailer had decided. A course of action that succeeded by a hair's breadth was applauded as daring and brilliant. If the same course of action failed by the same hair's breadth it was a rash blunder. There was no doubt in his mind that, so far, he had failed. He had lost three ships, in retrospect unnecessarily, without even seeing the enemy that had sunk them, and his remaining charges remained afloat only by the grace of God. If he lost them now, he could expect little sympathy from an Admiralty that had despatched them with so little regard for the consequences. Someone in Whitehall, with lunch at the club waiting, had hurriedly initialled a memo, barely having read it, and Hayes-Mailer was faced with a near-impossible commitment. He wished he could have the bloody fool on this bridge now, to explain how it should be done, because he, Hayes-Mailer, did not think he would reach Murmansk.

If he did, he must write some letters, to the parents of Sub-Lieutenant Coope and Able Seaman Foster, and to Bob Roper's wife, Joan, in Lee-on-Solent. He had been Bob Roper's best man and, later, had driven Joan to the hospital, during her husband's absence, when their first child was born. It had been the nearest thing to a family of his own that he had ever known.

And he must write to Vice-Admiral George Furloe, retired. It would be a letter that must be compiled with utmost care — brief, sympathetic but concise. On balance, he well knew, it would be wise if he did not write at all, but he knew he would. He detested the weakness in him, but the ugly thought refused to be thrust away. He was going to enjoy writing condolences to George Furloe.

Ordinary Signalman Ludd, of 7 Mess, was not on letter-writing terms with anyone except his mother, and she, he felt bound to concede, was not the most inspiring of confidantes. Each of her letters was an almost precise facsimile of her last — a brief discourse on the state of the weather, the black-out, queues and rationing, the frequency of air raids, if any, and the expressed hope that he remained in the pink. Writing back anything less prosaic to Mrs Ludd, Lobby had long concluded, was like trying to establish a conversation with a machine that spoke your weight. He would like to receive letters from a girl. Most of his fellows seemed to have 'parties', and had photographs to prove it, although the validity of their relationships with the beauty queens whose faces were pasted to their kit-locker doors was less than certain.

He retained, still, a mild guilt-complex with regard to his brother's death, or, more accurately, his own lack of emotion; he ought to feel bereaved, but he did not seem to have the time. His hours were too full, his environment too gregarious, and even when alone with his thoughts in those fleeting moments between waking and sleeping, when he decided to feel mournful, he was asleep before he could begin.

His few anxieties were minor and transitory. He was often miserably cold and wet, and almost always tired, but so was everyone else. Others, more experienced, cursed the destroyer-man's lot and spoke enviously of those lucky bastards in bigger ships, shore stations or coastal forces, but Lobby Ludd could only compare conditions with those of Boys' Service and *St George*, and they compared favourably. For him the most striking point in *Virtue*'s favour was that she carried no Jaunty or Regulating Petty Officer; defaulters were arraigned before the First Lieutenant by the Coxswain, Bogey Knight, to be allotted extra work or lose a period of pay, but at sea serious offences were rare simply because there were few situations in which to commit them. There was no leave to be broken, no opportunity for being drunk and disorderly, or for friction with civil police. Occasionally a man's patience, frayed by tired-ness or some imagined slight, would snap, but violent confrontation could not be tolerated in such an in-tegrated community, and cooler minds would prevail. When Lobby Ludd thought about it — and saving his brush with the First Lieutenant in Liverpool — he had never enjoyed such a long period without constant surveillance and frequent censure.

Campbell of *Pennyroyal* did not intend to invite another reprimand, and this time he gave ample warning. Prob-able aircraft were reported at twenty miles — a report which, in view of the unfavourable conditions, must have been the result of snap judgement by a radar operator, but it was sufficient to send all ships to action stations. Gun-muzzles were lifting, ready-use lockers were wrenched open, and magazine and damage-control parties closed up when, within minutes, *Pennyroyal* made an amplifying report. Four aircraft were approach-ing from almost dead ahead at 200 knots. Their course and speed would bring them within sight of the convoy at any moment.

The whole thing had happened so quickly that there

was almost no intervening period of waiting, during which men begin to calculate and their nerves tighten, no time to question how in hell's name the enemy had located the convoy with such pinpoint accuracy. It was happening. Fender, relieved by the Commander and the First Lieutenant, had barely flung himself off the bridge, trailing helmet and headset, and young Fairbrother, racing for the after four-inch gun, had hardly hauled himself, with clenched teeth, to his feet after falling and gashing his shin to the bone, when the four Focke-Wulf Condors snarled out of the grey-yellow cloud-base, four miles ahead.

Thank Christ for *Pennyroyal*'s radar, Rainbird gritted. Without it, the four aircraft could have made their first run at the convoy before a gun had replied. In the event, the merchant ships' short-range Lewis and Hotchkiss guns opened wild fire at the first moment of sighting. It was unfortunate; the two warships had been ready for that first hurried run by pilots who thought that they were making a surprise attack. The harmless spatter of machine-gun fire told them that their victims had been aware of the aircraft's approach for at least several minutes. That meant radar, and that changed matters.

They banked away, climbing to westward, turning their pale under-bellies to the ships, and below the guns turned with them, tracking. 'BWO. Make to all ships. Stand by to alter course together, eighty degrees to port.' The Commander lifted his binoculars. 'Cloud-base is not more than four thousand feet, Number One.' If they meant to attack, the aircraft would have to make a long, low-level approach into the teeth of the warships' anti-aircraft fire which, if modest, would still be sufficient to unsettle the concentration of pilots and bomb-aimers. Then, astern of *Virtue*, almost at the limit of visibility, the enemy had turned again. 'Here they come.'

The light guns of *Brazos River* and *Olympic Madison* sputtered immediately, and seconds later those of *Chessington* and *Empire Mandate* followed suit, the long ribbons of tracer smoke snaking alarmingly low over *Virtue*'s masthead. Instinctively, Rainbird ducked, then swore, as angry with his own involuntary action as with the undisciplined gunfire that had provoked it. He could hear Fender's voice, strained, on the gunnery circuit. 'Barrage — commence, commence, commence. . . .'

On the flag-deck Lobby Ludd flinched, stunned, as only feet below him both port and starboard two-pounder pom-poms opened fire together, pounding deafeningly. He clamped hands to his shocked ears, and in the next instant came the crack of the three-inch high-angle gun amidships. There was a stinging, acrid smell of burnt cordite, and he could see Yeoman Shaw, with an intensely twisted face, staring astern. For a fleeting moment he experienced panic. Jesus Christ! This wasn't just an air raid in which bombs might fall in Clapham North or Herne Hill. The aircraft, distant still, were just below the cloud-canopy in staggered form-ation, overhauling the ships with ominous speed. He could see them clearly, and they were very real. From below the barrage of flak seemed overwhelming, impenetrable, but most of the tracer was that of the merchant ships' small-calibre fire and was falling short. The pom-poms in *Virtue* and *Pennyroyal*, however, were reaching, and the destroyer's single three-inch gun, served by a team that worked like madmen, was blotch-ing the sky with shell bursts. But the four aircraft came on, straight and flat, with bomb doors open.

Hayes-Mailer, also, was watching astern, calculating the moment that the approaching aircraft had committed themselves to their bombing run with bomb-sights locked. He lowered his head. 'BWO. Executive signal. Executive signal.' Then he fixed his eyes on *Brazos River*, waited for the big tanker's frothing wake to begin its orbit. 'Port thirty.'

'*Check, check, check....*'

' 'Midships. Steady. Hold her there, Coxs'n — oh-one-oh....'

'Steady, sir. Course oh-one-oh....'

The six ships were turning under maximum rudder, excruciatingly slowly, it seemed to Lobby Ludd, but the enemy aircraft were to port now, almost abeam, and the guns were traversing, the pom-poms crump-crumping without pause, spilling expended cartridge-cases that rolled untidily as *Virtue* heeled, the three-pounder with its ear-stinging crack every four seconds. He saw the bombs leave the leading aircraft and float leisurely downward. He knew they were falling directly at *Virtue*, and pressed backward against the flag-locker with bile in his throat and his legs like water. Incredibly, a column of grey water lifted from the sea, 300 yards to starboard in the curving wake of *Olympic Madison*, and in that same moment the aircraft exploded into orange flame, disintegrated, spewing debris and thick smoke.

'We've *got* the bastard!' Signalman House bawled into his ear, and the Yeoman was half-crouched with fists clenched, like a boxer. The shattering hammer of the ship's guns was continuing, and a flurry of black soot, shaken from the galley chimney, whirled over the flag-deck. There were more convulsive water-spouts to starboard, rearing skyward and collapsing slowly — one so close to *Empire Mandate* that it seemed certain she had sustained a hit, but she ploughed on, her rust-streaked black hull and buff upperworks undamaged.

'*Check, check, check. Cease firing. Cease firing.*'

'They'll make another run, Number One. All stations report, please.' *Pennyroyal* was flashing, and Lobby Ludd, trembling, but glad of a distraction, reached for the Aldis. 'My bird, I think,' the corvette suggested. 'We gave it both barrels.'

Only the Commander's eyes showed momentary annoyance. He spoke to the BWO. 'To all ships — stand by to alter course together, sixty degrees to starboard.'

The Focke-Wulf Condors were prowling, low on the horizon with the grey blanket of cloud behind them. Their leader would be mouthing instructions to his fellow-pilots, Rainbird guessed, angry at having lost one of his flight in the face of comparatively light opposition, but achieving nothing. The German fliers would not like the low-altitude approach during which their aircraft filled the sights of the warships' guns, but there was no alternative. Together, they turned for the second time.

In the brief respite, steel boxes of pom-pom ammunition had been hoisted from the magazine, the litter of spent cartridge-cases kicked free of the guns, and an SBA had hastily bandaged Fairbrother's gashed leg. Laboriously, the wardroom steward had climbed to the bridge with a pail of tea, found that nobody had time for tea, and retreated to the pantry.

'*Target enemy aircraft starboard oh-three-oh, angle of sight oh-two-oh. Commence tracking. . . .*'

Lobby Ludd sucked his teeth. Soddin' hell, it was

going to start again. Nobody told anyone anything. He'd know next time. Ear-plugs for a bleedin' start.

'If we doant gi' this skylark finished wi',' Signalman House sniffed, 'it'll be past bloddy tot time.'

The three aircrafts' approach was fast, at a hazardous four thousand feet, toward *Virtue*'s starboard bow and the waiting guns. *Pennyroyal*, to eastward, had already opened fire, and for several seconds was almost hidden in a shroud of her own smoke. The ships turned, twisting away from the enemy's flight path. To anxious eyes below it seemed inconceivable that the massive and ponderous *Brazos River* and *Olympic Madison* should not be struck, if only by one of the pattern of bombs that fell lazily to tear great towers of water higher than the destroyer's masthead. And it would need only one bomb on the thin steel fo'c'sle of either tanker to turn it into a floating, raging furnace. And he'd gone deaf, Lobby Ludd decided. Stone bleedin' deaf. It'd mean his ticket, of course. Soddin' discharged deaf.

'Check, check, check. Cease firing. Cease firing.'

Rainbird was grinning. 'I think we've pulled it off, sir. The devils are turning away. They've shot their bolt.' Below them the gun-crews were jubilant. There were laughing, disputing oaths, the clatter of ammunition boxes. The wardroom steward had appeared again, apprehensively, with his bucket of tea.

The Commander's glasses were clamped to his eyes. *'Pennyroyal,'* he said. 'She's stopped.'

'BWO to bridge. From Pennyroyal, sir. "Have sustained damage from near-miss. Steering-shaft fractured with helm jammed twenty degrees to starboard. Suspect loss of screw. No casualties."'

Hayes-Mailer drew a long sibilant breath, turned

narrowed eyes toward Rainbird, then spoke back to the operator. 'Thank you. Please patch the trans-receiver to the bridge remote position.' He twisted open the tiny locker that housed a handset and loudspeaker. 'Camshaft, this is Lurcher. Captain to Captain. Your last transmission acknowledged. I am turning to close you. Please give me radar situation report and state your condition of seaworthiness.'

Campbell's brisk reply came immediately. 'This is Camshaft. Sorry, sir — we've had our arse pinched. Radar reports enemy aircraft clear of screen eastward. We are maintaining watch with operators double-banked. With regard to damage, one bomb during the enemy's second run fell under our stern just as we'd completed our starboard turn, fracturing the after section of the steering-shaft. We have a spare section, but it seems almost certain that we have lost our screw and A-bracket. The main shaft appears all right as far as the main gland, but there's no load inertia — the engine is turning nothing except the shaft.' Campbell's voice halted, then went on hurriedly. 'It's just been reported that we are making water fast, and my damage-control party has had to withdraw to the tiller flat. We'll get a pump on it.' He hesitated again. 'With your permission, sir, I'd like to begin to jettison depth-charges while I can. It will give me more buoyancy aft.'

Virtue had come up to within a hundred yards of *Pennyroyal*. The corvette's stubby, inelegant hull was wallowing in the long swell, her funnel still smoking. 'She's down by the stern, sir,' Rainbird said. An arm waved from *Pennyroyal*'s bridge, and Hayes-Mailer resorted to loud-hailer.

'Affirmative. Proceed immediately to jettison depth-charges and give me report on effects of pumping as soon as possible. Stand by with your wire. I shall take you in tow in the hope that you can effect repairs within a reasonable time. If you wish, my engineer officer can transfer to you. If repairs prove to be impossible, I shall take off your ship's company, and you will scuttle. Meanwhile, in the event of aircraft or submarine attack I will have to let you slip in order to manœuvre, but will do my best to stay with you. Are you ready?'

The First Lieutenant, amazed, said nothing. He just did not understand Hayes-Mailer. The man could abandon a sinking sister-ship, send two trawlers to almost certain destruction without a qualm, yet now he was taking a disabled vessel in tow under circumstances that could prove disastrous if the enemy reappeared. And, sooner or later, the enemy would reappear. Of that there was no doubt. Rainbird hurried aft as *Virtue* turned her stern toward *Pennyroyal*.

For the two small groups of shabbily muffled men, on *Pennyroyal*'s exposed fo'c'sle and *Virtue*'s stern, it was a viciously cold task to pass first a heaving line and then the 3½-inch wire, thick with ice, from one to the other, and Rainbird wondered if Campbell had men working to their waists in icy, swirling water below the deck-plates of the tiller flat. When a single-shafted vessel lost or damaged her screw she was a helpless thing, and Campbell would try anything, and keep trying until the last possible moment, to get his ship moving. The wire was hauled inboard and shackled up. Thank God there was no sea running; the penetrating cold was enough. He faced forward, crossed his hands above his head to indicate to the bridge that all was secure. Between the two ships the wire rose, jerked taut, hummed like a harp string. From *Pennyroyal*, Campbell's voice came to him through a gusting swirl of snow. 'Smartly done, John — thanks. I always say that following in the path of *Virtue* will bring its just reward.' Rainbird flung up a hand in acknowledgement as he made for the bridge, head lowered.

'Send one watch below for something hot, Number One,' Hayes-Mailer ordered, 'and do the same yourself. And pipe "Up Spirits". Issue it neat to all hands. The dutymen can have it at their stations. But I want all guns cleared and ready for instant action. If *Pennyroyal*'s electrical circuitry is intact, we've still got her radar.'

So that was it, Rainbird mused. He was towing *Pennyroyal* for her radar, intending to cast her loose, a helpless target, if attacked. 'Sir, couldn't we take off some of her men now? If we just left her with her radar personnel, a telegraphist and a signalman, say, a couple of officers and a few seamen to handle the tow—?'

'No, Number One. *Pennyroyal*'s still a fighting unit, and she needs every man to remain one. I'll give Campbell a chance to effect repairs first. We shall work up to an engine speed of sixteen knots, ten revs at a time, which should give us the equivalent of nine or ten. If we try any more, we might lose the wire. I've already ordered the merchantmen to reduce.' He paused. 'According to met. reports we should be in fog, but we're not. If we don't get fog within the next hour or two, Number One, it won't matter whether we're towing *Pennyroyal* or a box of dates.'

In the sanctuary of the messdeck, Lobby Ludd expounded. 'Near-miss, did yer say?' He snorted, eyes raised. 'It was a near-miss, orl right. If I'd put out my bleedin' 'and, I'd 'ave caught it.' He took an imaginary catch at first slip. ' 'Owzat, Umpire? Christ, I sez — 'ere it comes, and I ain't said me prayers. Then, SPER-LASH! — right in the 'ogwash. Talk about panic!'

'Anyway,' Lobby Ludd pressed on. 'It must 'ave taken the paint off the flag-locker. I wouldn't be surprised if orl the bleedin' flags ain't been bleached white.'

Bungy Williams nodded, rolling a cigarette. 'Yer was nearly a three-badge soddin' angel in 'eaven, Stripey.' He considered. 'No, come ter think of it, yer'd be down in the bleedin' stoke 'old. They wouldn't trust yer near the cherubs.'

After almost two hours of progressively increasing speed by a few engine revolutions, the two ships had barely achieved six knots. *Virtue*, of 1100 tons, and narrower in the beam than *Pennyroyal*, was hauling a deadweight of 925 tons and an unknown additional burden in the water that had penetrated the corvette's damaged hull. *Pennyroyal*'s stern was well down, suggesting that her pumps were not holding their own, and reluctantly Campbell confirmed it.

'We must have taken more damage than we thought, sir, and we can't get to it. Three men have tried, and they're lucky to be still alive. We've jettisoned forty depth-charges, and moved some ammunition forward, but we shall have to abandon the tiller flat. The after provision-store, magazine and shell-room are already flooded. If the bulkhead and doors hold, and if there's no damage further forward, we'll stay afloat.'

Then he added, 'If we don't get bad weather.'

Hayes-Mailer had not left the bridge for eleven hours, and had been on watch for twenty of the previous twenty-four. His muscles ached with fatigue and his eyelids were leaden; the cigarette he smoked tasted foul. But, he knew, he was not alone. Most of the dutymen in their dirty duffel-coats, with slumped shoulders at their guns, at the snow-swept stern-rails, or shivering in their exposed look-out positions, had not seen their mess-decks for nine or ten hours. They had stood their own watch, been retained at their stations for the next, and were now in their third, without relief — sustained, if they were lucky, by cocoa and the occasional solid food that the cooks, released briefly from their action duties in the magazine, could prepare in a cold galley. At least, he told himself, he could enjoy the luxury of a brandy in his cabin, change into dry clothing, even ask the Surgeon-Lieutenant for benzedrine; but he did none of these things. Like everyone else, he dipped a filthy cup into a bucket of cocoa, ate the same stale corned-beef sandwiches, and remained where he was, not even deigning to sit in his bridge chair.

'All right,' he replied to Campbell. 'I am going to increase speed; we must go faster and your weight is increasing. The wire may go, so prepare to pass your chain-cable, which we shall winch inboard. I shall keep you in tow for as long as possible for the benefit of your radar. Meanwhile, please pass across your confidential books, log, and other similar items. Begin that now. Jettison your charts in weighted bags — and anything else you wish. Prepare scuttling procedure, then stand by all men who are not required to fight ship. They must be ready to come over at a minute's notice.' He paused. 'In the event of threatened action, I shall slip the tow immediately and leave you to your own resources until the situation allows me to return. If we are both still afloat. Is that quite clear?'

It was very clear, and it became brutally clear ten seconds later.

'*Asdic to bridge. Reciprocating engines red oh-four-oh. Asdic to bridge. . . .*'

Rainbird had just lifted himself to the compass platform to check the course, and the Commander had turned, lifting his binoculars in the direction of *Chessington*, who, two cables abeam of *Empire Mandate*, was ahead of the two tankers, also abeam of each other with *Virtue* and *Pennyroyal* more than a mile astern. Fender and the Ordnance Artificer were at the three-inch gun amidships, and Prentice, Waddell, a leading wireman and a handful of seamen were grouped around the winch on the stern. In the sick bay the Surgeon-Lieutenant had just given Sub-Lieutenant Fairbrother an anti-tetanus injection and was threading a suture into a needle, telling his patient that he had rather hoped for an amputation, as he hadn't done one since Bart's.

Lobby Ludd had just collected the mess potatoes from the potato locker and returned to the messdeck, wondering how long he could drag out his absence from the flag-deck, and the Yeoman, on the flag-deck, was wondering how much longer Ordinary Signalman Ludd thought he could postpone scraping the ice from the twenty-inch lamp. In the Bridge Wireless Office, Bungy Williams had written in his operator's log, '1430: Quiet. Receiving Gear Correct,' and was rolling a cigarette.

The action alarm-bell exploded into shattering

thunder, reaching into every messdeck and flat, every compartment and cabin, the wardroom and pantry, the magazine, engine room, wireless office and sick bay, heads and bathrooms, every gun position and the depth-charge stowage, passageways and ladders. Lobby Ludd snatched for his steel helmet and life-belt. Jesus Christ, it just weren't true.

Yeoman Shaw stared. 'What have yer brought a bucket o' spuds for, boyo? In case we run short on ammo?'

'*Asdic to bridge. Target bearing red oh-five-oh, range one thousand yards and closing. . . .*'

'Let go towing-wire aft. Depth-charge crews stand by to fire pattern from stern and port side.' Hayes-Mailer, at the bridge-rail, was looking impatiently aft to where Waddell and several cursing seamen were struggling to release the taut wire that coupled *Virtue* to *Pennyroyal*, but the pin of the big securing shackle was frozen hard into its thread and was refusing to budge. 'Stand clear of the wire aft,' the Commander ordered, then, 'Full ahead both.'

Waddell and his men scattered. The wire strained, then snapped like a thread with the two severed ends flailing viciously. 'Get it in!' Hayes-Mailer roared. 'Don't let it foul the screws!' And the screws were clawing deep as, freed, *Virtue* surged away from the corvette. Waddell's party hauled madly, and between the two ships was a widening gap of white, churning froth. Then, with her wheel hard over, *Virtue* slewed, turning in her own length.

'Half-ahead both. Asdic — extent of target?'

'*Asdic to bridge. Only five degrees, sir, bearing red oh-oh-five, range eight hundred and closing. . . .*'

'Stand by to fire pattern, all charges minimum setting. We shall approach target fine on port bow. Asdic, switch to SRE.'

But in the tiny sound-proofed compartment on the forward lower deck the operator, whose straining ears had detected first the faint chukker of submarine motors and now listened tensely for the echo of his own probing transmissions, jerked upright in his seat as his headphones were filled with a sound he had rarely heard since passing out of the anti-submarine school at Portland — a chilling, sibilant roar that had only one possible meaning.

'ASDIC TO BRIDGE! TORPEDOES RUNNING!'

Virtue was still turning. Rainbird shouted, pointing. 'There, sir! Torpedo tracks — two! Almost dead ahead!'

' 'Midships. Starboard ten — 'midships — and meet her. Steady — steady. . . .'

Distinctly visible, the pale parallel lines of tiny bubbles streaked nearer, with ship and torpedoes meeting almost head-on at a combined speed of fifty-five knots. It was a passage of time to be measured in seconds, yet it seemed interminable. There was nothing, absolutely nothing, that anyone could do except stare with senses cringing as the lethal, whitening tracks vanished from view under *Virtue*'s bows, but then, 'Torpedoes running down port side, sir! The bastard's missed!'

'Jesus bleedin' Christ,' Lobby Ludd exploded, and Yeoman Shaw, with a white ring around his lips, snorted disdainfully. 'If yer can't stand excitement, boyo, yer shudn't have bloddy joined, see?'

'Asdic to bridge. Target bearing red oh-oh-five, moving from right to left, range six hundred. Torpedoes

still running. . . .'

'*Full ahead both. Depth-charge crews stand by —
stand by —* FIRE PATTERN!'

Without the wire, *Pennyroyal* slowed, then stopped,
rising and falling in the boiling wake of *Virtue*. The
crouched fo'c'sle party stared, uncertain, at the destroyer's stern, threshing to port, and the SRE shrieked
abrasively. '*All guns prepare to engage to port. Clear
lower deck, negative W/T, asdic and radar watchkeepers.
Hands muster starboard side, at the double. Clear lower
deck. Clear lower deck.*'

Impotently, Campbell watched the retiring stern of
Virtue, hazed by the smoke that poured from her
funnels, and then, beyond, saw the twin torpedo tracks
into which the destroyer was turning desperately. His
interpretation was detached and crystal clear; it was
beautifully simple. If *Virtue* avoided the speeding mis-
siles, they would hit *Pennyroyal* precisely amidships,
five seconds later.

Ah, well, he mused. Once your pants are down,
there's no point in being embarrassed about your
curlers, as the actress said to the bishop. . . .

The muffled thuds of the pattern's detonations were
clearly audible. The sea flattened momentarily and then
began to dome upward, but even before the giant
upheaval of whitened water had broken the surface
there was the roar of another explosion. A thousand
yards astern a colossal mushroom of leprous smoke
climbed for the sky, bursting outward and spilling
flaming debris. On *Virtue*'s stern, Petty Officer Arnold
and his depth-charge crew flung themselves to the deck

as, almost simultaneously, the sea beyond the rail
disintegrated.

Behind the falling thunder of spray, *Pennyroyal* had
disappeared, and beneath a pall of swirling dirty smoke
the sea writhed, floating with burning cordite, splintered
life-floats and timber, mess-stools, a shattered motor-
cutter, hammocks, oil drums and unidentifiable fragments of clothing. The 200-foot corvette had vanished,
leaving only sodden refuse to mark where she had
floated, seconds earlier.

It was incredible — totally and utterly incredible.
From bridge and fo'c'sle, gun position and flag-deck,
men stared, aghast and uncomprehending. That a ship
should be torpedoed was understandable, that it should
sink as the result was probable — but that it should
dematerialise like a soap bubble in a single instant was
inconceivable.

'Hard to port. Half-ahead both. We are going about.
Stand by with full pattern — stern-rails, port and starboard.' *Virtue* gyrated, her decks heeling crazily so that
both Hayes-Mailer and Rainbird stumbled, unbalanced,
and Lobby Ludd watched the mainmast lean fifty
degrees to starboard. Nothing could surprise him now.
He had seen it all. From deep below came the clatter of
dislodged tinware and crockery, the crash of lockers
torn from their weldings. In the Bridge Wireless Office,
Bungy Williams was flung from his chair. 'Sod this fer a
skylark,' he decided.

The amplified peenk-peenk of the asdic echo silenced
every voice. '*Asdic to bridge. Target dead ahead, range
three hundred and stationary. . . .*'

For only one second the First Lieutenant wanted to
shout that *Pennyroyal*'s floating debris was also dead

ahead, that there could be survivors in the path of *Virtue*'s bows, but the Commander's face was twisted into a snarl that Rainbird had never seen before, and he clenched his own teeth until they hurt.

'Full ahead both. All guns prepare to engage port quarter.'

'*Independent control. Stand by all guns for target port side astern, fire when ready.*'

'*Instantaneous echo!*'

'Stand by depth-charges. Fire pattern!'

From astern, and on both quarters, the depth-charges spun, curved against the sky, fell, disappeared. Arnold counted slowly. 'One, two, three—'

Two and a half thousand pounds of amatol and TNT tore the sea open with an effervescent roar. Hundreds of tons of white water rose slowly in three mountainous geysers, seemed to hang motionless in the grey sky, defying gravity, and then, equally slowly, fell back to the sea from which they had come, to subside in a convulsion of milky froth.

'Submarine surfacing, sir — port quarter!'

The U-boat broke surface exactly where Hayes-Mailer had prayed it might — astern and to port as *Virtue* turned. From the maelstrom of spume the dark grey bows thrust upward, like a steel finger, at forty-five degrees, exposing seventy feet of her forward length, knife-end bows, jumping wire, the dark mouths of her torpedo tubes, and a swelling under-belly streaked with oxydisation and slimed with green weed. Around the cascading pressure-hull the sea boiled.

For the after four-inch, the 'midships three-inch and the port pom-pom, already bearing, loaded and ready, it was a target impossible to miss.

'Target U-boat red one-four-oh. Range two hundred. Shoot, shoot, shoot!'

The submarine might slide back into the sea as quickly as she had emerged from it, and the pom-pom gunlayers, failing to compensate for the ship's sudden roll as she straightened course, aimed short, but the first screaming four-inch projectile struck square, followed almost simultaneously by a three-inch shell that ricocheted off the sea and burst at water level. Then the pom-pom crew found their mark just as the third and fourth shells from the heavier guns smashed into the rearing pressure-hull in rapid succession. Enveloped in smoke and spray, the great, helpless carcase lurched even higher, hesitated, then plunged. The sea pounced, whirlpooled, and the U-boat had gone.

There were no cheers, but almost complete silence as binoculars searched and *Virtue* circled, turned her bows towards the eddying area of sea where the enemy had sunk from sight. There was no sign of survivors from either submarine or corvette.

'Asdic to bridge. No contact, sir.'

'Thank you, and well done. Keep sweeping.' Hayes-Mailer drew a deep breath, nodded acknowledgement as Rainbird pointed to a small, grey shape that bobbed past the starboard side in a heavy slick of oil. 'It's a German life-raft container, from the forward casing. I think she'd bought it before she broke surface. That shallow pattern must have torn out her main ballast-tank, like gutting a herring.' He was silent, then, 'All right, Number One, bring us up with the convoy, please, as fast as you like. Take station two cables ahead, and we'd better keep our ears skinned. I've a feeling that the U-boat didn't meet us by accident.'

For a certainty the enemy aircraft had transmitted a course-and-speed report, and U-boat Command in Bergen had plotted an interception. The submarine captain must have smiled to see one escort vessel being towed by the second, and had decided to deal with the warships first. Having done so, he could easily overhaul the crawling merchant ships and sink them at leisure. Perhaps he had been over-confident, because he had fired two bow tubes when he might have made sure by firing all four, or he might have been merely conserving torpedoes; there was a lot of sinking to do, and reloading took time. In any event, the attack had gone wrong. The destroyer had wrenched free from her disabled companion and the submarine had been depth-charged, perhaps crash-diving from periscope depth. The first pattern may have damaged her, the second had killed her. If the U-boat's crew had even been aware that they had destroyed *Pennyroyal*, they and their knowledge were locked in a steel sepulchre at the bottom of the Arctic.

Eight

Chessington had signalled her intention to reduce speed further, to ten knots.

Lobby Ludd snorted his professional disgust. 'Ten knots! If we go any slower, we'll be goin' bleedin' backwards.'

'An' if we get much more bloody red lead,' Signalman House complained, 'the soddin' heads'll be bunged up wi' tomato pips.'

'In my day,' Stripey Albright told the mess, 'we got a Bluenose certificate when we crossed the Arctic Circle — like crossing the Line. There was a ceremony, with a bloke dressed up like Neptune, and a squeegee band.'

Bungy Williams pondered. 'Shave off. In your day they thought the bleedin' earth was flat, didn't they, Stripey? Yer got danger money fer goin' near the edge. I read it in a book.'

'In destroyers we got hard liers, mate — extra pay for discomfort—'

'Discomfort?' Signalman House retorted. 'If they was worse'n this floatin' bloody gash-bucket, sithee, they should ha' *jumped* over the soddin' edge.'

'Yer jes' wait till yer get ashore in Polyarnoe, Shit,' Bungy Williams advised, 'an' all will be fergiven. All the Russian wimmin break a bit off fer nothin'. It's state controlled, see. Yer jes' buy a stamp in the Post Office, then stop the first party in the street, an' say, " 'Ullo, darlingski. May I 'ave the pleasure o' sticking my stamp in your paybook? O' course I'm a party member." An' before yer know it, yer find yerself up 'omers, dangling from Olga be'ind the samovar. If yer give her a bar o' nutty, yer can 'ave her young sister as well. Shave off, even Stripey can dig 'is toes in — if he can remember 'ow ter do it. They 'ave a special Corps o' Veteran Wimmin, what fought in the Revolution. O' course, after all that time, some of 'em have 'ealed up.'

'*Virtue* from Admiralty repeated *Pennyroyal*: Operational Priority: U-boat callsign U-V has been ordered by Bergen to intercept four merchant ships and two escorts at utmost speed. Positional co-ordinates undecipherable. DNO has no information of your position and course. If you have not proceeded further east than longitude 15 you may at your discretion turn convoy for Iceland. This signal repeated to merchant ships in company on BAMS broadcast. Report your ETA when practicable.'

Hayes-Mailer raised his eyebrows. 'These Operations johnnies are a bit belated with their submarine warning, aren't they? They probably received it after five. And the Senior Met. Officer ought to be hanged from Admiralty Arch in thick fog.' He shrugged. 'Are we further east than longitude 15? I'd like to tell them that we are somewhere inside a circle drawn on the chart by the First Lieutenant, which means that we're roughly between Jan Mayen and the North Pole.'

Rainbird was stung, but made no comment. He was the First Lieutenant and Navigating Officer, and *Virtue*'s navigation was his responsibility even if, by necessity, it was frequently in the hands of the officer of the watch. The Commander, a brilliantly instinctive pilot, had never questioned Rainbird's calculations other than to periodically glance at the chart and deck-log, purse his lips and nod, perhaps span a pencilled line with dividers. Until now, there had never been cause for criticism and, Rainbird told himself, there was hardly cause now.

For three days there had been no opportunity to use a sextant in fixing position. There had been continuous low blanket cloud, periods of snow, elusive patches of floating mist. Navigation had been by dead reckoning, in addition to which the ships had turned and turned again, zig-zagged and back-tracked, increased speed and reduced speed, until every chart was criss-crossed with lines pencilled by frozen fingers. Five times in those three days they had heard the drone of aircraft, and had fled for the nearest curtain of fog, which, when reached, might thin and disappear in minutes or close around the ships for hours.

The First Lieutenant had asked for noon positions from all four merchantmen. All were different, none claimed to be better than approximate. The German Naval Command might know exactly where they were; *Virtue* and her companions did not.

'Course due east,' Hayes-Mailer ordered. 'We'll either enter Tromso tomorrow to the band of the Wehrmacht, miss North Cape and fetch up in the Polar ice, or, by a thousand-to-one chance, find ourselves off the Kola

Inlet.' But he stood for several moments, frowning, then, 'Send the chart and the deck-log down to the plot.'

For an hour Hayes-Mailer worked over the chart-table, to Rainbird's irritation replotting the convoy's course from Seydhisfjord, scribbling figures on a signal-pad, calculating, staring at the chart, grunting as he reached for his cigarette case and then selecting a cigarette with extreme care. Finally he was satisfied.

'Well,' he conceded, 'there's not much wrong with your arithmetic, Number One, but get a damn pencil sharpener for the bridge-table. Some of these lines are five miles wide, and I think Fender holds his pencil with his left foot. At 1500 precisely order the convoy to alter course to oh-eight-six. As from now, I want the EDR read every thirty minutes, and logged. At 2300 we shall alter course to oh-nine-five.

'If I've guessed right, we'll be passing very close to the Norwegian coast. The German Freya radar equipment has a range of about seventy-five miles, and if there are any coastal installations in the area we'll certainly be within that range. I'd like to think that, if their radar does pick us up, the enemy will assume that we can only be their own flotilla out of Tromso, but they can't all be stupid. They'll surely check with their naval HQ.

'All right, Number One. Tell the merchantmen, by light, that there must be *absolute* radio silence; the next twenty-four hours are vital. Inform Stevens that he must be ready to make smoke, and tell Fender to mount the Lewis guns.' The ship had two twin Lewis gun mountings which, because they impeded the bridge ladder and also because of their doubtful value against aircraft, were usually dismantled and stowed. 'If we go to action stations, the signalmen can man them.'

The fog was unpredictable. For periods it would wreath thinly above the floating ice, then thicken and climb around the ships' hulls and reach for their superstructures. Occasionally it was so dense that *Virtue* turned her searchlight aft to give the following vessels a point from which to take their bearings, and sometimes it would disperse magically, as if a curtain had been wrenched aside, to leave nothing but the low, heavy cloud and the slowly heaving sea swirling with icy vapour. It was at these moments that they felt nakedly exposed. They listened continually for the throb of aircraft engines above the chuckle of the fragmented dull-white ice that their bows jostled aside. It was soddin' ear-trumpets they needed, Signalman House complained, shivering and blue-lipped. Powdery snow accumulated, climbed coamings below doors and hatches, clogged ventilators. The cold pushed its fingers through the heaviest of clothes, and penetrated the lungs. Nobody moved more than necessary. They wedged themselves into sheltered corners, against a gun-heater or in the lee of deckhouse or funnel, and stopped thinking about anything except the end of their watch, when they could get below decks again to the stale air of the mess, to the smell of wet oilskins and duffel-coats, fuel oil and warm metal, the bulkheads and deckheads that streamed with condensation.

They heard the aircraft, then saw the five black hornets at the vague merging of horizon and cloud, and it was Sub-Lieutenant Waddell who identified them. 'Stukas!' he shouted, as he ran for the three-inch HA. Enemy warships, he had said, all looked the same to him, but aircraft were different. His bedroom at home

202

was still cluttered with the aircraft models of his schooldays — a Hawker Fury and a Blackburn Shark, a Fairey Battle and a Gloster Gladiator — and he could have told a great deal about the Stuka if the three-inch gun was not slewing, lifting its slim barrel, with the ready-use lockers already open.

'The Sub's right, sir,' the First Lieutenant said. 'Stukas. Five of 'em — but this cloud is going to cramp their style, I reckon. It'll have to be a low-level attack or nothing, and if they don't take their fingers out it'll be nothing.' Or a lethal game of hide-and-seek with the Stuka pilots stalking, snarling into an attack when a break in the cloud gave them altitude. This dive-bomber, the most detested of all enemy aircraft, carrying a 2200-pound bomb-load, preferred to peel off into a screaming dive from 8000 feet and release its bombs at 500 feet above its target. Accuracy was claimed to be within thirty yards, and it was a claim that few disputed.

Like the Focke-Wulfs earlier, however, the Stuka pilots did not relish a level flight, low-level approach, which reduced the speed of their aircraft to less than 200 miles per hour, but in a few minutes the fog could close in again, and the opportunity could be lost. They circled, out of range, and then, together, climbed into the cloud.

Hayes-Mailer swore, then whirled. 'Director! Fender? Be ready for aircraft to come at us from any bearing, straight out of cloud-base. Independent firing by all guns, targets of opportunity.' He had seen an attack force of Stukas do this once before, and an 8000-ton cruiser, with 700 men, had gone to the bottom. Having calculated the target's distance before climbing into the

cloud, they then dived — blindly, and watching their
altimeters, but with a good chance of emerging with a
ship in their target-view windows. There would be only
two or three seconds for them to pull out of their dive,
and pilots might momentarily black out, but their
bombs would be gone, and before the guns below could
turn frantically to meet them the aircraft would have
regained the safety of the very cloud that had made a
dive attack seemingly impossible.

'BWO. To all ships. Emergency — alter course
together ninety degrees to starboard. Executive signal.
Executive signal.' They could play for time, but only a
short time. In those few vulnerable seconds during
which the screaming Stukas flattened and climbed again,
Virtue's guns could hit back — but five were too many
for one old destroyer that should have been scrapped
years ago.

'This is no place for a bloddy married man, boyo,' the
Yeoman said, but nobody heard him. House and Ludd
were manning the Lewis guns, with neither of them
knowing their arse from their elbow, and Shaw was
alone. It was just his soddin' luck, and him a time-
expired man. He looked beyond the shimmer of smoke
above the after funnel. The ensign was bloddy filthy; it
had been flying since Liverpool. It was just his soddin'
luck. He had already written to the brewers about that
little whitewashed pub by the level crossing that old Mrs
Lloyd was relinquishing as soon as the war was over.
With his gratuity, he and Marge would have made a go
of it. A nautical pub in unnautical mid-Wales, with a
ship's wheel and a brass binnacle, a ship's bell to ring
drinking-up time, and thirty years of spinning yarns over

the bar.

In the Main W/T Office, Coder Crowthorne wrote the Fleet Code groups that were changed every four hours. KPR NFO SST LMU. *I have been struck by bomb(s). . . . I am sinking. . . . My position at 1900 was. . . .* It might never be sent, of course, but behind Crowthorne the PO Telegraphist had turned the transmitter output control to full power. If it was going to happen, it had to be first time. Operators sat at all receiving bays — Admiralty Broadcast HD, Ship—Shore H/F, Merchant Ship Distress, and the RDF goniometer. If the ship were lethally injured they might reach the upper deck or they might not, but it hardly mattered. In the sub-zero Arctic temperature the lightly clad dutymen from below decks would survive for only a short time. In the sea, they said, a man died within two minutes. On a life-raft, with the wind at twenty degrees below freezing-point, death would come almost as quickly.

With legs braced against the ship's roll, Sub-Lieutenant Waddell watched the layers cranking the three-inch gun in a slow rotation with the muzzle high. There was a shell in the breech and another in the crooked elbow of the waiting loader. The drone of aircraft engines seemed to come from immediately overhead. There could be only seconds to go, and there was nowhere to hide. He was of no consequence here, Waddell told himself. The gun-crew would fire, reload, and keep firing, like high-speed clockwork automata, without any help from him, until ordered to cease fire or until they were cut down. For all that the Sub-Lieutenant contributed, he may as well not be here. *It is with deep regret that I have to inform you that*

205

Sub-Lieutenant Brian Waddell was killed in action on 11 July.... He supposed his name would be added to the alphabetical list on the Watford war-memorial. Nobody ever read through the entire list, name by name, and Waddell would be almost the last, before West and Wood. *At the going down of the sun and in the morning....* All he was really doing was trying to keep out of the way of the three-inch HA gun-crew, who did not require his presence. He might as well be in an air-raid shelter, if there was such a thing.

It was always cold in the magazine. 'As cold as charity,' someone said, 'and that's bleedin' chilly.' The sweating, rivet-seamed bulkheads were lined with racks, of QF shells, boxes of pom-pom ammunition, .303 ball and tracer, flares, scuttling charges, detonators. In this ill-lit, dank cavern all sounds were localised — the clatter and whine of the hoist, the quick voice of a gunner's mate, the screech of boxes on the raw steel of the deck. Here worked the men who had no fighting station — seamen, cooks, storemen, the Commander's writer. They would feed the guns whose noise they could hear, but could gauge the progress of an action only by the SRE's fragmented commentary, and if a bomb or shell, or even an explosion flash, penetrated the magazine their end was immediate.

Twenty-one years in the Andrew, Stripey Albright mused, and all he had achieved was a magazine station. Well, at least it was out of the rain, but if he had used his loaf he should never have left RNB; there were quiet numbers in barracks for old stanchions, in the Duty Watch Office or the Victualling Office, a slinging space in the gymnasium, regular meals, and shore leave three nights out of four. With his years, a man didn't want sea-time, unless it was the Torpoint ferry. When a man got stiff in his joints, and couldn't read the print on daily orders, it was time to stop pretending. When this lot was over, he'd spin a yarn to the Commander and get himself a draft chit.

Below the bridge ladder, Lobby Ludd peered through the sights of two Lewis guns, loaded and cocked. Aim off ten degrees, the Chief had warned, and don't swing across the ship or yer'll knock someone's soddin' head off; it was a right pot-mess when bleedin' bunting-tossers were put on guns. In *Dawn Patrol*, Lobby Ludd recalled, Errol Flynn had gunned German aircraft out of the sky with nonchalant ease. The enemy planes had placed themselves conveniently in front of the hero's gun-muzzles, just asking to be shot to pieces. He just wished, that's all, that Eileen Wilkins could see him now, and if it wasn't so bleedin' cold. . . .

Incredibly, the roar of aircraft engines, already muffled by cloud, seemed to be fading. 'They've overshot, sir,' Rainbird offered, uncertain, 'or perhaps they were expecting to attract AA fire, to give them a fix. They'll not pull out now they've got us nicely tied up with pink ribbon.'

'Then they'll have to make another sighting.' Hayes-Mailer turned his binoculars slowly. 'It's thicker ahead, Number One. With just a little luck—'

'*BWO to Bridge. From* Chessington, *sir. Have stripped turbine. Must reduce to dead slow or cannot answer for consequences. Intend to act independently of convoy.*'

'Like hell she will,' the Commander gritted. 'I've not nursed that arthritic scow for 1500 miles, and lost four escorts, to let her cut loose now. BWO — make to all ships, "Increase to maximum speed on present course.

Ignore my movements." Number One, bring us about. We'll come up to windward of *Chessington* and make smoke. I don't care a damn if she tears her engines to scrap. She's going to stay in company.'

'Bridge! Enemy aircraft!' Several shouts from aft, tangling, reached the bridge. 'Aircraft, port quarter – almost dead astern and closing!'

'Three of the bastards, and low,' the First Lieutenant rasped. 'They've broken up. Where are the other two?'

'Target enemy aircraft red one-seven-five, angle of sight oh-oh-five. Commence tracking. . . .'

Another voice exploded across the gunnery circuit. It was Waddell's, and it was desperate. 'Bridge! Those aren't Stukas! Bridge? Those aren't Stukas! They're Fulmars!'

For the first time, Rainbird saw perplexity in the other's tired face. 'Fulmars? *Here?*' They stared at each other. *'Victorious?'*

The Commander whirled. 'BWO. Make to all ships – *immediately* – "Disregard aircraft approaching from northward. They are friendly repeat friendly." ' He turned back to Rainbird. 'They can't be from *Victorious*, Number One. She's 500 miles away, but *Argus* flew off aircraft some months ago, to operate from Murmansk, if the Russians allowed them – Hurricanes, I thought, probably some Fulmars – but who the hell cares?' He heaved a breath. 'And thank God young Waddell screamed out when he did – or our Wings over the Navy might have had a few feathers plucked.'

The Fulmars came low, almost wave-hopping, rose over *Chessington* and then *Brazos River* with a throaty surge of their Rolls-Royce engines. From the leader a light was blinking.

'Your Stuka friends have run off sulking. Did you bring any Plymouth Gin? Pinkers made with vodka ain't the same.'

'Yeoman. Ask him, "Please give me course for Kola Inlet. Short on Plymouth, it will have to be Scotch."'

The aircraft's lamp flickered a reply. 'First on the right past the lighthouse. Please set watch on 364 M/cs. I will point you in right direction and continue air cover. Scotch will be fine. Will provide own ice.'

'Another five seconds,' Lobby Ludd said, eyes narrowed, 'and I'd 'ave let 'em have it. They were soddin' lucky. I was jes' waiting, see, ter make sure. They wouldn't 'ave had a bleedin' chance — it'd 'ave been murder.'

'It might,' Signalman House nodded, 'if yer'd taken tha' bloody safety catch off.'

Bungy Williams had reached the mess with the latest news. 'We've jes' taken on a pilot an' a Russian liaison bloke. The merchant packets are goin' upstream ter Murmansk; we're mooring alongside *Northumberland* at Polyarnoe. Yer know what that means — bleedin' dress o' the day and mornin' divisions.' *Northumberland* was a County Class cruiser of 10,000 tons. 'Scapa Flow,' he pronounced, 'is goin' ter seem like New York after this soddin' place. Shave off.'

On both sides of the Tuloma estuary the snow-covered landscape was flat, bleak and featureless, with the near shore-line, sliding past, fringed with sedge and spiky broom against which the dark water lapped sadly. There were no signs of human life, no movement, no familiar screek of gulls, only white and silent wastes under a cold grey sky. 'If this is soddin' Russia,' Bungy

Williams decided, 'they can stuff it right up Stalin's jacksie.'

In view of conditions in Polyarnoe, SBNO had advised, libertymen would be permitted to land in sea-boots and oilskins or duffel-coats. There would be no currency exchange; there was nothing to buy. Personnel should be warned to remain on recognised thoroughfares, strictly to observe notices that forbade entrance to certain roads and areas, and immediately to obey instructions given by Russian sentries, who were posted everywhere. No, the notices were in Russian and the sentries did not speak English, but to ignore either could mean a bullet.

Personnel should fraternise with caution, particularly with women. It was not the women who objected so much, it was the men, but all Russians were less than cordial in their feelings towards their British allies. There should be no requests for alcohol; there were no bars or shops, and houses, barracks or community centres should not be entered. Libertymen should take ashore cigarettes or tobacco sufficient only for their own needs; the Russian authorities firmly forbade foreigners to give cigarettes, foodstuffs, tinned goods or confectionery to Russian nationals. If this proscription was ignored, both British donor and Russian recipient would be arrested.

Virtue's libertymen, SBNO continued, could proceed ashore in *Northumberland*'s drifter. There would be ample room. As an alternative to shore leave, a Soviet

Navy choir was giving a performance aboard *Northumberland*, and *Virtue*'s ship's company were welcome to attend.

The Polyarnoe Naval office was right about the drifter. Under normal circumstances *Northumberland* might be expected to land 200 libertymen, anxious to escape the confines of the ship for a few hours, but not more than a dozen came down the big cruiser's ladder to join the sixty from *Virtue* on the drifter's deck. *Northumberland* had been in Polyarnoe for a week; her crew had been ashore, and most of them agreed that even a male choir could not fail to be more entertaining.

It was all a little discouraging, but Lobby Ludd was determined that he would set foot on foreign soil. He had seen Iceland from a distance but could not truthfully claim that he had been there, while the Isle of Man hardly counted. He had been unqualified to participate in those exchanges which always began with the words 'When I was in . . .' There was a certain prestige about Russia that could not be equalled by Scapa Flow, Gibraltar or even Malta.

They had to take some groundbait, Bungy Williams insisted. They would never get a nibble without groundbait. The trouble was, if they were apprehended by the OGPU with their pockets filled with bars of nutty, they could clew up in Siberia. Twelve years in the Andrew was bad enough, but sod Siberia.

Lobby Ludd had grinned. It was a subject he knew something about. When it came to confrontations, the OGPU had nothing on the instructors in *St George*. And he still had the same overcoat.

At Fleetwood, returning from leave, he had boarded the *Snaefell* ferry with hundreds of others, all frantically smoking their remaining cigarettes and loudly telling embroidered stories of the previous fourteen days. On the jetty at Douglas the chatter had begun to die, and on the quarterdeck of *St George*, a mile distant, they were faced with the familiar line of instructors, waiting to search cases, parcels and clothing.

'Ah, Boy Ludd!' The Master-at-Arms had beckoned ominously. 'I'll search you myself. Turn out your case.'

The contents of the case, disappointingly, included no forbidden items. 'All right, now your cap.' Charlie Ludd surrendered his cap.

' 'Ullo, 'ullo, 'ullo!' The Master-at-Arms was triumphant. 'Ten Woodbines in the lining. Yer didn't really think you'd get away with *that*, did you, Ludd?' He shook his head sorrowfully. 'You know what that means? I mean, you do *know*?'

'Yessir.' Charlie Ludd was contrite.

'Yessir,' the Master-at-Arms retorted. 'Caught in possession! All right, Ludd. Get changed into Number Threes, then report to the Regulating Office. At the double!'

Charlie Ludd had trotted away with a suitable hangdog expression, congratulating himself. He had fully expected the ten cigarettes to be found in his cap, even hoped they would be. They had been calculated to distract the attention of any searcher from the 500 cigarettes carefully dispersed in the lining of his overcoat.

There was a ramshackle timber jetty, its piles a trap for floating garbage and drifting oil, strolled by soldiers with rifles, some of them thronged around a fire burning smokily in an old paint-drum. A half-dozen trawler-type vessels, dilapidated and filthy, were moored with their bows to the jetty, in company with a submarine, flying the Russian ensign, but in an advanced state of rust and corrosion. By comparison, the sea-stained *Northumberland* and *Virtue*, in mid-stream, were immaculate.

From the jetty there was no obvious direction in which to walk. Snow blanketed everything, churned by footprints in the immediate vicinity. In the near distance was a vast area of disembarked war-cargoes — lines and lines of aircraft under tarpaulins, tanks, field-guns, snow-obscured crates stretching beyond vision. There were people, trudging through the snow — walking apparently from nowhere and proceeding toward no identifiable point. Groups of both sexes were clearing snow with long-handled shovels in several locations seemingly selected at random, and having no discernible relationship with any other. An open motor-truck, of appearance not dissimilar to that of a Model T Ford, and crammed tightly with standing passengers, lurched past in the slush.

'I saw a bleedin' film like this once,' Bungy Williams said, 'but I ferget what it was called. It was about Paul Muni and a chain gang. I ferget 'ow it ended.'

The soldiers eyed the foreign sailors with expressionless faces. They were all either very youthful or rather elderly, Lobby Ludd noted. No two wore similar uniforms, if uniform was the right word for ragged, quilted jackets or drab, ankle-length coats, shapeless hats with ear-flaps, broken gloves and clumsy felt boots.

Bungy Williams addressed himself to the nearest. 'Wotcher, Townie. Which way do we go fer the 'Igh Street — the local Kremlin an' all that?' Aside, to Lobby Ludd, he cautioned, 'I'll betcha he sez he's a stranger 'ere 'imself. They always bleedin' do.'

The soldier regarded them woodenly, then, 'You got a cigarette?'

Bungy Williams opened a new packet, from which the soldier extracted half the contents to stow beneath his coat. 'Fill yer boots,' Bungy grimaced. They waited, and the Russian stared back at them. 'Well, which way, me ol' commissar? Where's the soddin' Town 'All an' the bus station?'

The soldier's eyes were vacant. He frowned, then shrugged. 'You got a cigarette?' he asked.

Northumberland's contingent, however, had struck off across the snow with the purposeful air of those who had done it all before. Lobby Ludd and Bungy Williams followed. There was, they now perceived, a track through the snow that was more trampled, tyre-scored and slushy than the snow on either side, but which was becoming progressively wider as more and more pedestrians moved to its fringes to seek drier footing or avoid the cranky motor-trucks that sputtered wetly in both directions, heavily laden with clinging people. It was still impossible to guess where anyone was going to, or coming from. Then, ahead, a mile distant and indistinct, was a clutter of buildings.

It was a fatiguing mile, and the reward was frustratingly disappointing. There were no recognisable streets, but regimented rows of two-floored timber dwellings with windows heavily shuttered, interposed by other, unidentifiable buildings which, however, included one which was obviously a small cinema. Its doors were closed, but crudely coloured posters depicted symbolically handsome Russian soldiers bloodily defying overwhelming numbers of cowering ape-like Germans, and a throng of people studied them gravely. Another was an austere brick-built barracks. Telegraph wires sagged from leaning poles, many of them fixed with trumpet-like loudspeakers from which issued faint, discordant music and, at intervals, a voice that shouted in unintelligible Russian.

There was a depressing similarity about the people who trod through the dirty slush — their shapeless, shabby and often ragged clothing tied with string, felt boots and scarved heads, their unsmiling, unemotional faces. Groups of both men and women worked with shovels or hauled handcarts and improvised sleds, or simply walked for no apparent purpose. Soldiers, with rifles slung, were as numerous and equally ill-clothed.

'It's a regular bleedin' Butlin's, ain't it?' Bungy Williams sniffed. 'I ain't seen a female that don't look like a dirty sack o' spuds on two big feet.'

They had noticed that at several intersections stood small circular buildings, each with a single door and high, slotted windows from which, intriguingly, escaped trickles of steam. People of both sexes were entering, remaining for minutes, and then reappearing. They watched.

'They ain't taking nothing in,' Lobby Ludd calculated, 'an' they ain't bringing nothin' out. They ain't 'ad a 'aircut, an' it's too small fer a knocking shop, ain't it?'

Bungy Williams decided. 'I reckon it's one o' them steam baths, where naked parties give yer a massage, then whips yer with sticks. It's bleedin' marvellous.

That's why the picture 'ouse is shut, Lobby. 'Oo wants ter watch bleedin' pictures when yer can be massaged by a naked party?'

Lobby Ludd agreed. 'And 'oo wants ter listen ter the Red Fleet choir when yer can be whipped wi' bleedin' sticks?'

They watched the arrivals and departures for several more minutes. 'Do they *all* get a massage from a naked party?' Lobby asked. 'It don't take long, does it? I mean, that ol' man was in an' out like a bleedin' jack-rabbit.'

'It depends what yer pay for,' Bungy shrugged. 'Yer can 'ave steam and massage, or jes' massage. I suppose there's some blokes that has jes' steam, though I can't soddin' think why.' He considered. 'There's no 'arm in us having a *look*, is there? If they get stroppy, offer 'em a bar o' nutty crunch.'

Beyond the door there was semi-darkness, and the stench met them like a blow in the face. There was a circled seat of heavy slate, pierced by open, rounded vents at three-foot intervals. Several were obscured by the people that sat over them, half-crouched and gravely resigned. Below the seat was a vast common pit, which steamed. . . .

'Shave off,' said Bungy Williams, at a safe distance. 'I've a good mind ter write ter "Live Letters". 'Ave yer ever seen anything like it? That's where all the flies go in winter — down soddin' great 'oles in Russia.'

'You got a cigarette?' enquired a muddy small boy. 'Spam? Mitt loff? 'Errins-in?'

'Do I *look* like a bleedin' canteen manager?' Bungy countered. He took a single cigarette from his packet. 'It'll stunt yer growth, son. Look at me. I was

216

six-foot-three once — before I started smokin'. Now piss off.'

The cigarette disappeared. 'Spam? Mitt loff? 'Errins-in?'

Lobby Ludd relented. He reached into the lining of his overcoat. ' 'Er — 'ave a bar o' fruit an' bleedin' nut. 'Ave yer got a big sister that don't look a female Robinson Crusoe?'

The boy shot a quick glance in several directions; there was more in the foreigner's coat-lining than one chocolate bar. He pointed to a door twenty yards away and beckoned.

'Well, I'll kiss a pig's arse,' Bungy Williams marvelled. 'Would yer soddin' believe it? Yer'd never know if yer didn't ask, would yer? I mean, if they can't 'ave a red light, there oughter be some way o' letting bonified blokes know.'

Inside, things were not quite as they had expected, but they had resigned themselves to the unpredictable. It was a sizeable bare messroom with unpainted walls and two lines of long wooden tables. At the rear was a serving-counter beyond which could be seen a kitchen, a large black stove, pans and kettles. There was a smell that was suspiciously like that of boiling cabbage, and there were two women — short and thickset, but passably clean, each with her hair hidden by a white head-scarf, each wearing the inevitable felt boots. They eyed the newcomers with sullen faces as the boy offered an introduction in which only the words 'Spam' and 'Mitt loff' were comprehensible.

'Yer wouldn't say either of 'em reminded yer of Dorothy Lamour, would yer, Lobby?' Bungy Williams observed. 'More like Marie Dressler. Still, yer can't 'ave everything. 'Ave yer got the groundbait? Try a packet o' Fudge Delights an' a tin o' sardines — jes' ter start the ball rollin'.'

The offerings vanished instantly, and one of the women grinned. 'Borsch?' she asked conspiratorially. Bungy Williams nodded. 'Me and my mate, darlin'.' He turned to Lobby Ludd. 'What did I tell yer, Lobby? Every woman's got 'er price. Meself, I fancy the one in the rubber apron an' the army shirt.'

'The other one's got black teeth,' Lobby Ludd objected. 'It's a bit public, ain't it?'

'What do yer bleedin' expect fer a packet o' Fudge Delights an' a tin o' sardines? Soddin' Claridges?'

The woman with the rubber apron ladled thin soup into two tin basins and placed down a pair of spoons. 'Borsch,' she said.

The men glanced at each other. 'It's probably some old Russian custom,' Bungy Williams explained. 'Like a ritual, see. Try ter act natural.' With commendable *sang froid* he took a mouthful of soup. 'Shave off,' he gritted. 'It's like bleedin' boiled paint-brushes.' But he smiled at the woman. 'Soddin' marvellous, darlin'. I can see yer the essence o' Russian woman'ood. Under them boots, I bet yer legs go right up ter the top.'

'Bungy,' Lobby Ludd insisted. 'They ain't jes' black. They're *iron false teeth*.'

'Yer lucky bastard, Lobby. There's blokes that's been in the Andrew fer twenty soddin' years, an' never 'ad a grind with a party that 'ad iron teeth.' The women regarded them impassively. 'All right, Lobby. Now play yer trump card — a packet o' Liquorice Allsorts an' a bottle o' OK Sauce. When these Russian wimmin get started, they're soddin' sex animals.'

218

Lobby Ludd was unconvinced, but he complied. The proffered items disappeared immediately and the woman with the rubber apron filled two more basins with soup. 'Shave off,' Bungy Williams breathed, 'they're playing 'ard ter get. If yer didn't know better, it'd make yer want ter scrub round the 'ole thing, wouldn't it?'

Lobby Ludd was more than willing to scrub round the whole thing. The short, stocky woman with blackened steel dentures smelled strongly of boiled cabbage, and the prospect of an intimate exchange with her had failed to arouse the vaguest sexual appetite. 'Well,' he shrugged, 'I ain't fussy. I can take it or leave it—'

'Yer've got ter persevere, Lobby,' Bungy Williams advised. 'Faint 'eart never screwed a pig, see. What groundbait 'ave yer got left?'

'Brylcreem, baked beans, an' a packet o' Olde English Toffees. If I'd known, I'd 'ave brought a soddin' toothbrush an' some metal polish—'

The door of the messroom opened, admitting a flood of icy air, and a dozen heavily muffled soldiers filed in, stamping the snow from their boots, wrenching off gloves and blowing on their fingers. They shot disinterested glances at the sailors, then hammered noisily on the serving-counter, shouting. The two women were filling bowls with soup, shouting back. One of the soldiers peered more closely at Bungy Williams. 'You got a cigarette—?' He was the man to whom they had spoken on the jetty.

'Lobby,' confessed Bungy Williams, 'suddenly, all the magic's gorn.'

'Spam?' enquired the small boy. 'Mitt loff? 'Errins -in?'

'The Red Navy choir? I bet that was a soddin' riot.'
Bungy Williams surveyed his listeners. 'Yer should 'ave
been ashore with me an' Lobby. Bleedin' marvellous! We
came alongside these two parties, see, in this restaurant
— two crackers. Ain't that right, Lobby? If we didn't
'ave ter get back, we'd 'ave been all night in, easy. As it
was. . . .' He drew a deep breath, meaningfully.

'Did tha *get* a bit?' Signalman House asked.

Bungy ignored the question. 'O' course, a soddin'
choir's all right, if yer like that sort o' thing. What was
that, Shit? If yer watch ashore tomorrow' — he considered — 'but it ain't easy ter find. Yer've got ter know
yer way around. Mind, these ain't the sort o' parties
yer'd pick up in the bleedin' Scotswood Road, Shit —
they've got Cossack blood, see.' His eyes narrowed.
'Talk about bare-back ridin'. Shave off.'

Nine

Virtue steamed in wide circles off the estuary, waiting for *Northumberland* to emerge. When the heavy cruiser did appear, there would be no time to waste. She was capable of better than thirty-two knots, and her captain had been less than pleased with the orders that reduced him to the economical speed of the elderly escort destroyer. With her eight eight-inch and eight four-inch guns, sixteen two-pounders, eight torpedo tubes, radar, and a Walrus amphibian aircraft, *Northumberland* did not need *Virtue*, but at least there were to be no accompanying merchantmen. Could *Virtue* sustain twenty-two knots?

The destroyer had been tied alongside the cruiser, in mid-stream, for several days. There had been film shows in *Northumberland*'s office flat, tombola, freshly baked bread from her bakery, a well-stocked dry canteen, a bookstall and a modest library — all rare luxuries for the destroyer men, but they were ill at ease in the comparatively spacious below-decks of the bigger ship, and with the proximity of a quarterdeck and its duty officer, midshipmen, quartermaster and marine bugler the well-meaning but annoying condescension in the hundreds of eyes that gazed down on *Virtue*'s worn deck. They had been glad to slip their lines, to refuel, and then nose slowly for the open sea.

The ship teemed with new rumours. They were going to land sled-dogs in Spitzbergen; hundreds of boxes of dog biscuits had been loaded aboard the cruiser. They had been detached to the South Atlantic to bring gold bullion from Freetown. *Northumberland* was embarking several hundred Russian sailors for the Forth, where they would be given a battleship with which to fight their own war. *Virtue* was going to the Mediterranean, to Brooklyn Navy Yard, to Australia for troop convoying. . . .

As they idled offshore, Hayes-Mailer ended all further speculation.

'We are ordered to accompany *Northumberland* by the shortest practicable route to Scapa Flow.' He knew that the statement would be generating groans from his ship's company. Scapa Flow was a joyless destination — a vast, dreary anchorage where it always seemed to be drizzling with rain, with moored battleships, carriers, cruisers, shabby Flotta with its beer canteen, shore patrols, dirty liberty-drifters, the long lines of fleet destroyers in Gutta Sound among which *Virtue* would be just another arrival, to stagnate, week by endless week. Almost anywhere was better than Scapa Flow.

But the Commander was still smiling as he went on. 'We shall not, however, remain with *Northumberland*. We shall be proceeding direct to Hebburn, on the Tyne, where we shall be dry-docked for three weeks. I think we shall manage ten days' leave for each watch.'

There was a moment of uncomprehending silence,

and then he heard the whoops and cheers he expected, from every corner of the ship. Leave? Did the Old Man say *leave*? 'Hebburn?' Signalman House gaped. 'Does tha' know I can get home on a bloddy *tram* from Hebburn?'

'Hebburn?' Bungy Williams enquired. 'That's in England, ain't it? What money do they use?'

Hayes-Mailer had known two days earlier, but there had been a flurry of letter-writing in Polyarnoe, and he had resisted releasing the news until the ships were at sea. In the event, *Virtue*'s mailbags were in *Northumberland*, whose chaplain would censor them. It was possible that many of *Virtue*'s crew would reach their homes before their letters.

'Although less important than the times of the trains from Newcastle,' the Commander said, 'you may be interested in knowing what is happening to the ship. She is to have her fo'c'sle strengthened, and fitted with a recently developed forward throwing weapon, Hedgehog, installed with radar and a new TBS radio-telephone—'

'Hedgehog?' Stripey Albright shook his head. There had been nothing like that in his day.

'Hedgehog,' the Commander explained, 'is an equipment for launching twenty-four anti-submarine bombs simultaneously, 250 yards ahead, so that once the ship is in asdic contact, it is not necessary to run over the submarine's submerged position to make a first attack.' That was about the sum total of his own knowledge, gleaned in *Northumberland*'s wardroom. 'This will mean a brief period of training with the new weapon, after leaving the dockyard, before resuming normal sea duties.'

It was better and better — days at sea, and back to harbour each evening, shore leave and all nights in. 'Shave off,' Bungy Williams decided, 'I'm going ter get measured fer a new suit from Bernards — Canadian serge an' twenty-eight-inch bottoms, gold badges—'

'I have no information yet on the ship's ultimate programme,' Hayes-Mailer resumed, 'but we can be certain that there will be drafts leaving and joining. There is one appointment I can tell you about. *Virtue*'s new commanding officer will be Lieutenant-Commander Rainbird — and I can think of no officer into whose hands I could more confidently relinquish this ship and her company. Those of you who remain aboard will, I know, give to him all the loyalty and goodwill you have always shown to me.'

Rainbird was on the bridge with young Fairbrother, both watching for *Northumberland* to emerge from the estuary. The First Lieutenant had assumed he knew all that the Commander was to tell the ship's company, and he was listening only casually. He was completely unprepared, however, for the last-spoken piece of information. 'Good God,' he swallowed. Hayes-Mailer must have known two days ago, but had said nothing until now. Fairbrother grinned at him. 'Congratulations, sir.' The bridge messenger was grinning, too, and the Yeoman. Rainbird choked back a confusion of emotions which included stinging annoyance and explosive elation. 'Thanks, Sub,' he nodded, and drew a deep breath. Damn Hayes-Mailer.

But this was no moment for thinking about anything. 'Here she is, sir,' Fairbrother said.

It was *Northumberland*, majestic and powerful, the sea creaming away from her bows, a haze of blue smoke lifting from three tall funnels that remained serenely steady against the sky while *Virtue* rolled ten degrees in the long swell. The cruiser's signal-lamp was blinking.

'Take station three cables astern, sir,' the Yeoman shouted. 'Course three-four-oh, speed twenty-two knots.'

Rainbird leaned over a voice-pipe with the feeling that something was oddly wrong, then realised what it was. This was one of those occasions when, normally, the Commander would infallibly be on the bridge, standing at the screen or sitting in his high chair. Today he was not.

'Port twenty. Full ahead both.' He raised himself, lifted his binoculars. 'Sub, ask the pantry to send up some coffee, will you?'

She wasn't one of the new 'M' Class 2000-ton pocket cruisers with almost 50,000 shaft horse-power that Bob Roper had enthused over, but an emasculated old-timer that only the war had kept from the breaker's yard. Still, with her modifications, Hayes-Mailer mused, she would have a new lease of life, and to Rainbird, from this moment, she would be the finest little ship in the Navy. A first command always was. He remembered his first car — a third- or fourth-hand bull-nosed Morris that had every defect imaginable, but which had inspired a pride in him that had never been repeated in any vehicle he had driven since. They didn't make cars like that anymore, he had told himself — and they didn't build ships like *Virtue* anymore, Rainbird would console himself when the water seeped through the scuttle of his sea-cabin, or the old generator's wiring burned out, or a green sea tore every boat from its davits. Who wanted a glossy, pretentious 'M' Class destroyer when one could have a real 'V & W' that had served in two wars and pushed her battered bows through every sea in the world?

In Polyarnoe he had written to Joan Roper and to the parents of Sub-Lieutenant Coope and Able Seaman Foster. He had written also to Vice-Admiral George Furloe, but had not mailed the letter; it still lay on his cabin-table. He had, as he guiltily anticipated, enjoyed writing it, but now he would never send it. The writing had been sufficient.

Below the Saltash bridge, near Devonport, six new 'Hunt' Class boats waited for their new Captain D. Their commanding officers would be wondering who the hell this Hayes-Mailer was. Six new destroyers with new crews, half of them straight from training, from *Collingwood* and *Raleigh*, green young officers from *King Alfred* in their new Moss Bros uniforms. Well, he had a couple of summer months in which to shake them down, to turn them into something like a co-ordinated flotilla before leading them into the U-boat war of the Atlantic. It was impossible, but it had to be done.

Vagrant, Pennyroyal, Trooper and *Truelove* had gone, and with them, more important, the lives of 280 men — trained and experienced men who could not be replaced by a few weeks of exercising between Falmouth and the Needles. They could never be replaced.

Why was it, the Russian liaison officer had enquired politely, that the English had so many ships sunk? The Red Navy did not have their ships sunk. Why, only last week a Russian submarine returned to harbour after having torpedoed six German warships, including a heavy cruiser. . . .

'It ain't bloddy reet,' Signalman House complained, 'goin' on leave wi'out any rabbits.' Home-going men felt morally obliged to take gifts for their familes. 'Coming from bloddy Russia, my party'll be expectin' a soddin' fur coat.'

'Take 'er a tin o' corned dog, Shit,' offered Bungy Williams, 'an' tell 'er yer caught it yerself. An' a slab o' kye — then every night yer can sit on the scullery roof and prertend yer on the flag-deck.'

'Gib's the best place fer rabbits,' Stripey Albright said. 'Watches, cigarette lighters, wimmin's scanties—'

'Scanties?' Bungy Williams frowned. 'D'yer bleedin' mean yer buy *scanties* fer your party, Stripey? Shave off. Does she wear 'em under or over 'er combinations? If I was you, mate, I'd get 'er one of them lockets that yer put a piece of 'air in. Yer've still got a bit at the sides.'

This time, Lobby Ludd told himself, ten days' leave was going to be bleedin' marvellous. This time he didn't have to flannel; he had done it all. The odd thing was that he didn't really feel like telling people much — that is, people at home. Their world, he realised, was so entirely different, so limited, that it was difficult to communicate meaningfully. If he told Mrs Ludd how *Pennyroyal* and eighty-five men had been blown to pieces in a single terrible moment she would nod sympathetically, but would not comprehend. There were more tangible things like rationing, bus queues and the black-out. Owen Melville of the Borough Engineer's Department struggled with the problems of waste collection and the local drains; his nearest impression of the icy, white-shot depths of the Arctic, in which men died and stiffened in agonising minutes, was the deep end of the Fulham Baths when the heating was reduced because of the annoying fuel shortage. How could someone like Freda Harris understand the tense killing hate of a depth-charge attack, or the bloody-minded gloating when an enemy submarine was smashed to its death? Would Eileen Wilkins understand that men could be so fatigued that they could not find their mouths with their dinner-forks?

He knew now, vaguely, why sailors on leave were so apparently nonchalant, easy-going but never wholly confiding, with stories about golden rivets and rollicking experiences in foreign ports. There was nothing much else to tell that would be understood. Better to spin a yarn about green oil for the starboard lamps, or getting a bucketful of revs from the engine room.

He could tell Mrs Ludd something about William's going. He recalled what the Commander had said — if it was any consolation, it was a quick and easy way to go. It would comfort Mrs Ludd to know that Charlie's captain had done all he could to search for *Vagrant*'s survivors, and doubtless she would always envisage a ship sinking sedately with William saluting the grand old flag while an orchestra brayed 'Anchors Aweigh'. That was exactly what Clark Gable had done in *Send Us More Japs* at the Odeon.

'If yer ram it tight,' Stripey Albright was explaining, 'yer can get a pound o' tickler into an 'arf-pound tin, and the dockyard police don't know the difference — 'specially in a civvy dockyard. It ain't the same as coming out o' RNB, where the crushers want ter look up yer arse wi' a periscope.'

'They oughter 'ave Wren crushers,' Bungy Williams said. 'And they could search fer my tickler any time they bleedin' liked. Jes' fancy bein' shook in yer 'ammock by a smashin' little Wren crusher. Wakey, wakey, lash up an' stow, or I'll smack your botty. Shave off.'

Sixteen immaculate kits were laid in a long line in the gymnasium, each of sixty-one items precisely rolled and tied, hammocks, lashings and clews, seamanship manual, hymnbook and signal card, cap box and brushes. Commander Wilkins walked slowly along the line, pausing before each rigid owner.

'Ludd, sir,' the Master-at-Arms said ominously. 'Rated Ordinary Signalman this mornin'.'

Commander Wilkins raised his eyebrows. 'Ah, yes. So we're losing you at last, are we, Ludd? I must say that my defaulters' table won't seem quite the same again.'

The Master-at-Arms agreed. 'Twelve cuts for insolent complaining, sir. Twelve cuts for smoking, an' a total of sixty-three days 8a punishment.'

The Commander frowned. 'Thank you, Master-at-Arms. I didn't ask.' He turned back to Charlie Ludd. 'You'll be pleased to know, Ludd, that on completion of Boys' Training, your conduct record is destroyed, so you start with a clean sheet from today. I'd like to think you can keep it that way.' He thumbed musingly through the youngster's service documents.

'You've got good school-marks, Ludd, which means you can do well in the Service if you put your mind to it; but you'll get nowhere by trying to fight authority, because you can never win. If you conform, and work at it, there's every chance that you can end up with rings on your cuff like these.' He held up his arm.

'Yessir,' Charlie Ludd said. In only a few minutes he

would be finished with *St George,* the Master-at-Arms, jankers, and perpetual double-marching. He had only to keep his nose clean for a few more minutes.

'That's it, Ludd,' Commander Wilkins nodded. 'Good luck.' He offered a casual hand, then passed on.

The Master-at-Arms spoke from the corner of his mouth. 'You jes' watch it, Ludd, all right? You needn't start warbling yet. Jes' put a foot wrong before you're out o' that gate, see, and there'll be a charge waiting for yer in barracks. Understand?'

'Yessir,' Charlie Ludd said.

'If you work hard,' the Commander was saying to the next draftee, 'there's every chance that you can end up with rings on your cuff like these. . . .'

At the establishment gates the Master-at-Arms waited until all kit-bags and hammocks had been loaded into the waiting truck. 'Ludd,' he ordered, 'lift up the bottoms of yer trousers.' Charlie Ludd sighed.

'I thought so,' the Master-at-Arms nodded. 'You're wearing shoes. While you're inside these walls, Ludd, yer'll wear *boots*, see. Where are yer boots?'

'At the bottom o' my kit-bag—'

'At the bottom of yer kit-bag,' the Master-at-Arms nodded again. 'All right. Get yer kit-bag out o' the truck, unpack yer kit, and put yer boots on. Then yer can re-pack yer kit-bag and put it back in the truck. Yer can start being a Jolly Jack when yer get out of them gates.'

Thirty miles to the east of Fair Isle, *Northumberland* flashed her last signal. 'Thank you for your company. Have a good leave.' She turned to starboard, increasing speed as if to shake the destroyer from her coat-tails, and in twenty minutes she was hull down and dis-appearing into the horizon haze. Hayes-Mailer stretched in his tall chair. 'Reduce to twenty knots, please, Number One.' He would have liked to reduce further after the several days of hard pounding in the wake of the cruiser, but they were still in dangerous waters. The ship's company, too, was anxious to reach the Tyne. Leave passes and travel warrants had already been prepared, suitcases were packed, and there had been a flurry of clothes-pressing and shoe-polishing in the confined messdecks. The first leave-party would want to be ashore within minutes of berthing, to race for their trains, for London, Glasgow, Liverpool. There would be mail waiting at Hebburn, too — weeks old — and per-haps a jaded Canadian lieutenant who had been living out of his valise for a month.

'ETA about 1000 tomorrow forenoon, sir,' Rainbird said. The passage from Polyarnoe had been fast and uneventful, the proximity of *Northumberland* and her big guns comforting. Tensions had relaxed, the galley was functioning normally, and tonight, the Commander decided, the men could sling their hammocks; they would be passing close to Aberdeen. During the morning watch he would transmit their time of arrival and request gate and berth, after which it would be only a matter of elbowing their way through a congestion of shipping to their designated jetty, and by this time tomorrow *Virtue*'s old hull would be in dry dock.

It was a beautiful day, the sky showing blue between cumulus cloud, the sea crests glittering silver in the sunshine. There were men on deck for the pleasure of it, laughing, grateful for the warming freshness of the wind, open scuttles and clean air below decks. Yer've got ter change at York. If yer don't change at York, it's slow ter Grantham. It'll be opening time in the Smoke, mate — time for a few jars. Yer'd better not be in the family way, I said. Paddington's on the Met. Line, ain't it? Anyway, I told the chef — there's too many 'oles and not enough bleedin' toad. You an' me, an' Taff Shaw an' Bogey. No. Nobby's stayin' at the UJC. That's right, yer can walk from Lime Street to Exchange, easy. O' course I love yer, I said, but what's that got ter do with gettin' bleedin' spliced? That's all wimmin think about. It splits in 'arf at Leeds, so make sure yer in the right 'arf, or yer'll clew up in Manchester. . . .

In the asdic cabinet Sub-Lieutenant Fairbrother sat before the AP125 with the leading hand at his shoulder. Both wore headphones. 'No, sir,' the man was saying, 'there's no "ping" because yer not transmitting — jes' listening. When yer transmit' — he made the switch — 'there, see. Jes' the one "ping", unless the impulse strikes an object and is reflected back. Now, sir, if yer'll sweep from beam to forward in five-degree steps — that's right. If yer do get an echo, it don't necessarily mean a submarine. It can be turbulence, a shoal o' fish, a whale, or jes' one o' them things. Now *there*'s an echo, sir, see? That's right. Now, if yer listen. . . .'

Hayes-Mailer had just descended to the fo'c'sle deck when he saw Ordinary Signalman Ludd at the foot of the bridge ladder. He hesitated. 'Ah, Ludd—' There was something he wished to tell the youngster, and he would probably never see him again after tomorrow. It may as well be now. Perhaps Ludd already knew; the Yeoman did.

Lobby Ludd turned, startled. 'Yessir?' He wished he had been somewhere else.

At that moment the action alarm-bell burst into a frenzied tattoo, deafening.

The Commander whirled, to fling himself up the bridge ladder, but he had mounted only three rungs when the first of two torpedoes struck *Virtue* at the junction of fo'c'sle and upper deck, below the forward funnel. There was a rending crash that shuddered the entire ship, a dull red eruption of flame, and an explosion that wrenched skyward in a massive vomit of twisted steel, splintered boats, spray, sparks and black smoke. Seconds later the second torpedo struck further aft, between the three-inch gun and the searchlight platform, wrecking both and scything down their crews.

In the wardroom Surgeon-Lieutenant Nicols and the SBA had been packing instruments and drugs into the big grey transit-chest when the ship staggered and the deck tilted. They reached the upper deck through the pantry hatch. They could not see far forward because of a fire that burned in the waist, and beyond the shredded after funnel the entire bridge structure was hidden in a pall of thick smoke. *Virtue* was already leaning heavily to port, her back broken.

Commissioned Engineer Stevens, the Chief ERA and two stokers died in a hell of twisting, scalding steam-pipes. Lieutenant Prentice and Petty Officer Arnold, in the tiller flat, worked frantically to render the depth-charges safe, and they succeeded just as the ship's stern, joined to the main hull by only trailing wreckage, lurched free with a screech of tortured metal, and plunged. They clawed themselves to the ladder, but got no further.

Sub-Lieutenant Waddell and the crew of the forward

four-inch gun had achieved their station, loaded, and were traversing to port. There was no communication with the bridge or director — if either were still manned. The port side of the bridge structure was afire. Waddell could hear shouts and the crack-crack of exploding ammunition boxes, but could see little in the smoke except vague, unrecognisable figures. *Virtue* tilted suddenly; the four-inch gun was useless now.

Then Fender appeared. Half of his head was soot-black, one eye a pit of blood, and an arm hung, swinging uselessly like a rag doll's. 'All right, Sub,' he shouted. 'Abandon ship — from the starboard side. At the bloody rush. She's going to go, any second.'

'The Commander—?'

'Nobody's seen the Commander. The First Lieutenant's still on the bridge. Now, get going — all of you — and fast.' He turned and disappeared into the smoke.

'We're loaded, sir,' a gunlayer objected. 'We might as well fire the ol' beauty before we leave 'er.' Waddell nodded. The gun belched, recoiled, and the aimless projectile hurtled into oblivion. 'It ain't as if we're wastin' money,' the gunlayer said.

In the asdic cabinet, Fairbrother and the leading hand had been flung to the deck in a tangled heap. The lights failed immediately, but the rating groped for the emergency Nife lamp. 'In case you ain't guessed, sir,' he said, 'that echo weren't a shoal o' fish.'

The deck was inclining with alarming speed. Fairbrother, nearer the door, hauled on the big locking clip, but without success. His nose was bleeding. 'Let me try, sir,' the leading hand said. 'That door always was comical. There's a knack.' It was a soundproof door, seven inches thick, of laminated timber, wadding and lead sheet. He strained, his full weight against the clip handle. 'It ain't going to budge, sir. I reckon the bulkhead's distorted. It always was a lash-up.' He turned an apologetic face, seemingly more disturbed by the door's inadequacy than the hazardous situation they shared.

There was a distant, shuddering rumble as if massive machinery had shifted, deep in the ship's vitals, and the deck tilted further. Fairbrother reached the voice-pipe. 'Asdic to bridge! Is anyone there? Bridge?' He waited, palmed the blood from his face. Above him, a shelf spilled books, papers, two dirty cups. 'The voice-pipe's gone,' he gritted. Odd, he thought, how quiet it was. This was a sound-proofed coffin.

Stripey Albright, in only underclothes and boiler-suit, carefully inflated his life-belt in the galley flat, then clambered to the starboard side of the fo'c'sle deck, where 'A' gun-crew, with Sub-Lieutenant Waddell, were struggling to free a Carley float, but the toggled retaining cords were wet and unyielding. *Virtue* was continuing to list, and there could be only seconds remaining before she capsized. The air was thick with smoke and swirling sparks. A seaman cursed, and Stripey Albright thumbed open his clasp-knife. 'I've 'ad this,' he said, 'since I was an OD. In my day nobody went aroun' without their knife.'

Rainbird, dazed, pulled himself to his feet, grappling for comprehension. The screen was shattered and the compass smashed, there was glass underfoot and a bridge messenger was on his hands and knees, moaning. The after bridge and flag-deck were a shambles, and dense smoke enveloped everything aft, but from beyond the flash shield below he could hear shouted orders, the clatter of a gun breech. Something, then, was functioning among this chaos.

When it happened, he had felt the ship lift under his feet. Asdic had just shouted, the action alarm-bell was hammering, and the Commander must have just reached the fo'c'sle deck.

'Are you all right, sir?' It was Fender, grotesquely blackened, bleeding from the face, but upright. Rainbird nodded. The engine-room telephone was dead and there was no response from the wheelhouse. 'What's the score, Fender?'

'I thought you'd bought it, sir,' Fender said. 'The boiler and engine room have gone, and there's an oil fuel-fire, but the magazines are safe. The Surgeon is with the damage-control party, dealing with the injured. There's a lot of dead, sir. The whaler's intact, and all the rafts on the starboard side, but I don't think we've got much more time, and the ready-use ammunition's a danger. I'm just going to order off the forward gun-crew.'

The concussed bridge messenger was staring at them blankly, his mouth loose, and Rainbird knew exactly how he felt. He compelled himself to think. 'Prentice? Waddell? Fairbrother?'

Fender shook his head. 'None of them.' He began to vomit.

Rainbird released his grip on the wheelhouse voice-pipe, swayed, but did not fall. 'All right. Get A gun-crew away, then see to yourself — and no heroics. I'll work aft.' His ears sang and his eyes were focusing oddly, he felt drained of all strength; his legs were like water, their muscles jerking uncontrollably. 'And you, lad,' he told the bridge messenger. 'Over the side.'

The BWO was smoke-filled but empty. On the flag-deck there was more glass, a tangle of bunting, fallen halyards and aerials, the twenty-inch lamp torn from its mounting. He stumbled over softness; it was the Yeoman, dead and blood-drenched. Another shape, contorted and duffel-coated, lay under the halyard cleats. Signalman House. The after bridge must have sustained the full concussion of the first torpedo. Hayes-Mailer had been only feet from the impact.

There was another corpse in the wheelhouse, identifiable only by a pair of fur-lined flying-boots. The smoke was choking. He could see men further aft, and shouted for them to abandon ship. He saw one raise an arm in acknowledgement, and he turned into the galley flat. There could surely be nobody remaining on the messdeck, but he would make certain. The deck was tilting impossibly, and there was not much time.

He lowered himself over the leaning messdeck ladder, only vaguely aware that to reclimb it would be difficult in the extreme. It was weirdly silent down here, peaceful, almost dark. White-scrubbed tables, messlockers, stowed hammocks, oilskins, an untidy clutter of crockery and buckets in the angle of deck and bulkhead, sea-boots, scattered clothing. There was nobody here. That left the paint store and the asdic cabinet.

The asdic cabinet? No, the operator would have had ample time to get clear. He turned away, then changed his mind. It was just the sort of place that got overlooked. . . .

The varnished, plywood-faced door inclined forty degrees from the vertical. It was closed, and the heavy locking clip was as tightly clinched as if welded. He hammered with the ball of a fist. 'Asdic! Is anyone there?' If anyone was, and the bulkhead had shifted only fractionally, then it was a task for an acetylene cutter, but there was no time, no time.

From beyond the door came an answering thud-thud-thud, a faint, almost inaudible shout. Fairbrother. Fairbrother and someone. What the hell was Fairbrother doing in the asdic compartment? Fairbrother and Phillips.

The deck lurched and he fell to his knees. It was dark, but there was a hydrant here somewhere, he knew, a reeled hose-pipe and a fire-axe. He groped, found the axe, wrenched it down. There was no point in shouting for help; nobody would hear. And he would never regain the fo'c'sle in time. The axe would be useless. He knew it. It would take one man an hour to hack through seven inches of wood and lead with a blunt fire-axe. It was one of those things that a First Lieutenant never thought about, until it was too late.

The deck slewed, climbed crazily, and his legs were plucked from under him. He sprawled in the darkness, hearing the roar of the sea as *Virtue* plunged.

'Don't rock the bleedin' boat, Lobby,' he heard a voice say. 'Shave off. Remember the soddin' watch-keepers.'

The voice had a familiar ring, but the words meant nothing. Nothing at all. Then he couldn't remember the words, anyway. He stopped thinking about the words and concentrated on being something. Perhaps he was dead. Was this all there was to it? He would have to wait and see. Did you feel cold and pain when you were dead? Well, cold, he supposed. That was logical. Don't

rock the bleedin' boat, that was it. Jesus Christ, it hurt.
What hurt? His legs hurt. *Legs?* He wanted to withdraw
into oblivion again, but could not. It was incomprehensible. No, he was *waking up*, that was it. Waking up? It
was like when he'd had his appendix out in
Hammersmith Hospital, and he'd spewed in a basin.
Wake up, a voice had said. Wake up, then you can go to
sleep again.

He opened his eyes, and the face of Bungy Williams
grinned at him, a chalk-white, skull-drawn face with
mauve lips, hair wetly plastered and ludicrous. 'Wotcher,
me ol' Lobby. 'Ave yer 'eard the buzz? We're all gettin'
three weeks bleedin' survivors' leave.'

Lobby Ludd took stock, slowly because he could
apply his mind to only one thing at a time. He was half
lying, half sitting in a Carley float, which swilled with
several inches of icy water. His legs hurt. His legs were
outstretched on the duckboards and were tied together.
He was sodden to the skin and very cold. The Carley
float was filled with other men, but for the moment he
did not wish to embark upon the mental process of
identifying them. The Carley float was surrounded by a
heaving green sea, and there were more men in the sea,
clinging to the sides of the Carley float. One of them
was Bungy Williams.

Ten yards away another Carley float rose and fell,
similarly filled with men, and further still was the ship's
whaler. He supposed it all meant something. He returned his attention to Bungy Williams and decided to
experiment with speech.

'Soddin' 'ell.'

'That's the 'ammer, Lobby.' Between his blue lips,
Bungy's teeth chattered. 'I'd make yer a cup o' tea,' he

gasped, 'but we've run out o' bleedin' sugar. I can't stand tea wi'out bleedin' sugar.'

Lobby Ludd tried again. 'What's 'appened?'

'We was tinfished, me ol' cocker.' Bungy Williams grappled for a fresh handhold. 'And yer've got two broken legs, mate. Don't panic — the Surgeon-Lieutenant's roped 'em up, and yer'll be all right. He's in the whaler with the worst injured — and the SBA. All yer've got ter do is keep still, see. Shave off, with all the leave yer'll be gettin', the bleedin' war 'll be over by the time yer get back.'

He tried to remember. The Commander had swung up the bridge ladder, and the action alarm-bell was ringing. That was all. And they'd been tinfished. 'How did I get 'ere?' he asked.

Bungy Williams needed time to answer. His eyes were clenched and his teeth bared. 'Lieutenant Fender found yer,' he jerked, 'but we never saw 'im after. There was you an' me, an' Stripey Albright, an' Crowthorne from our mess. An' Sub-Lieutenant Waddell.' He paused to suck breath. 'I've got Stripey 'ere. I keep telling 'im ter push, not pull. That's why we ain't going very fast.'

Stripey? Did that contorting, pipe-clay face and cavernous mouth belong to Stripey? Christ. 'Can't yer get in, Stripey?' It was a soddin' stupid question. Stripey turned red-shot eyes towards him, retched, shook his head. One Carley float, twelve men for the use of, and twenty-five inboard already.

'Don't put yer feet down too far, Stripey,' Bungy Williams advised. 'There might be bleedin' crabs.' Stripey croaked a response, unintelligible, choked as the sea broke over him, and retched again. Inside the waterlogged float all but the slightest movement was

240

impossible; the shocked and sodden men lay entangled, rocking with the sea's movement, eyes closed in bleached faces wet with spray and mucus. There was a hand and a sleeve across Lobby Ludd's chest that were not his. He watched the hand redden with blood, saw it washed clean, then fill with blood again. He wanted to push it away, but could not. Someone was hailing from the distant whaler. Try not to drift apart. Try to keep together. Nobody in the two floats did anything about it.

'I s'pose we all oughter be telling jokes an' singing bleedin' songs,' Bungy Williams panted. 'Stripey will now give 'is famous impression o' George Formby and 'is banjo. All right, Stripey? If yer watch careful, yer'll see 'is mouth never leaves 'is face—'

The Carley float rolled suddenly and violently, smashed through a wall of green brine, and Lobby Ludd yelped with the pain of it. He heard Bungy Williams' startled shout. 'Stripey — yer silly ol' sod! Jes' *'ang on*, will yer? Shave off—' Sleeting, stinging spray exploded over the side, and both Stripey and Bungy had disappeared. Lobby Ludd's throat knotted. He tried to raise himself, but his muscles refused to function, and he choked helplessly, pain-racked. Jesus Christ. Didn't anyone care?

Bungy Williams' ashen face rose above the kerb of the float. He sobbed for breath, then, 'Stripey's gone under. I couldn't do anythin'. *He didn't want ter bleedin' try.*' Sputum dribbled from his slate-coloured mouth and he spat an obscenity. 'What was a soddin' old stanchion like Stripey doing in a bleedin' destroyer in the Arctic? He ought ter 'ave finished wi' this skylark years ago.' His voice broke into hoarseness. 'An' he was a decent ol' sod. . . .'

Lobby Ludd wanted to close his eyes and shut out the shuddering misery that enveloped him, to sink back into the amnesia from which he had emerged, but that would be crass cowardice when there were others in the sea clinging to survival with torn fingers and desperate lungs. If only there was something, some contribution he could make.

'After this lot,' he jerked, 'I ain't even 'aving a bath without tying meself ter the door-'andle.'

The aircraft came out of the blue sky, westward, a Catalina with British markings that seemed for several excruciating moments to have passed unseeing, but then it banked and turned, lost height, and came low over the sea toward them. It gleamed white, with its hull gun-blisters glittering in the sun, and in the distant whaler there were waving arms. The Catalina circled again, lower still, but if the pilot had been debating the possibility of putting the amphibian down into the long, white-crested rollers, he now dismissed it. The aircraft climbed away, and from its belly a dark shape tore loose, fell, tumbling, to the untidy sea below, vanishing from sight.

'Bungy,' Lobby Ludd exulted. 'Soddin' 'ell, he's dropped a life-raft. Did yer see it?' But they had all seen, and the elation of seconds before had drained. 'The stupid, useless bastards,' someone snarled. 'It's a bleedin' mile away. Do they think we're soddin' trained seals?' Hardly a mile, but all of a thousand yards. It might as well be a thousand miles.

The Catalina circled for a second and then a third time. The coast of Scotland could not be far away,

Lobby Ludd calculated, and the aircrew would be in radio touch with base. An air-sea rescue launch or the duty destroyer could be no more than minutes away. An hour at most, say. The pain in his legs had gone; there was only a numbing coldness that pushed upward into his abdomen. An hour at most. The aircraft was still circling, and Bungy Williams was a sodden huddle, his eyes clenched and mouth agape as the float wallowed. 'Bungy,' Lobby Ludd offered. 'It won't be long, mate.'

The other lifted an exhausted face. 'I ain't *got* any longer, Lobby. Shave off. It's times like these when yer wonder why yer ever joined—'

'Bungy!' Lobby Ludd gritted. 'Fer Chris' sake!'

Bungy Williams suddenly chuckled. 'Come in, Number Nine,' he decided, 'yer bleedin' time's up.' He turned away, and the sea closed over him.

'The Admiralty has reported that one of our destroyers was lost off the north-east coast of Scotland yesterday. There were some casualties. Next of kin have been informed.'

Postscript

'What you need is a few early nights, dear,' Mrs Ludd assured him. 'And feeding up. You don't have to tell me about hospitals. When I was in Queen Charlotte's with you, the husbands had to bring food in every night. When the lights went out, all you could hear was people eating. No, I'll clean those shoes, dear — just leave them there. I always did say that half the food never gets to the patients. It goes out of the side door, mark my words. Three weeks! You won't know what to do with yourself. Mrs Godber had a broken leg. Well, it was her ankle, really. I've got a nice piece of hake. With parsley sauce. I was going to fry it with chips, but it's the fat. Anyway, she would polish under the mats, and she had one of them sticks for weeks. I'll show you the letter I had from the Admiralty, about William. I had a telegram first, and another letter from the Mayor of Fulham. Of course, I 'spose they're all written the same. It's like the soap, it's all the same. And coupons all the time. I don't know where all the offal goes to. I've pressed your best suit, dear, on the bed — the one you got from Fifty Shillings. And prices! I was only saying to Mrs Franks

— you know Mrs Franks, dear. She went to her daughter in Horsham for the Blitz, but she's back now. She said she couldn't stand Horsham, and I don't wonder. . . .'

There were still stalls in the North End Road, buses with methane-gas trailers, off-ration rabbit, mutton selling for lamb, and doubtful sausages, utility stockings, strange cigarette brands, black-out torches, stick-on soles and remoulded tyres, powdered egg, queues for oranges, for whale-meat, for children's shoes. Policemen were stunted by steel helmets. There were barrage balloons, surface shelters, water tanks, sandbags, and Elsie and Doris Waters at the old Granville Theatre. It seemed to him that everything was smaller and shabbier; Walham Green had shrunk. There was no war atmosphere, only a pervading obsession over coupons and dockets, of getting a little extra. Nobody talked about Stalingrad, or Burma, or Tobruk, only of streaky bacon, the cheese ration, or utilising pipe-cleaners as hair-curlers, the inadequate gas pressure, the coal problem. It was very odd.

Owen Melville, with official-business urgency, descended the dusty steps of the Town Hall. 'Why, hello — er—' He frowned. 'Hello. Home on leave again? My word, I wish I was in the Navy.' He chuckled. 'Still, we're always glad to see you lads. When do you go back?' He did not wait for an answer. 'Sorry — I must fly. Staff canteen committee, y'know— Deputy Clerk—' He had gone.

The bar of the Britannia was thronged with midday drinkers — a bus driver, workmen in overalls, old ladies with glasses of stout, old men playing cribbage, and a young man in seaman's uniform, talking.

'O' course,' he was saying as Lobby Ludd entered, 'this civvy rum ain't the same as yer get in the Navy. When yer've drunk Navy rum fer a few years, this stuff's nothing. When yer on Russian convoys, I can tell yer' — he sniffed — 'yer need the real thing. . . .' From the clumsy cut of his suit, his boots, and his stores-new jean collar, the young man was almost certainly enjoying his first leave from a training establishment.

'Wotcher, mate,' Lobby Ludd nodded. The other nodded back, unspeaking, suddenly interested in a door marked Gentlemen. Lobby called for a pint of beer.

'What you were saying about being torpedoed,' the bus driver said. 'What's it feel like? I mean, suppose yer can't swim?'

'Ah — well—' The young seaman frowned, and Lobby Ludd's eyes widened. 'Shave off,' he blinked. 'Yer've been tinfished?' His face was gravely respectful. 'I might 'ave guessed them clothes was survivor's kit, mate. Nobody wears clobber like that unless he's a bleedin' survivor, or jes' joined last week.' He chuckled sympathetically. 'If yer fell off them boots yer could do yerself a damage.'

The young seaman drained his glass, coughed, then glanced at the clock. 'Is that the right time?' he enquired.

Lobby Ludd sniffed. 'Clocks in pubs are always ten minutes fast, mate. They ain't piped cooks ter the galley yet.' He groped in a pocket. ' 'Ave another of them grogs — Navy size. It ain't like the real stuff, but it's better'n the beer. Where did yer get it — the tin fish, I mean?'

'Well, as a matter o' fact—' The young man eyed the large glass of rum bleakly.

'All right, mate, don't tell me. Walls 'ave bleedin' ears. I know 'ow yer feel.' He leaned forward confidentially. 'I thought I recognised yer when I came in. Didn't I see yer in barracks, in the drill shed, when *Virtue*'s lot was drawing their loan bedding? "Pore bastards," I said. "Jes' look at them pore bastards." ' He shook his head. 'I suppose yer lost everythin'?'

'Well, not *everythin'*—'

'I know. Shave off.' Lobby Ludd sucked his teeth. 'If I 'adn't recognised yer, I might 'ave thought yer was jes' some green sprog up from training, full o' bullshit. Yer do get 'em, mate.' He sighed. '*Virtue*, did yer say? Roll on. Them soddin' destroyers is murder — corned dog and 'ard tack, watch-an'-watch about, an' cold as bleedin' charity. There oughter be a law.'

The other drank his rum as if it was quinine. 'Well—'

'I 'ad an ol' mate in *Virtue*,' Lobby Ludd reminisced sadly. 'Yer must 'ave known 'im, o' course. Name o' Williams — Bungy Williams. An' there was another bloke — Albright. Yer *must* 'ave known Stripey Albright?'

The young seaman had difficulty in remembering the names, but he did suddenly remember that he had a pressing appointment in Hammersmith. 'Tell 'em on the bus yer a survivor,' was Lobby Ludd's parting advice, 'and yer won't 'ave ter pay.'

'When yer think about it,' the bus driver considered, 'we don't know arf of what goes on.'

'Too true, mate,' Lobby Ludd agreed. 'Yer could write a bleedin' book.' He pushed his nose into his beer.

Glossary of Naval Lower-deck Terminology and Technical Terms

Many Naval expressions have passed into common use and their original meanings have become blurred. Many others, from sailing-ship days, have passed into misuse. Those listed below were common during the Second World War, and undoubtedly some still survive.

The list is, of course, by no means complete, but expressions and abbreviations used in the text are included, together with one or two others which give the flavour of the period.

Nicknames have not been included because they were so numerous. A Williams was inevitably a 'Bungy', Wilson a 'Tug', Bell a 'Dinger' and every Knight a 'Bogey'. Ships also had their nicknames. *Royal Sovereign* was the 'Tiddley Quid', *Vengeance* was the 'Lord's Own' ('Vengeance is Mine, saith the Lord. I will repay') and *Weston-super-Mare* became 'Aggie on Horseback' — a subtlety that the reader can unravel for himself by referring to the notation against 'Aggie Weston'.

Active Service. Term applied to ratings of the regular Navy although, contrarily, they were of peacetime recruitment.

adrift. Late, particularly when mustering or returning from leave.

Aggie Weston. Loosely applied to all seamen's temperance hostels ashore, but particularly those originally introduced by Dame Agnes Weston, the 'sailors' best friend', who, however, also persuaded the Admiralty to stop issuing rum to ratings of under twenty years.

all night in. For watchkeeping sailors, the occasion on which they enjoyed an entire night in their hammocks. Ashore, all night abed with a woman.

Ally Sloper's Favourite Relish. A particularly racy bottled sauce, available from ship's stores, reputed to be excellent for cleaning brasswork.

Andrew (The). The lower deck's name for the Royal Navy. During the Napoleonic Wars, Andrew Miller was a notorious press-gang officer who impressed so many seamen that he was said to own the Navy.

asdic. Submarine-detection branch, equipment and techniques. From the initial letters of the Anti-Submarine Detection Investigation Committee of 1917.

baby's head. See 'dead baby'.

back teeth awash. Drunken, or the process of becoming so.

BAMS. Wireless broadcast service for British and Allied merchant ships.

baron. One with modest accumulation of money, usually by saving, and a target for borrowers.

battle-wagon. Battleship.

bear pit. The stokers' messdeck.

belay. Stop or cancel. To 'belay the last pipe' would be a cancellation of the last order given.

bells. Bell-bottomed trousers, sometimes worn extravagantly wide in defiance of regulations.

Blue Label. Popular brand of bottled beer, brewed in Malta.

Bluenose. One who has travelled north of the Arctic Circle. Circumstances permitting, first-timers are subjected to a light-hearted ceremony similar to that when crossing the Equator, and presented with a 'Bluenose certificate' signed by the ship's captain.

BN. Continuous wireless broadcast for warships, 107

kc/s.

Bootnecks. Royal Marines, for whom sailors had little affection.

breathing licence. Station card — an identity card held by all ratings, deprival of which meant loss of leave and limitation of leisure activities.

bubbly. Rum, issued to eligible ratings daily.

Buffer; Chief Buffer. Bosun's Mate; Chief Bosun's Mate.

bulkheads. The dividing walls of below-decks compartments.

bunting. General term for flags of all kinds.

Bunting Tosser, Bunts. Rating of Visual Signalling Branch.

buzz. Rumour, often distorted by repetition or completely unfounded.

buzzer. Closed-circuit morse code for practice purposes.

BWO. Bridge Wireless Office.

cable (length). Unit of distance, about 200 yards.

Captain D. Senior officer of destroyer flotilla.

Carley floats. Life rafts of varying sizes, often made of balsa.

caterer. Senior rating in mess, once responsible for victualling arrangements.

Charlie (Chaplin). Ship's chaplain. Padre.

Chinese wedding-cake. Boiled rice, laced with currants.

Chippy. Ship's carpenter.

chocker. Fed up, frustrated. Abbreviation of 'chock-ablock', meaning a rope that is jammed tightly into its block.

civvies. Civilian clothes.

Civvy Street. Civilian life, the yearned-for end of a service engagement.

clacker. Pastry or pie crust.

cleaning station. Appointed location for daily cleaning duties.

clew up. Finish, end up. A defaulter might 'clew up' in gaol.

coaming. Vertical erection around hatch or at base of door to prevent entrance of water.

Cook of the Mess. Rating(s) responsible for bringing food from galley, washing up, cleaning messdeck.

corned dog. Corned beef.

cowboys. Bacon and beans.

crusher. Regulating Petty Officer (R.P.O.), member of Naval police branch, allegedly the last resort of the moronic or illiterate.

daymen. Ratings who do no watchkeeping and work during day hours only, thus enjoying 'all night in' every night.

dead baby. Sometimes 'baby's head'. Meat pudding.

deckhead. The ceiling of any below-deck area.

depot. Devonport, Portsmouth and Chatham were depots, also port divisions, to one of which every rating belonged, defined by the letter D, P or C prefixing his official number.

DFs. Duty Frees, referring to duty-free cigarettes or tobacco.

D/F. Direction finding.

dhobeying. The process of washing clothes.

dickie. White linen bib-like item, secured by tapes, worn instead of a standard seaman's shirt.

dip, at the. 'At the dip!' was a response when addressed or called; an acknowledgement. An ensign was dipped in salute or acknowledgement of another.

ditty box. Small box of scrubbed white wood, with brass name-plate and lock, in which a rating kept his most private possessions, letters, photographs, etc.

divisions. Morning muster of ship's company.

DNO. Director of Naval Operations.

DO. Divisional Officer, of which there might be a number in a ship, each responsible for different professional branches.

draft chit. Drafting instructions to or from a ship or foreign station.

drills. White drill uniform.

drink, the. The sea, particularly that in close proximity; e.g., '. . . fell into the drink'.

ducks. See 'Number Threes' for definitions of naval kit.

EA. Electrical Artificer.

EDR. Electrical Distance Recorder.

ERA. Engine Room Artificer.

ETA. Estimated Time of Arrival.

Fill your boots! Help yourself!

filled in. Suffer bruises or beating in fight or brawl.

fish-heads. Aircraft carrier's ship's company, as opposed to Fleet Air Arm personnel. (See 'pin-heads'.)

flakers. Exhausted. To 'flake out' is to collapse.

flannel. (1) Seamen's white flannel shirt, with square-cut neck edged with blue jean. (2) Nonsense, unconvincing bluster.

flat aback. Cap worn on back of head, contrary to regulations.

foo-foo. Talcum powder, used to limit perspiration and prickly heat, sometimes violently scented.

fore and aft rig. Naval uniform involving peaked cap, jacket, and trousers creased at front and back.

gannet. One with a voracious or greedy appetite.

gash. Refuse or garbage. This must be disposed of with caution in wartime as it can betray a ship's presence to a submarine, and discarded written material may impart useful information.

Gestapo. Regulating Branch personnel.

goofers. Idlers and off-duty men who congregate to watch some interesting procedure, sometimes in hazardous circumstances.

green rub. Misfortune, an undeserved penalty.

groundbait. Small gift, such as stockings or cosmetics, given to female acquaintance, with ulterior motive.

guard and steerage. Watchkeepers and other personnel with arduous duties who are allowed extra sleep periods and other privileges.

gulpers. A gulp of another's tot of rum, conceded as payment for some service, or as a gambling debt. (See 'sippers'.)

Gut. Notorious street of bars and places of entertainment in Valetta, Malta, riotously frequented by sailors.

Guzz. Devonport depot, dockyard and barracks. When affiliated to the Devonport port division, a man is a 'Guzz rating'.

HA. High Angle, with particular reference to high-angle anti-aircraft guns.

hard liers. Small bonus once paid in compensation for the hard conditions of small ships.

HD. Continuous wireless broadcast for warships, 78 K/cs. See also 'BN'.

HE. High Explosive; also Hydrophone Effect.

heads. Latrines, in earlier times always in the head, or bows, of a ship.

herrings-in. Tinned herrings in tomato sauce, a frequent breakfast dish.

H/F. High Frequency.

HO. 'Hostilities Only'; a rating conscripted for the duration of hostilities.

hogwash (hoggin'). Sea, sea water.

homers. A domestic environment ashore, not necessarily a rating's own home, which he visits. He is then said to be 'up 'omers'.

Hooky. Term of address for a leading rating, identified by an anchor badge on his left arm.

Jack Dusty. Rating of the Stores Branch; any rating employed in storekeeping.

Jack Strop. Belligerent or impertinent rating.

jankers. Punishment routine imposed on defaulters.

Jaunty. Master-at-Arms, senior rating of naval police branch and probably the most unpopular person in any ship or establishment.

Jimmy, Jimmy the One. First Lieutenant, responsible for the smooth running of ship's routine and daily work-programme. See also 'Number One'.

killick. Leading rating of any branch; e.g., killick sparker, killick of the mess, etc.

KUA. Kit Upkeep Allowance; a small supplement to cover the replacement of uniform kit which, after the first issue, must be purchased by the rating.

kye. Cocoa, made from solid bricks of unsweetened chocolate which must be grated or crushed before adding hot water.

lamp swinging. Boastful reminiscing.

lamps trimmed. Suffer injury or punishment in fight or brawl.

L and PA. Lodging and Provision Allowance. Additional payment to ratings who are quartered in private accommodation ashore.

liberty boat. Boat (occasionally a road vehicle) taking men ashore for leave.

Lobs! Peculiar to Boys' Service, a shout of warning at the approach of danger, e.g., an officer or instructor.

make and mend. A period of no duties, usually a half-day, originally given to seamen for the purpose of making or mending clothes, but in more recent times for sleeping, shore-going or recreation.

matelot. Lower-deck sailor.

messdeck lawyer. The equivalent of a barrackroom lawyer; one able to quote chapter and verse of regulations.

mess traps. Crockery and utensils used on messdecks.

Mickey Mouse. Motor Mechanic (Naval), from the initials MM.

muzzle velocity. Tinned meat and vegetables, from the initials M&V.

nap hand. Veneral Disease.

Navvy. Navigating Officer.

neaters. Rum issued undiluted (neat) as opposed to grog, which has water added, and is classified as one-and-one, two-and-one, etc.

Nife lamp. Emergency, battery-fed lamp, switched on either manually or automatically when main electrical supply fails.

north-easter. Stoppage of pay, from the initials 'NE' in the pay ledger, meaning 'not entitled', and imposing a cold wind of poverty.

nozzer. A recently enlisted boy; a raw recruit.

Number One. First Lieutenant. See 'Jimmy the One'.

Number Threes. A rating's third-best blue suit. A full kit should include four blue suits, numbered one to four; number fives, white ducks; number six, white drills — through working rigs, overalls, tropical shorts, etc. The 'rig of the day' is specified daily, or for certain duties. Only 'number ones' has gold badges.

nutty. Any kind of sweetmeat or confection. The terms 'chocolate', 'toffee', etc., are almost never used.

OA. Ordnance Artificer.

OD. Ordinary Rating; the lowest rating in men's service.

'Oggie. Hot cornish pasty, often eaten ashore or in canteen, particularly in Devonport.

onion. A fraction of a knot (nautical measurement of speed). Thus 'ten knots and an onion' would mean something between ten and eleven knots. One knot is a speed of 2,000 yards, a nautical mile, per hour.

OOD. Officer of the Day.

OOW. Officer of the Watch.

oppo. Friend or shore-going companion, from 'opposite number'.

Out pipes. Order given to indicate a resumption of work, or shortly before night retirement. Originally meaning that tobacco pipes should be extinguished.

party. Any woman, but usually an acquaintance, casual or formal.

Pay Bob. Paymaster.

paid off. On completion of a commission, possibly of several years, a ship returned to its home port and 'paid off' its company, who returned to depot to await further drafting.

pea doo. Pea soup.

pierhead jump. Orders to join a ship at extremely short notice.

pigs. Officers.

pin-heads. Fleet Air Arm personnel, as opposed to ship's company, in aircraft carrier.

Pipe down. Order imposing silence, the last routine order of the day, following 'Out pipes'.

P/L. Plain language, as opposed to code or cipher.

Pompey. Portsmouth depot, dockyard and barracks. Men affiliated to the Portsmouth port division are 'Pompey ratings'.

pom-pom. Two-pounder Maxim gun, for both high and low-angle firing.

pongo. Soldier.

pusher. Woman, usually one of casual acquaintance.

pusser. Corruption of 'purser', denoting any item of service issue, whether food, clothing or equipment; the word also describes anything that is correct or conforming to regulations. A 'pusser' ship or person is one that is strict and highly disciplined.

QF. Quick Firing.

rabbits. Gifts or souvenirs, usually purchased ashore, intended for family or friends at home. A 'rabbit run' is an excursion ashore primarily for the purpose of gift-buying.

rate of knots. At high speed. Any journey or activity undertaken speedily is said to be done 'at a rate of knots'.

rattle, in the. Faced with disciplinary action.

RDF. Radio Direction Finding, by which the bearing of a ship's radio transmission can be determined.

red lead. Tinned tomatoes.

red ink. A character assessment of 'Excellent', which is written in records in red ink. More normal assessments, in black ink, were 'Very Good', 'Good' or merely 'Satisfactory'.

requestmen. Men submitting a request (for leave, advancement, etc.) through official channels. They were interviewed prior to, but on the same occasion as, defaulters.

RNB. Royal Naval Barracks.

Roll on my twelve! Frequent *cri de cœur*, referring to the longed-for expiry of a service engagement, of twelve years or any other period.

Rose Cottage. The Venereal Diseases ward in Sick Quarters.

rounds. Inspection of ship or establishment by duty officer during late evening; Captain's rounds occurred during Saturday forenoons, following an intensive cleaning programme.

Royals. Royal Marines.

R/T. Radio Telephony. Voice transmissions, as opposed to morse code (W/T).

rum bosun. Rating in mess responsible for collecting and distributing rum issue.

rum rat. One with insatiable appetite for rum, both his own and others'.

salt horse. An officer of solely seamanship qualifications, as opposed to those with specialist training, e.g., communications, flying, torpedoes, gunnery, etc.

Saturday night sailors. Officers and ratings of the Royal Naval Volunteer Reserve.

Sally, The. The Salvation Army.

SBA. Sick Berth Attendant.

SBNO. Senior British Naval Officer.

scran bag. All items of kit and clothing left unstowed were confiscated and put into a 'scran bag'. They were subsequently redeemed by their owners on payment of an inch of soap for each item. The soap was used for common cleaning purposes.

scribe. Writer; rating of the Navy's clerical branch.

scrub round. Ignore, cancel, or take no further action.

set. A beard, for the growth of which it was necessary to obtain official permission.

Shave off. To shave off beard, the removal of which must also be officially approved. Also, the expression 'Shave off!' indicates surprise, frustration or disgust.

shite hawks. Seagulls, unpopular for their depredation of paintwork and polished brass.

shamfered. Damaged. A ship suffering damage in action was said to have been 'shamfered'.

shock. To cook. A dish taken to the galley would be accompanied by a request to 'give it a shock'.

short arm inspection. Medical Officer's examination of genitals.

sippers. A sip of another's rum, conceded as payment for favour or gambling debt. Two sippers equalled one gulpers.

skate. Rating with a bad disciplinary record, spending frequent periods under punishment.

slops. Items of uniform kit purchased from ship's stores; pusser's issue.

Smoke, The. London.

snottie. Midshipman, who wears three brass buttons on each cuff, allegedly to prevent them being used to wipe nose.

sparker, Sparks. Telegraphist Rating.

spin a yarn. To tell a story in defence of misdemeanour; to deceive by verbosity; boastful reminiscence.

Spithead Pheasant. Kipper.

sprog. Infant; anyone of immature years.

square rig. Naval uniform involving blue jean collar, jumper and bell-bottomed trousers.

squeegee band. Improvised musical group utilising mouth organs, combs, clappers, and unusual percussion media.

SRE. Sound Reproduction Equipment, for amplifying orders throughout ship, and for radio programmes.

stanchion. Rating who has held a comfortable shore posting for unusually long lime.

stand easy. Brief cessation of work during forenoon and afternoon, usually giving time for a smoke and cup of tea.

station card. Small identity card held by all ratings, withdrawn during loss of leave and other privileges.

Stokes. Stoker.

stone frigate. Any Naval barracks or shore establishment.

Stringbag. Swordfish torpedo-carrying biplane.

Stripey. Rating with three good-conduct badges (stripes) indicating lengthy service and particularly one who has achieved no promotion. They represent at least thirteen years 'undetected crime'.

stroppy. Belligerent, insubordinate. The description of a 'Jack Strop'.

Sub. Variously, a sub-lieutenant, a submarine, a loan of money.

tailor-made. Manufactured cigarette, as opposed to one rolled by hand.

TBS. Radiotelephone for 'Talk Between Ships'.

T, G, or UA. Temperance, Grog, or Under Age. A rating is Under Age until twenty, when he may opt to draw rum (in which case he is defined as 'G') or to draw a small payment in lieu (and so become 'T'). A temperance rating was a *rara avis*.

three-badger. See 'Stripey'.

ticket. Discharge from the service. To get one's ticket was an enviable achievement.

tickler. Cigarette and pipe tobacco allowance, packed in ½lb tins, a duty-free purchase. A hand-rolled cigarette was also a 'tickler'. The name comes from that of a manufacturer of tinned jam.

tiddley. Neat, or of good appearance. Applied equally to the tie of a cap ribbon, the cut of a suit, or the lines of a ship.

tiffy. Artificer, either Engine Room, Ordnance or Electrical.

tiller flat. Aftermost compartment of ship, housing emergency steering position and, when applicable, depth-charge stowage.

tinfish. Torpedo.

Tombola. The Naval equivalent of 'Bingo'.

Torps. Torpedo officer or rating.

tot. Measure of rum issued to eligible ratings daily, at midday. Rum is denied to defaulters.

Townie. Specifically, another rating who originates from the same home town, but often used as a friendly form of address.

train smash. Tinned tomatoes and bacon.

Uckers. A complex version of the table game Ludo, widely played on messdecks.

UJC. Union Jack Club; servicemen's hostel near Waterloo Station.

up the line. To travel home on leave, as opposed to

local leave ashore.

victualled. To be officially listed for maintenance by a ship or mess, on permanent or temporary basis, so that accommodation, food and rum can be issued.

V/S. Visual Signalling.

watchkeepers'. Extended shore leave and/or sleeping periods allowed to watchkeeping personnel in compensation for long working hours.

Wavy Navy. Royal Naval Volunteer Reserve, from the wavy gold bands on the cuff of an RNVR officer which distinguish him from a colleague of the regular Navy.

winger. Chosen friend or shore-going companion.

W/T. Wireless Telegraphy, generally assumed to mean morse code transmissions as opposed to voice telephony (R/T).

Convoy PQ17

Convoy PQ17, of thirty-three merchant ships loaded with 200,000 tons of war supplies for Russia, sailed from Iceland in late June 1942. Its immediate escort, under Commander J. E. Broome in the destroyer *Keppel*, comprised six destroyers, two anti-aircraft ships, two submarines, and eleven armed trawlers, minesweepers and corvettes. A hundred miles ahead of the convoy was a screen of four heavy cruisers — two British and two American — under Rear-Admiral Dalrymple-Hamilton, and distant cover was provided by the battleship *Duke of York*, the American battleship *Washington*, the aircraft carrier *Victorious*, three cruisers and a number of destroyers, commanded by Admiral Tovey, C-in-C Home Fleet. Additionally, no less than twelve British, one French and several Russian submarines patrolled North Cape and the Norwegian coast.

This massive deployment was intended to balance the threat of the German battle fleet in Trondheim and Narvik — the super-battleship *Tirpitz*, the pocket battleships *Admiral Scheer* and *Lützow* (formerly *Deutschland*), the heavy cruiser *Admiral Hipper* and a half dozen large destroyers.

Attacks by U-boats and bombers began on 2 July, when the convoy was five days out, but these were beaten off. On the same day the German battle units left their anchorages to move further north, nearer to the convoy route. Information of this movement had reached the Admiralty, but could not be confirmed by air reconnaissance, and the ships at sea were not informed. On the 4th, however, against the consensus of expert advice, the First Sea Lord in London, Sir Dudley Pound, ordered that the convoy should scatter.

There was no amplifying information, but to Rear-Admiral Dalrymple-Hamilton and Commander Broome the order meant only one thing — that an attack by the enemy battle fleet was imminent. In fact, the German ships had re-anchored in Alten fjord, more than 400 miles away. Dalrymple-Hamilton had already exceeded his orders by accompanying the convoy as far east as longitude 30, but now his orders were unequivocal; he must withdraw westward at utmost speed. Expecting to meet an overwhelmingly superior enemy force at any moment, he took Commander Broome's destroyers under his command so that he could at least attempt a torpedo attack against *Tirpitz*.

The merchant ships, scattered, and deprived of the escort that had hitherto successfully defended them, were helpless targets for the enemy bombers and submarines that hounded them. Only eleven survived.

Tirpitz and her consorts did sally from Alten fjord on 5 July with the intention of intercepting the convoy, but were sighted and reported by a Russian submarine. Aware that their position was known, that there were submarines in the vicinity and, worse, that Admiral Tovey's heavy squadron would subsequently be racing to meet them, the German ships returned to the anchorage. They had never approached within striking distance of a British vessel, but the damage had been done. PQ17 had been massacred.

The disaster generated anger and shame throughout the Royal Navy, which resented the inference that its warships had deserted the convoy. In retrospect, how-ever, there can be no doubt that the blame must be directed at the Admiralty's practice of issuing orders without supporting information. Neither Dalrymple-Hamilton nor Broome could dispute their orders and, starved of intelligence, Dalrymple-Hamilton's decision to join Broome's destroyer force to his own in order to engage the German battle fleet is beyond criticism.

Admiral Sir John Tovey, C-in-C Home Fleet, had repeatedly suggested to the Admiralty that mid-summer convoys to Russia, whose own Navy contributed little or nothing, did not justify the heavy toll in British ships and lives, but political considerations prevailed. When PQ17 sailed, Tovey had telephoned Sir Dudley Pound from Scapa Flow, warning that if the convoy were ordered to scatter, the consequences would be 'sheer, bloody murder'. They were.